Checked Out

Daniel Harris

PAGE PUBLISHING, INC.
New York, NY

First originally published by Page Publishing, Inc. 2015

ISBN 978-1-68213-493-1 (pbk)
ISBN 978-1-68213-494-8 (digital)
ISBN 978-1-68213-792-5 (hardcover)

Printed in the United States of America

For my wife, Joy, the love of my life
and the light in my life.

You can check out anytime you like, but you can never leave.

—The Eagles, "Hotel California"

Author's Note

This work is fiction. All of the events, people, and places are drawn from my own experiences or from stories that were passed on to me by friends or coworkers. I borrowed liberally from both sources for the express purpose of creating a story that the reader might become a part of as he/she continues to turn the pages of this novel. In summary, this novel is a literary work whose content is produced by the imagination.

Also by Daniel Harris

FICTION

Goodbye, Dearie

Capital Crimes

Blood Feud

SHORT STORIES

The Cowboy

The Closer

The Russell Riley Series

Blood Feud, a recent novel by Boston-native Daniel Harris published by RoseDog Books, a division of Dorrance Publishers, is the first book in a fictional series about working in closely held family businesses. This novel introduces narrator Russell Riley as the highest-ranking nonfamily executive of a large local supermarket chain. *Blood Feud* tells a simple story. It begins with an immigrant grocer selling vegetables from a pushcart and ends in a court case with two billion at risk. Two brothers, sons of the founder, inherit equal share of a burgeoning food chain. One dies, and his widow, suspecting that she has been shortchanged from profits, sues to recover.

Now it becomes complicated. The author, an insider with over thirty years working in the food industry, spins a yarn of a twisting, turning labyrinth that features a love tryst, intrigue, betrayal, and greed. The characters and dialogue are real, authentic, and they draw you from the printed page into the middle of this fast-moving action.

Russell Riley is the highest-ranking "outsider" in this company, and it's his job to protect and grow the business while the two families duke it out in court. But even he can't stay entirely above the fray because he owns stock that could provide the swing vote for control.

If you are in the mood for an insider's take on a nasty and vitriolic family food fight that ends in a celebrated court case the *Boston Globe* called "the longest and most expensive in state history," *Blood Feud* is it.

The sequel, *Checked Out*, opens in a tony section of the East Side of Providence at the corner of Hope and Angell Street in a fashionable New England colonial. The stunning second wife of the CEO of Food Basket supermarket chain opens her kitchen door to a man she knows. Together they walk into the living room, where her husband is passed out in his chair. The man steps behind the chair and pumps two bullets into the back of his head.

A month later, our narrator, Russell Riley, gets the career call of a lifetime from a former collegiate baseball buddy who consistently stuck him out with his curveball. His uncle, the former CEO of the family firm, has died unexpectedly and offers Russell the chance to head the company. Russell and his advisers huddle after he visits with the C-suite members of Food Basket in Providence. Despite what his eyes see and his ears hear—misgivings about its business practices, the competence of the CFO, the declining market share, enough red flags if he were sailing to signal, "Hurricane-force winds, return to shore or take shelter!"—Russell takes the job. And so the next chapter of Russell Riley's professional career begins.

Many of the Galetti characters from *Blood Feud* return, including Russell's nemesis, Joe Galetti; Dom's wife, Maria; her son Trip; plus a coterie of professionals whom Russell has trained in key positions to help even the playing field in a game of deception, greed, and betrayal. Russell himself falls under suspicion when the CFO's suicide is ruled a murder by the highly competent duo of Providence police captain Alan Cummings and assistant district attorney Donna Mitchner. Russell soon realizes that this crack twosome have the know-how to uncover the malevolence that hovers over Food Basket like a classic nor'easter.

Besides a great yarn, *Checked Out* reinforces the reader's faith in Russell innate sense of higher ground and their belief in karmic forces deciding Joe Galetti's fate.

Introduction

I saw this one coming, and I still didn't duck. My wife, Holly, much smarter than I, thought it was a bad idea, and my partner in our food brokerage business, Bill Hartman, told me that the last of my marbles had made a daring escape. The blame lay squarely with me. I was about to consider a job that was eerily similar to one that ended in my termination.

Stick with me here: I can put this catastrophic blunder into a short version. My name is Russell Riley, and my last job was president of Galetti Supermarkets. I worked there for thirty years to include the time when the Galetti family became embroiled in a two-billion-dollar family food fight that one publication reported was "the costliest and nastiest court case in state history."

My job during this courtside fiasco was to keep the organization working as efficiently and effectively as it did before this major distraction. While the family wrestled for control, I, in my own mind, thought I did a terrific job building dollar volume while keeping competition and the takeover crowd at a comfortable distance. However, the CEO of Galetti Supermarkets felt I was a little light in the profit column and showed me the door.

Here's where my thinking becomes a little suspect. A friend from college, Bob Santone, called me with a proposition. We had played baseball against each other, and we kept running into each other in places such as the Cape Cod Baseball League. He was a pitcher, and I was an outfielder. Even though it was a long time ago, we both knew exactly how we did against each other. In my first six at bats facing Bob, he struck me out five times. In the next six, I had two singles, a double, and two home runs. What happened? He stopped throwing me the curveball.

Bob Santone was a very successful money manager in Providence, Rhode Island, but he was calling me about his family business. His uncle, the CEO of an eighty-store supermarket chain headquartered in Providence, was gunned down in his home, and it sent shockwaves throughout the six-state New England area. I had written Bob a note of condolence over his uncle's demise and attended the funeral.

He was on the other end of the phone and greeted me in his usual kindly way, "Oh, Russ, if I'd only remembered the curveball."

"Yeah, but that's the reason that Ted Williams said all pitchers were stupid!" I said.

"Williams, what the hell did he know about hitting?" Bob asked.

"What did Robert Oppenheimer know about the bomb?" I replied.

"Okay, okay, you have a point. Maybe. I'm not the sharpest knife in the drawer. Actually, that brings me to why I'm calling. I need your services for as long as a year."

CHAPTER I

Corner of Hope and Angell

She was understandably nervous. Many hours of planning were about to come to fruition, and in her darkened mood, she felt as if a building might fall on her no matter the outcome. Her husband had had too much to drink and was passed out in his chair in the living room.

She let him in the kitchen door, and she nodded at him and pointed toward the living room. He stepped around her, moved to the living room, approached the man from behind, and put two bullets in his brain as calmly as if he had just entered the room to say hello.

She looked up at him and said, "Is he…"

"He's dead, and you need to get this gun back to its owner now," he said.

"I'm meeting him in half an hour at his place," she said.

"Good," he replied. "Are you comfortable that you can get the piece back where it belongs?"

"Yes," she said. "I'm only distracted by one thing."

"Oh, what?" he said. "I need you to really focus."

"I want you to make hard love to me right now on the floor!"

"You're turned on because I just shot somebody?" he asked.

"Yes, because you just restarted my life," she said.

"I hear what you are saying, but we are in a critical stage right now. This, in a very short time, will be a murder scene. Have you planted those things we talked about?"

"Done," she said.

"Good," he said. "Let's move out. Get your part done and stick to your knitting. No communication of any kind from now on."

CHAPTER 2

Life in the Fast Lane

B ob Santone wanted me to up and leave my job for a year.

"Seriously, Bob, you may not have noticed, but I have a job that occupies a good part of a working week."

"Yeah, yeah," Bob responded, clearly not buying my filled-to-capacity workweek yarn. "You can dump your responsibility on your partner, Bill Hartman. Everyone knows he's been carrying you for years."

"Jesus, I forgot what a smooth operator you are. But then I know most of your clientele are folks born just after the big war who you have sold worthless annuities and who can no longer see or hear. I'm guessing if Hartman takes over my nonexistent responsibilities, he'll want my very real and existing salary, which I currently use to support my family."

"Details," Santone said. "You can name your salary for this job I'm going to ask you to take. And while we are on the subject of money, I'm pretty sure your wife, Holly, makes more than the average American. My people say she is formidable competition."

"I'm impressed. You have done your homework. I think you are wasting your time, but fire away, it's your nickel," I said.

"I need you to come down here and run Food Basket until we can get back on level ground. I anticipate this to be a minimum of a year," Bob said.

"Why? Doesn't Food Basket have a succession plan?" I asked.

"Does Warren Buffet have a succession plan? My uncle has three children, none of whom work in the business or have any interest. Additionally, he had become more hands-off in recent years, divorced his wife, and married a woman half his age. I am clearly not qualified to take over the reign of an eighty-store food chain that does several billion dollars a year."

"Very messy," I responded. "Sounds to me as if his hands had drifted to more exotic pursuits, but how did the bottle spin and point to my name?"

"Oh c'mon, Riley, this is déjà vu all over again! You successfully steered Galetti Supermarkets through the nastiest family food fight in the history of the state. This shouldn't be tough for you," Santone said.

"Okay, you sweet talker, let me summarize this venture you are proposing. You want someone to come in to save a sinking ship who apparently is not holding up his end of his current corporate assignment and who was unceremoniously fired by the Galetti CEO for the job he did during the food fight fiasco."

"Sticks and stones. Are we a little touchy?" Bob asked. "My G-2, without exception, says you did an excellent job of managing the chain while the Galettis duked it out in court. You actually built the business during this distracting time, and that's exactly what I want you to do for Food Basket."

"You know what I really like about you, Bob?" I asked.

"What?" he replied.

"You have more bullshit than a Christmas turkey. But it's working. You really want to hire a guy who is in the twilight of a mediocre career!"

"Call me crazy," Bob said, "but I want a guy who has been there and done that, and you are it."

"Listen, Bob, I've got to run. Let me leave it with you this way. Call the industry's very best headhunter, Jim Sneed, and have him work up a list of the most capable candidates. And recheck your Galetti sources for their opinion of my time during the major distraction at Galetti Supermarkets."

"Okay, Russ, but you could get stiffed."

"I really don't want to know, but why?"

"Sneed might recommend Hartman, and then you'd really be screwed!" he said.

"Good-bye, Bob."

CHAPTER 3

Buck Naked on Facebook

Doubts shuddered through me as I sat paralyzed in my chair. What was I thinking? I hadn't been on that side of the aisle for several years. I was the combatant now, the enemy storming the retail grocery barricades with my presentation to sell more of my principal's macaroni and cheese, bobbing and weaving through objections such as "Your stuff tastes like shit, Riley" and "It doesn't sell."

And my response was always the same: "So you know what shit tastes like, Larry?"

That either brought a big belly laugh and a sale or a quick exit stage left.

But seriously, things had changed since I was president of Galetti Supermarkets—technology and the consumer to name two of the major ones. I was in the saddle before Amazon, mobile technology, and apps. If I were on Facebook buck naked in Macy's window, I couldn't get on it to delete it. The consumer was more cautious than she was a decade ago, and the shift in the customer base was seismic. When I slipped away from Galetti with my cardboard box of personal belongings in my hand, Walmart didn't sell groceries. Now it sold 3 percent of the nation's grocery volume. CVS, Costco, and

Target were mauling the traditional and major stalwarts of the industry such as Grocery Wholesalers and SuperValu, to name the largest, which were teetering on the brink of bankruptcy.

My partner, Bill Hartman, a former Procter & Gamble manager, had taken on the "iron piano" complications early. He embraced social media, spent time with major advertising agencies on Madison Avenue, and helped our principals and customers to embrace it. He was also trained in what we in grocery called the nonfood channel. He held a seminar for our principals on how to approach these not-so-traditional customers, which was a huge advantage to us. With many of these companies, Hartman was thought of as an insider rather than the enemy.

It suddenly occurred to me—maybe Bob Santone was right. Hartman was running the show, and I was the eye candy. Truthfully, we were actually a good match. Some large grocery customers felt more comfortable with me than Hartman because they knew him in his other life when he was a hard-charging sales guy for P&G, giving no quarter and asking for none. I'm not sure how he would react to this new turn of events, but I was pretty sure he'd be on an even keel.

"You did what!?" Hartman barked in our office the next day. "Jesus, Russell, I don't see you for twenty-four hours and you start playing with razor blades while walking on the highway! Who in the hell is going to sub for you here, Smokey the Bear? Did it occur to you while you were in this trance that Food Basket is a customer of ours and that this could be considered a conflict of interest? Can you see the headline: FOOD BROKER REP BECOMES CEO OF FOOD BASKET AND, COINCIDENTALLY, DISCONTINUES ALL OF THE BROKER'S COMPETITIVE PRODUCTS?"

"So you're okay with this then?" I asked.

"I'm as okay as a Bernie Madoff shareholder," Hartman said. "Who will call on your accounts while you're on hiatus—sabbatical boondoggle?"

"Well, it can't be you unless you bring a food taster along," I said. "But I think Arnold Cable would do a terrific job."

"Have you put this scheme in front of the big boss yet?" Hartman asked.

"I'm still working on that presentation, and based on your reaction, I have a bit more work to do," I said.

"I seldom make predictions, but when she hears this one, you'll be sleeping in the Hotel Acura," Hartman said.

CHAPTER 4

Sneaking a Fastball by Henry Aaron

B ill Hartman was a rock. He was bigger than a bread box, more powerful than a locomotive, and able to leap over potholes that I fell into with frightening regularity. He had a great philosophy, which I had learned from him when I was with Galetti and he was with P&G. He was polite and respectful to everyone, but he took very little crap from people who mistook his calm demeanor for weakness.

I asked him about this philosophy, and he said, "What's the worst that could happen? At P&G they could fire me, but we're survivors, and we will always land on our feet. But now, hell, we can't even be fired. We own the joint."

I was trying to apply this fearless rationale to my chat tonight with my wife, Holly. I am madly in love with this woman. She's bright, beautiful, and 95 percent responsible for how our two children are turning out. My mother adores her, she's on the board of the local bank, a portfolio manager for a very successful mutual fund company, has time to play with her friends, reads two books a week, and can fix a leaky gutter while attending to me. See my problem?

Using my guile, skill, daring, and mental acuity to blow this by her would be as likely as Congress passing something—anything—on a timely basis. They said sneaking a fastball past Henry Aaron was like trying to sneak a sunrise by a rooster. This was a serious mismatch, but falling on the mercy of the court was an option. Pushing the blame on a third party had some appeal, or maybe I could break the news at a party, hoping that there would be safety in numbers. If I miscalculated, a number of witnesses could record my demise.

As I drove up my driveway after work, I was clear-eyed, calm, confident, full of snappy retorts. It reminded me of when we were kids and a buddy said something we didn't like. We'd say something snappy back like, "I saw your grandmother's underwear."

I pulled into the garage, opened the back door to the kitchen. There she was, working on a salad. She walked over to me, gave me a kiss, and said, "Hello, sailor, I have been really missing you!"

Beaten like a drum! How was I going to put her grandmother's underwear into a retort after that wonderful greeting? I did the next best thing and threw myself on the mercy of the court by blurting out, "I think I may have really screwed up today."

"You mean the Food Basket offer?" Holly asked with a huge smile on her face.

"What? How? Who? Jesus!" I declared.

"He didn't have anything to do with it. In order, your favorite headhunter called, followed by Bob Santone, followed by Bill Hartman, and finishing off out of the money in fourth place was Trip Galetti."

"Wow, security is really tight on this one!" I said. "The only people that haven't called are the Boston Globe, Supermarket News, and the Rockettes."

"Here's what I was thinking," Holly said. "The kids are off at a concert. I've prepared a nice dinner featuring scallops, a watermelon salad, a lovely white wine, and a dessert to be named later. I thought you might want to bounce off me what you're thinking, and I could give you a cursory report on their financials?"

"Sure, sure, but can you darn a sock?"

"I'd rather buy you a new pair," Holly said.

"I know I say this all the time, but you are amazing. I was riding home from the office wondering how to break the news to you while at the same time you are breaking down Food Basket's financials. Awesome! For the record, I have an offer, can name my salary, but I haven't committed to do anything," I said.

"Yeah, that's what Hartman was calling me about. He felt as if he went over the line. He said he likened you to Smokey the Bear, a Bernie Madoff shareholder, a drawer full of not-so-sharp knives while having the FTC lock you up for conflict of interest."

"That about covers it," I said. "Honestly, I don't know what is driving me. It's a crazy idea. I have a wonderful business surrounded by people I like and trust. I really don't need this aggravation."

"Well, let me fill in some of the blanks for you, and that might help this quandary. First, Food Basket is losing share of market. Its stock is pretty unspectacular and could take a nosedive when the next quarter's results are made public," she said. Holly suddenly looked at me. "Enough of this stuff. Get out of that suit while I get dinner ready."

No use calling anybody back tonight. I knew the executive search person, Jim Sneed, because he had worked with Hartman at P&G, and they, to include wives, were great buddies. Bob Santone was a friend but just over the line from an acquaintance. But Trip Galetti, the CEO of Galetti Supermarkets, I knew extremely well. I had trained him, and he reported to me when I was president of Galetti Supermarkets, and I had a high regard for him. His uncle had fired me a couple of times, including the final time just before he lost the court case and was removed from the board of directors.

I don't think I mentioned this before, but in the interest of full disclosure, when I slipped away from Galetti with my box of personal belongings, in my hand I also cashed in private family stock worth twenty-five million dollars. From a personal point of view, that engenders a deep-seated loyalty to my former employer, especially Trip's side of the family, who had signed off on this particular transaction. If this new job opportunity competed in any way with Galetti, I would have to dismiss it out of hand. I heard Holly calling me for dinner, so I headed downstairs to do my part by opening a bottle of white wine. The meal looked great, tasted better, and we stuck to other subjects until I had cleared the plates and we were ensuring that none of the wine would be left for another day.

"Holly, why don't you pick up on the Food Basket financials where you left off? So far I know it is losing market share, the stock is not exciting, and the current quarter's results will only add to those woes," I said.

"Yes, you have the picture, but let me ask you a question. Why is Bob Santone running the show instead of one of his uncle's children?" Holly asked.

"Because he is the executor of his uncle's will, and the children are not connected in any way to Food Basket," I said.

"Okay," Holly said. "While we are on this subject, being CEO of Food Basket is a whole lot different than it was at Galetti. This is a publicly held company, unlike Galetti, and you would report to the board."

"How would that affect me in a different way than being at Galetti?" I asked.

"Remember the masterful promotion you ran while the court case was ongoing that cost several million dollars?" she asked.

"I do. It got me fired," I replied.

"It's my guess that to spend that kind of dough at Food Basket, you would have to run it by the finance committee on the board," Holly said.

"Anything else, my beautiful financial wizard?" I asked.

"One last thing—people," Holly said. "Food Basket is big and not well managed. You can't do this job by yourself. You need to go to Trip Galetti and borrow people from finance, buying, and distribution, Arnold Cable and Hartman too. Turning this around by yourself right now is like turning the *QE2* around with a canoe."

"Great thought," I said. "Speaking of being attended to, I'd like to attend to you upstairs before the kids get home."

"Lucky you," Holly said. "You were the dessert to be named later."

CHAPTER 5

The Elusive Brass Ring

She breezed into the bar, took a seat at the far end, and signaled the bartender, and he walked quickly down to her.

"Where have you been?" he asked. "I was expecting you earlier."

"I was waiting for him to pass out. It took longer than usual," she replied. "How long have you been at work?"

"About an hour. I was waiting for you at the apartment, but I had to be here to relieve the boss. I was hoping to have some time alone with you before work," he said.

"When do you get off? Maybe I can make it up to you," she said as she rubbed her fingers on his forearm.

"I'm closing, so I won't be back to the apartment until one thirty," he said.

"I'll see you then," she said. "He's sleeping it off and won't even turn over until well past sunrise."

"Great. Want a drink?"

"The usual."

"A stinger?" he asked.

"Yes, indeed."

The bartender shuffled off reluctantly to service his other customers while she sipped her drink. It was the first time all day she had let down, and she could feel the tension draining from her neck and shoulders. She couldn't remember when she wasn't on the run, grasping for the brass ring, but never quite having a secure grip on it. Married twice, once for love, once for money, now she felt as if she were in a no-man's land, neither fish nor fowl, one blind alley after another. Not helpful to reach too far in the future, but for the present, all she wanted was to feel his big, burly arms around her while making love like two teenagers on the beach.

She signaled him at the end of the bar, and he immediately responded by saying, "Yes, missy."

"One more of the vegetables before I make my way to your place," she said.

"As you wish," he said, squeezing her hand ever so slightly.

She couldn't see him, but she felt him slide onto the stool next to her. When the bartender returned with her second drink, he ordered a Bud Light and a shot of rye. He drank in silence, but the reverie for her was broken. She wasn't a high-profile socialite by any means, but hanging out in a bar was an exposure that probably wasn't worth the risk.

Turning to her left, she slid off her stool and headed for the ladies' room. When she came back, the man was gone, and on a drink napkin he had written, "I hope it wasn't something I said." She smiled at the note, finished her second stinger, and left a fifty-dollar bill folded under her empty glass. She was feeling slightly inebriated, but as she opened the door and stepped into the night air, she became more alert.

She arrived at his apartment fifteen minutes later and went about straightening it up, including wiping down his revolver and returning it to its rightful location. She picked up the living room, made the bed with fresh sheets, and started a load of laundry. She vacuumed the living room and dusted the end tables. As she removed her clothes and headed for the shower, she was thinking to herself that she couldn't live with a slob.

She crawled into bed and drifted off to sleep very quickly. Later, she felt someone slip into bed and start nuzzling her neck. He was rubbing her left nipple very lightly, and she felt something hard pressing against her backside.

She moaned and whispered, "Give it to me now. I can't wait another second."

But she couldn't turn toward him quickly enough, and he entered her from behind, and she screamed in equal parts of ecstasy and pain.

"Jesus Christ, Bruno, more, more!"

CHAPTER 6

Bernie Madoff Shareholder

At the office the following day, the turmoil in my mind about the events of the previous day seemed greatly diminished. Most importantly, Holly was supportive, even enthusiastic, about this opportunity at Food Basket. She hadn't gilded the lily in her research of Food Basket. It was an uphill struggle, especially in contrast to Galetti when I took over there during the infamous food fight. Competitors were afraid of Galetti, and only the brave and/or the foolish would take that beast on one-on-one. Not true in the present circumstance. The recently murdered CEO had taken his hand off the wheel and, by omission, had let the stores slowly start to decay.

Truth be told, if he had lived, he would have been replaced within six months. He became distracted by extravagant toys: a 32-year-old wife, a jet plane, and a 180-foot cabin cruiser. It didn't take a PhD from Yeshiva to know where the store remodeling budget had disappeared to in the scheme of business interfering with pleasure. Not a kind thing to say, but Alex Santone, the deceased CEO of Food Basket, had become a drunk and a wastrel. Competitors thought of this chain as an easy mark, the redheaded stepchild of the grocery industry.

But to me that was the challenge. If I were offered and took the job, I thought my training at Galetti would allow me to turn this chain around. The great unknown to me was would the board of directors allow me to do it.

My intercom interrupted my thoughts, and my secretary told me that Jim Sneed was on the line and wanted to talk to me.

I picked it up and said, "Hello, Jim. How are you doing?"

"Hey, Russ, I'm doing well. How are you and your lovely bride, Holly?"

"Better now. Not so good yesterday when I learned from her that you, Bob, Hartman, and Trip Galetti had all called me at home," I said.

"Uh-oh, let me guess. You hadn't had a chance to talk to her about the Food Basket opportunity."

"Bingo. You, Bob, and Trip were very discreet. Unfortunately, that big hump, Hartman, told her everything."

Sneed burst out laughing and said, "Telephone, television, tell-a-Hartman. Man, that guy was not cut out for CIA work."

"Amen, brother. What can I do for you?" I asked.

"I wanted to talk to you about the Food Basket job. Do you know how things work at the CEO/president executive search level?"

"Not a clue," I said, "except at some point you carry off a wheelbarrow full of coin."

"First, I don't make money when I place someone as CEO of Food Basket. I've already been paid. Unlike searches at a lower level, headhunters don't get paid for the body they produce. But they do guarantee the success of the person they place, and if he doesn't work out, I'm on the hook to produce his successor for free," Sneed said.

"Interesting," I responded. "So if I screw up, you are working for free."

"Indeed," Sneed responded.

"What else is unique at this level?" I asked.

"Okay," he said, "I meet with the board of directors, and they specify what kind of a candidate they are looking for to take on a job of this import."

"What is the typical criteria they are looking for?" I asked.

"Wait a minute, Riley. I'm supposed to be asking the questions," he said.

"Humor me. I want to go into this thing with my eyes open," I responded.

"Well, every attribute begins with 'a strong demonstrated track record of...' What follows that phrase are things such as achieving goals, influencing others, problem solving, developing cooperative relationships, and viewing the importance of financial awareness in creating a profitable entity," Sneed said.

"Very helpful. And this leads you to where, Jim?"

"Simple. I am looking for things that are 'translatable' to the position I'm trying to fill. For instance, in your case, we don't need a translatable. You have already demonstrated that you can do this job and, by most accounts, do it very well."

"Okay, so I'm a shoo-in, right?" I asked.

"Not so fast, señor!" Sneed said with a laugh. "The retailing landscape has changed, and most customers are trying to deal with the elephant in the room, Walmart."

"Uh-oh, I think I hear the jail doors closing behind me," I said. "Bob Santone had a theory that I'm about to hear again."

"Maybe. The traditional grocery folks are looking to their suppliers for answers and people," Sneed said. "Bill Hartman would be an ideal candidate for a job like CEO of Food Basket."

"Who would you pick?" I asked.

"I'll get back to you, Russ," Sneed said. "I've got to go."

"Jim, Jim," I said, but he was gone.

I punched my intercom, and Bill Hartman answered, "At your service, My Liege."

"As Bob Barker would say, c'mon down!"

"On the way," he responded.

Hartman lumbered into my office with this big shit-eating grin on his face and flopped into a chair. He just wasn't a candidate for *GQ*. He had a pencil eraser facing out protruding from his left ear, he looked clean-shaven on the left side of his face, his shirt pocket had a pen in it that was leaking oil badly, and his tie, which had once been a solid gray, now had various stains on it of every size and description so that it looked like a vertical Jackson Pollock. He really wasn't an outright slob, but he was way over the line to be considered a casual dresser. But as I grew to know him better, I began to think this confused attempt at spotty attire was a show so that one would be distracted from his major gift. He had the rare combination of strong mental acuity balanced with incredible practical judgment. Such a rare combination. I knew lots of smart people and many street-smart folks, but rarely do they come in one package. Hartman was such a fellow.

"You know that job that I was considering—the one where you described me as a Bernie Madoff shareholder?" I said.

"Yeah," Hartman said.

The master of understatement, I thought.

"Well, you could end up getting it and leave me here holding the bag," I said.

"Are you saying in there somewhere that if I take the job, you'll be holding the bag?" he asked.

"Don't confuse me with the facts, you...you Benedict Arnold," I responded.

"Benedict Arnold? I'm the poor schlep that's left here holding the company together while you gallop off to save Food Basket," Hartman said.

"What exactly is a schlep?" I asked.

"Okay, I'll give you an example: I'm sitting at a buyer's desk in Queens, introducing Charmin. I have a four-pack of it on his desk. Halfway through my pitch, the Pepsi retail guy goes by his door with a two-wheeler full of Pepsi two-liter bottles. The buyer flags down the two-wheeler, and my buyer gives the Pepsi guy my Charmin sample, and the Pepsi guy gives him a two-liter bottle of Pepsi. That's a schlep!" Hartman explained.

"What did you do when the Pepsi guy left?" I asked, laughing at Hartman's story.

"I picked up the two-liter bottle of Pepsi, put it in my briefcase, and left his office," he responded. "Hey, want to talk this Food Basket fiasco?"

"Sure," I said. "What's your take?"

"Food Basket has the same inventory problems that A&P was having when Arnold Cable was working there," he said.

"Are you talking LIFO, FIFO, or what?" I asked.

"FIST," Hartman responded.

"I don't know that system," I said, somewhat puzzled.

"First In Stays There," Hartman said as he burst out laughing.

I couldn't help smiling at the doubled-over Hartman.

I don't think I knew anyone who enjoyed his own humor more than Hartman.

"Seriously, Russ, I know Sneed thinks I could do this job. No way. If they were flying high, I might be able to take them even higher, but this job is for a guy who knows the basics, has extensive grocery experience, and can spot the half-steppers quickly and get rid of them. You can do it, but go in with your eyes open. Get Arnold Cable and his Lawyers Weekly buddies digging for dirt. I hope I am not profiling here, but not so long ago Providence led the nation in murders per capita. Couple that with a heavy Italian population and some of the world's best restaurants and I want to be sure you don't get shipped to a local landfill on a pallet."

"A grisly thought indeed," I said. "But your view of the internals matches Holly's view of the financials. Can you check with your buddies at P&G to see if they are paying their bills?"

"Can do," Hartman said. "This is way out there, but I know you will be talking to Trip Galetti. It might be smart to ask him if he has any designs on Food Basket, and if he does, you may want to eliminate yourself as a candidate for this job."

"Great advice, Bill," I said. "I'm about to have lunch with him at our favorite restaurant."

"Let me guess," Hartman said, "that steak-and-cheese place that has a front window view of a Dempsey-Dumpster."

"Yes, sir," I replied. "Nothing is too grand for executives of our ilk! Thanks for the counsel, as usual."

As I entered the restaurant, Trip Galetti waved at me from a booth that had an excellent view of the back of a Dunkin' Donuts. I always took a double take when I saw Trip because I'd known him almost his entire life. However, he was no longer this gregarious kid who was dressed in jeans and a T-shirt, his face covered in peach fuzz, heading for his first year at Dartmouth. He was now a grown man dressed in a suit and a tie who was the CEO of a thriving grocery chain doing an excess of two billion dollars a year. He was about six feet tall with black hair and a smile that lit up the room. He looked like his mother, Maria, and for that happenstance of nature, he should be grateful. The combination of high mental acuity, a warm, open smile, and his natural good looks helped him in becoming an outstanding communicator. I thought what set him apart as a communicator was that he was the best listener I knew.

"Ordered you a steak and cheese fully loaded and a Coke," Trip said as I slid into the booth and simultaneously shook his hand.

"Perfect. Who's buying?"

"Bought and paid for in advance," he responded.

"In advance of what?" I asked.

"In advance of you giving me the complete lowdown on what the fuck, pardon my French, you are doing!" he said with a big smile on his face.

"Fair enough. You think I can be bought for a steak and cheese, and it happens you're right! But first tell me how Maria is and give me the lowdown on your family."

"Mom is thriving at work. I don't know if you've seen our store over the Bourne Bridge on the way to the Cape, but it's kicking some major butt. I'd like to take credit for it, but it was entirely Maria's doing. I wouldn't dare tell you what it's doing a week, but Maria found the site, schmoozed the politicos, and, get this, arranged for the store to have its own exit off Route 28. So in summary, she's doing great, has a boyfriend, but they never last that long. I know she's my mom, but she's a little too intense for most people."

"Not for me. I adored the woman," I said.

"She feels the same about you, pal," Trip said. "The family—Melissa is a jewel, but the girls are in middle school, and they are a giant pain in my ass."

"Oh yeah. Say no more. Been there, rough sledding," I replied. "But hang in there. They come back to you."

Our sandwiches were on the table, and we were both talking while pieces of onion, tomato, pickles, and hots escaped our lips in every direction.

"I suppose you want to know why I called you last night," Trip said.

"I think I know the general subject because my phone was ringing off the hook last night," I responded. "How did you pick it up?"

"Bob Santone called last week and asked me if I had any candidates who could take that job and turn Food Basket around. Hell, I thought he was feeling me out, but that simply wasn't the case. I mentioned you, but told Bob that you had a nice little business going and that I thought there wasn't a chance in hell you would have any interest. The next thing I know, a headhunter calls me yesterday, and he has no interest in me either. All he wants to talk about is Russell Riley. I told him I thought we had a guy by that name working here back in the day when my granddad had a one-store operation."

Trip had me laughing and reaching for multiple napkins.

"He didn't call to recruit you?" I asked with my eyebrows at their highest peak. "Suppose he knows that you have more money than the gross national product of the twenty-fifth largest economy in the world?"

It was Trip's turn to grab for the napkins as he laughed, and soda was coming out of his nose.

"Okay, okay, I wasn't that upset that he didn't offer me a job. But later in the day, Maria comes in and asks me if I've heard that you may become the CEO of Food Basket. Russ, this news is not on the down low. For Christ's sake, I'm expecting to hear about it on the CBS news tonight."

"What's your take on Food Basket?" I asked.

"Deadwood" was Trip's one-word answer.

"Do you know the specifics?" I asked.

"Macober, Pondorf, Williams, and Cable could give you chapter and verse."

"Would you mind if I had a chat with them?" I asked.

"Those guys love you. They'd be happy to give you a hand. And you know Cable lives in that neck of the woods, has been retired for about six months, and is probably itching to get back into the action."

"Thanks for the help, Trip," I said. "Let's play what if."

"Okay," Trip responded.

"What if I take this job, and by happenstance my team is able to turn Food Basket around, build volume and profit, and start filling up those parking lots and stores with cars and people, would Galetti have any interest in making a bid for this chain?"

"Can't give you an answer on the spot," Trip said. "We don't like to borrow money, and we usually own the shopping centers that we are in. It's way less than fifty-fifty, but not out of the question."

"Fair enough," I said. "Next time we meet, I'm buying."

"Deal," Trip said.

CHAPTER 7

No Weapon, No Shells, and Nobody Home

Even to the most obtuse citizen, it was apparent that something was going on at this estate near Brown University that extended beyond business as usual. There were a half-dozen police cars, an ambulance, and a large van with Police Forensics plastered across the side of it in big block letters. The scene looked more like the vehicles lined up for a four-alarm fire.

Police captain Alan Cummings was talking with the detectives on hand while carefully trying to avoid stepping on any potential evidence as he was well within the crime scene, which was marked off in bright yellow tape. He didn't want to distract his detectives, but his job was to talk to each of them and try to piece together facts that led them to a suspect. It really was true: if something didn't pop out of the woodwork in forty-eight hours, the trail grew cold very quickly.

Cummings wasn't a big man, but he was solid. He looked older than his thirty-six years, but that may have been because he had a permanent scowl on his face. But this was all for show. In fact, he was glib, moved like an athlete on the balls of his feet, and in his spare time, which was ample as he was recently divorced, he was a primary mover in the boys' club activities and the police league in the city of Providence. He had an old-fashioned buzz cut that disguised a handsome face. This penchant for trying to look older than his years may have had something to do with the fact that he was one of the youngest detectives in Rhode Island to be promoted to captain.

"What have you got, O'Malley?" he barked at his lead detective.

He didn't know if O'Malley owned a dog, but if he did, he was sure it would be a big old bulldog with three chins and jowls that flapped up and down in perfect unison as the beast attempted to run.

"Looks like a professional job. No weapon, no shells, and nobody home," O'Malley responded.

"Have you checked with the other detectives? Because if they don't have more than what you just told me, someone is going to be scrubbing latrines in town hall."

O'Malley smiled. They all liked Cummings, not because he was such a great guy, but because he treated everybody the same—like shit. But when push came to shove, he always had his people's backs.

"Not to be disrespectful, Captain, but we found something in the confines of the crime scene that will make you do a jig at the Thanksgiving parade."

"I'll be the judge of that," Cummings said.

O'Malley handed a letter to Cummings and stepped aside. Cummings read the letter, turned on his heel, and did a jig right in front of O'Malley.

He then turned to O'Malley and said, "Take this guy's name and address and put a patrol on him 24-7 'til I tell you to stop."

"Aye, aye, my captain," O'Malley said.

CHAPTER 8

Arnold Cable

I felt like the guy who rode facing backward while in an automobile. He wanted to see where he had been rather than where he was going. Here I was, recruiting people for a job I didn't have.

It reminded me of a story Hartman told me about a P&G manager in New York. He had proposed a Hispanic unit of one manager and five sales representatives to call on the bodegas in New York. Headquarters couldn't seem to push the proposal to the finish line, so working under the old adage of asking forgiveness instead of permission, he went ahead and hired the people. By the time management realized what had happened, the unit had shipped over a million cases of product to these outlets, and they had two and three times the market share they had in Anglo New York. They say failure is an orphan, but in this case, there was a stampede of people trying to take credit for this brilliant marketing stroke.

That's what I was grasping for: a brilliant marketing stroke. To that end, I called my old friend and fellow employee, Arnold Cable. I'd first met Cable many years ago; I was in my first to second year at Galetti, and he was a vice president of A&P. I was calling on A&P's national headquarters in New York because we were convinced that they were using their marketing muscle with over one thousand stores to try to run us (eight stores) out of business by lowering prices on popular items below the Mendoza line. We didn't have a scintilla of evidence to back us up, but we were hoping that a David-and-Goliath look would make them raise their prices if they thought we might take this grievance to the FTC or some other organization.

To this day, I remember exactly what Arnold had said to me: "Russ, you look like you're fresh out of school."

"Yes, sir, I just graduated from Boston University last year, and as a matter of fact, I'm thinking about going back to graduate school."

"Oh, to study what?" Arnold Cable asked.

"Price fixing," I said, looking directly at Cable.

Cable looked at me, threw his hands up in the air, and burst out laughing. We have been fast friends ever since that conversation.

Years later, Arnold called me. He was eligible for early retirement from A&P and wanted to know if he could come work for Galetti. He wanted to come back to New England, specifically Providence, Rhode Island, and I jumped at the chance to hire him. During my years at Galetti, when I was stuck on an internal problem at the firm, Arnold was the first person I consulted with to try to find a solution. Externally, particularly with suppliers, Bill Hartman would be the first person I called.

I had him on the line, and my objective was to coax him out of retirement and put him to work with me at Food Basket. I thought it might be a tough sell because he had a myriad of friends and projects that clamored for his attention.

I opened by saying, "Arnold, I hope you didn't give all your suits away to the Vietnam vets."

"No, I kept a couple, but there's a lot more space in that closet now than there used to be. What are you up to? The last time I checked in, you went rogue and joined the supplier side of the business."

"You've got the right skinny, as usual, but I may be veering back to your side of the table, Arnold. And that's why I'm calling," I said.

"Okay, as long as you didn't sign on to have anything to do with that sinking ship Food Basket," Arnold said. "It's a disaster in the making!"

"Son of a bitch," I said. "How did you hear about it?"

Cable was chuckling on the other end of the line.

"C'mon, Russ, man, don't be so naïve. I've had a dozen calls from people all over New England and New York wanting to know if you are dumb enough to stick your finger in the dike at Food Basket."

"You're kidding me," I said.

"I kid you not. One of those calls was from Supermarket News," Arnold said.

"Man, I wish I could get pub like this on something that was really important," I said. "Arnold, I need you on this one, which means I've already given you two jobs to do simultaneously."

"Two jobs?" Arnold asked.

"Yeah, I already told Hartman that you could help him with my grocery customers in my absence, but then I quickly also came to the conclusion, thanks to a gentle push from Holly, that you'd be a hell of a lot more valuable inside the Food Basket building."

"I know that you and Holly know I'm retired because you came to my retirement party," Arnold said. "By the way, I love Holly, but you can take—"

"Wait a minute, Cable. You're not bailing on me after all we've been through together," I said.

"Precisely why I am bailing. Don't want my last working assignment to sink like the *Andrea Doria*."

"You're working me for something, Arnold," I said with some suspicion.

"Not really. I just wanted to see you sweat a little for telling me you were doing graduate work on price fixing."

It was my turn to laugh at Arnold.

"Thanks, Arnold. I really do need your help. This should be just up your alley. It's in your backyard. Get together with your lawyer buddies, grocery contacts, neighbors, friends, clergy—"

"All right, already, I get the idea. What do you want to know?" he asked.

"What is really going on? How bad is it really? Who is the major stockholder? What can you tell me about the folks on the board? Why aren't the children involved? Any ties to an unsavory element? You know the drill," I said.

"I'm on it," Arnold said. "What's my title?"
"I'll tell you if I get the job," I said.
"Fair enough," Arnold said, and he hung up.

CHAPTER 9

Losing a One-Person Race

I had been summoned to Food Basket headquarters in Providence, Rhode Island, for a face-to-face with the board of directors. In the past week, I'd made some store visits to try to get a feel for what I was up against. As I walked into the waiting room and began to approach the receptionist, I saw Jim Sneed stand up and start moving toward me.

I smiled, put out my hand, and said, "Fancy meeting you here."

"Doing my job, Russ. How are you?" Jim inquired.

"Good. A little nervous actually that this group might think I don't play well with others," I responded.

"Butterflies are a good thing. I've just been up with the board and gave them a one-hour review of the candidates. There were only three including you. One of them has already been interviewed and fell on his sword."

"How did that happen?" I asked.

"They asked him what his biggest achievement was. He told them chapter and verse about what he did to launch this great product. A wonderful story, really," Sneed said.

"So what went wrong?" I asked.

"One of the board members asked, 'Where is this product now?'" Sneed said. "And the answer was it's in the rather sizeable pile of forgotten brands that went to an untimely demise."

"Jesus, Sneed, you set that poor bugger up to be annihilated, didn't you?" I asked.

"Well, I will say this: I never make the candidate I think is most qualified for the job be the first interview."

"Man, at first glance you don't look that Machiavellian to me," I said, only half joking.

Sneed was tall, slim, but not gangly. He was handsome, no doubt about it, but if he knew it, it didn't show. He was self-effacing, not a slap-on-the-back fellow well met, but he had a way about him that made you want to level with him. In a word, he was disarming, but behind the blond hair and piercing blue eyes was considerable intellect. Even though I'd never played cards with him, I thought he'd be a terrific cardplayer. He elicited scads of information from people but at the same time gave no clue as to his opinion on the matter.

He had worked with Hartman when they were both at Procter & Gamble. It was said—but never substantiated—that the coeds really took a shine to those two when they were college recruiting. Hartman said that Sneed was the kind of guy who would call a restaurant where they were to dine at together with their spouses and order a birthday cake for Jenny Hartman even though her actual birthday was months later. He still had a lot of kid in him. But Sneed was deadly serious about his career.

Although he was on the fast track at P&G, it wasn't fast enough. He jumped ship and started his own company. Initially, his office was his kitchen, and his wife was his CFO. From this no-frills beginning, he built one of the premier boutique management consulting companies in the nation. I always admired his decision to jump off the P&G gravy train after almost two decades into the deep end of the unknown.

He was the perfect person to have on your board of directors because this was the level of player he recruited. He was comfortable with top executives, well-read, up to the minute on new critical thinking, and he wasn't afraid to ask a question that others might avoid. But what I liked about him most was that Hartman trusted him with his life, and that was enough for me. He had all the tools to drag our operation into the twenty-first century.

"Who is the second candidate?"

"Hartman," Sneed said. "But he told Bob Santone he didn't have an interest. Further, he said that in his opinion Food Basket, in its current state of disrepair, needed a grocery guy who could deal with getting the chain's head above water before considering frills such as social media. He was pretty blunt. He told Bob that Food Basket was leaking water pretty badly, and the pumps couldn't keep up."

"Who am I talking to up there?" I asked.

"Bob Santone, who you know, Joe Snyder, the CFO, and Garth Brewster, who is the CEO of a large chain of discount drugstores that could be snapped up by CVS or Walgreens at any time," Sneed said.

"That's it?" I asked. "Seems like a pretty small board."

"Think of it as the executive committee of the board. These are the folks who make the decisions," Sneed replied. "Ready to roll?"

"Ready as I'll ever be," I said.

We took the elevator to the top floor, and when it opened, Bob Santone was there to greet us.

"Russ, welcome to Food Basket."

"Thanks, Bob, delighted to be here," I said.

He looked to me as if he could still pitch a few innings. He was lanky, built like a track guy; I was sure his body fat number was in the single digits and that with all that hedge fund money, he had a gym in his basement and a trainer on call. He wasn't handsome, but on the other hand, you wouldn't turn into a pillar of salt if you looked him square in the face. He didn't do that much—look me in the eye—but he was amiable and not hard to talk to. Maybe it was our sports backgrounds, but through no fault of his own, I felt I had to compete with him. This wasn't a "compete" situation. He was the boss, and I was the interviewee!

"Let's go in and meet the others," Bob said.

We entered a room that could seat a company of army personnel in full combat gear. It had a 360-degree view of Providence, and given the size of Rhode Island, I was pretty well convinced that we could see some other state line out there somewhere as well. My shoes sank into a two-inch-thick carpet as I approached the two men I had not met. Joe Snyder was in his early fifties, a shade under six feet, and seemed to be in excellent shape. I had this image that at any minute he might drop to the floor and do a half-dozen one-armed push-ups. He grabbed my hand to shake it, and I made sure I didn't leave any of my fingers in harm's way as he squeezed like a man getting the last drop out of a recalcitrant orange.

He looked me in the eye and said, "A pleasure, Russ."

I knew I was going to like Garth Brewster right away. He was about Hartman's size and shape, and they had the same tailor. He was just big all over. He had a ruddy complexion, a face that was open, disarming, friendly, except for the big brown eyes that seemed to see right through me. He had huge hands, and his arm length was thirty-seven or thirty-eight inches. He had a little bit of a beer gut, but he wasn't fat, just big. He wore cowboy boots and a string tie.

He had a blue sports coat on that had enough cloth in it to cover a small car completely, and his voice seemed as if it was booming out of a fifty-five-gallon drum as he shook my hand, patted me on the shoulder, and said, "Jesus, you must be a dumb fuck. We ran this job on Craigslist and didn't get a nibble!"

I doubled over laughing and said, "If I take this job, you better head for the hills because I'm going to wear you out!"

"I'll look forward to it," he said.

Just as we were sitting down, one of the most gorgeous women I had ever seen burst into the room. She looked at Bob Santone and said, "Shouldn't I be at this meeting representing my dead husband, Bob?"

Bob Santone was stunned.

"What are you doing here, Lucy? No, you shouldn't be here, and no, you would not be representing your husband. That's my job as the executor of the will. Now please leave."

"Bullshit. I'm not going. I want to see for myself who is going to pull a rabbit out of a hat after my husband did his best to run the company into the ground," she said.

"Lucy, you have a minute to leave voluntarily, or I will call security and have you forcibly removed," Bob Santone said as he reached for the phone.

I was ashamed to admit it, but during the entire time she was standing in the room, the only thing I could do was stare at her ass. This woman may have been tougher than a dollar-ninety-eight steak, but she had a great ass. I know, I'm a pervert, but Garth was looking right where I was. I just didn't want her to catch me staring at it. Damn, busted. A slight smile escaped her lips as she exited the room very slowly.

"Jesus," Jim Sneed said, "I thought I'd seen everything in the book, but she's an original."

We dove right into it now that Lucy Santone had made an early exit. Bob started the proceedings by saying, "Let's turn it around since the meeting has had a bizarre start and ask Russ what questions he has."

"What are your problems?" I asked.

"Who said we had problems?" Joe Snyder responded.

"Okay, one vote for no problems. Anybody else?" I asked.

"Let me count the ways," Garth Brewster said. "The stores are antiquated—make that shabby. Competition is chipping away at our share of market, the stock is at a standstill, our employees are older than our competition, so wages are higher, we currently have no leadership, and realistically, we haven't had any for more than five years, and morale is terrible as indicated by an employee turnover rate twice the industry standard. Banks have become reluctant to lend us money at the best rate, indicating that they think we might fold, and frankly, we have too many layers of management that are deadwood, including this board, which put up with Alex Santone's extravagances way too long. There's more, but I'm out of breath!"

"Bob?" I queried, looking at Bob Santone.

"I think Garth nailed it except that from a financial basis, I think we could be a target for a takeover."

"Very helpful," I said. "What I see is the board doesn't agree about the status of Food Basket as it exists today. That means that no clear direction is being passed down to the employees. Next, if the board can't identify what needs to be fixed, how are they going to find the person who has the skill to fix the problems? So why would I step into this hornet's nest?"

"What a minute," Bob said. "We brought you here today to offer you the job based on what you did for Galetti when their shorts were all bunched up over a family food fight."

"I get it, Bob," I said. "But honestly, it was a very different condition. Galetti was the hunter, not the prey. I was able to flex the company's muscles and promote the hell out of the stores during the court fight for control. I knew everyone in the building and the stores, and I knew what our capacity to succeed was, and I took advantage of it. Even though this is what Jim Sneed would call a translatable to your current situation, your plight is somewhat darker, and your chance of survival is much slimmer."

"Are you working us for more salary and compensation?" Joe Snyder asked.

I hadn't known Joe for very long, but I really didn't like him. Maybe it was the "one-armed push-ups" thing, but I was beginning to believe there was nothing but an airstream between his ears.

"Oh, Joe, believe me, you would pay through the nose for my services, but right now I'm leaning toward not taking the job."

"What would turn you around?" Garth asked.

"First, we need to hire Jim Sneed to bring us into the twenty-first century. He needs to educate us on the best practices for running a successful shop. Additionally, he will become a one-man restructure arm of the board with the mission of dumping the deadwood and hiring people who can compete and win in the marketplace. That includes the board of directors.

"Next, I'll need to bring a team in to analyze every department. They won't be consultants. They will be grocery and retail people. Last and most importantly, I need the full support of the board 100 percent of the time. To be blunt, that means if I turn to you with an idea, I'm not asking for permission—I'm telling you to get it done.

"And now to your question, Joe. If I'm not able to put Food Basket in better shape than I found it, my annual salary will be one dollar. If I am successful, I'll still take the dollar, but along with it I'll take three million dollars of stock options to vest over ten years at today's price. Gentlemen, it's been real, but I have another appointment."

I gave Garth a pat on the back on my way out the door.

CHAPTER 10

Jimmy Carter Was a Peanut Farmer

Police captain Alan Cummings and his squad of homicide detectives had been busy. From the letter they found at the crime scene, they had identified Bruno Jethroe, a bartender who worked at the Town Jug in Pawtucket. They checked his criminal record, and it was quite lengthy but mostly filled with nickel-and-dime misdemeanors. They obtained a search warrant, found the gun that killed Alex Santone, and felt like they were beginning to build an airtight case.

There was one problem that Detective O'Malley really didn't want to share with Captain Cummings.

"What is it, O'Malley? You look like you lost your best friend," Cummings said.

"The suspect, Bruno Jethroe, is in the wind. We lost him in Boston three days ago, and he hasn't been to work or to his apartment since."

"Okay, let's put out the APB and see if we can find him. That would include putting a tail on Mrs. Santone," Cummings said.

"Do we have enough to indict?" O'Malley asked.

"I think we do, and I will be with the ADA tomorrow," Cummings said.

The next day, Cummings was in front of a young ADA named Donna Mitchner. He didn't want to blow his cover as a career curmudgeon, but he really liked her. She reminded him of the two-time Academy Award winner whose name escaped him, but he knew she had played Amelia Earhart. Donna had that same overbite and expressive eyes, but he'd seen those eyes turn to green cords of steel when confronting a felon in court. Truth be told, Captain Cummings was just a little bit intimidated by her, but you couldn't tell that from his opening line.

"I've got another lay down for you, Counselor. If you don't make district attorney, don't blame it on me. I've done all I can in giving you cases that Little Girl Blue could prosecute."

"I don't mean to be crude, Alan, but blow it out your ass. The last time you extended a hand to help somebody, Jimmy Carter was a peanut farmer that nobody ever heard of," Mitchner said.

"And I wish it had stayed that way," Cummings said with a smile.

"We finally agree on something," Donna said. "Tell me about this marvy case that will rocket me to fame and fortune."

"It's the East Side murder of a prominent businessman, Alex Santone, the CEO of Food Basket stores. Shot twice in the back of the head with a .38 pistol. No sign of forced entry, no weapon, no shells, nobody home."

"This is sounding as airtight as a bunch of squirrels in an open laundry bag," Donna said.

"Hold your horses. I'm getting to that part," the captain said. "The lady of the hour left a letter on her bureau to a lover telling him how much she loved him and what a jerk her husband was."

"That's going to be an issue," Donna said. "The other side is going to claim we needed a search warrant to secure the letter."

"Bullshit," he replied. "For Christ's sake, it was an active crime scene."

"What else have you got?"

"We went to the address on the letter, the home of one Bruno Jethroe, with a search warrant and found the handgun that killed Alex Santone," Cummings said.

"And this Bruno Jethroe, he's in custody?" she asked.

"He's in the wind," Cummings replied.

"Great," she responded. "You didn't come all the way up here to make yourself look foolish, Alan. What do you want?"

"Easy for you. I need you to go to the judge and obtain a wire-tap on Mrs. Santone's phone. I'm betting money she is corresponding with Mr. Jethroe, and if she is, we will be able to track him down."

"Let me have the letter," Donna said matter-of-factly. She read it for what seemed a very long time and turned to Cummings. "Pretty thin gruel, Cummings, but I'll run it up the flagpole with Judge Bascomb. After all, he's a legman."

Cummings got up to leave, sniffed, and said, "Wear something short."

CHAPTER 11

The Great Wallenda

As I drove up my driveway after the meeting with the Food Basket board, I reflected objectively about how I had approached the board. In the clear light of day, I had to ask myself if I would have hired me. Absolutely not. It was not dissimilar to hiring a czar, maybe a potentate of some ancient civilization. I thoroughly pissed off the CFO, Joe Snyder, tried to give Jim Sneed two jobs he hadn't asked for, and asked the board of directors, my potential bosses, to stand out of the way and rubber-stamp any half-assed plan that I might endorse.

"How did it go?" Holly asked.

"Terrific. I think I had them eating out of my hand," I said with conviction.

"That's good. I was afraid it would be an unmitigated disaster because you actually never interviewed for a job in your life," Holly said.

"Once you've ridden a bike," I said.

"Russ, in this example, you never rode a bike. *Comprendez?*" Holly asked.

"Got it," I said. "Maybe not terrific. They may have been eating my hand instead of eating out of it. But the good news is that somebody else will get the job, and our food brokerage company likely will prosper."

"That bad?" Holly asked.

"Yeah, it was bad. But if I had been picked for the job working with Garth Brewster, it would have been fun. He runs a chain of discount drugstores, and I think he would be a terrific resource and friend."

"Tell me the dirt about the murder. Did you find anything out that isn't in the paper?" Holly asked.

"No, but I saw Lucy Santone, the wife of the late Alex Santone, as she tried to bust into the directors' meeting," I said.

"Let this be a lesson to you, Russ. This is the important stuff. What's she like?"

"Arresting. Really. I can see why the old man threw in the towel at Food Basket and chased her until she let him catch her."

"What did she look like?" Holly asked.

"All cats are gray at night," I responded.

"Russ?" Holly asked in a slightly higher octave than usual.

"The entire board was staring at one part of her anatomy," I responded.

"Her butt?" Holly asked.

"Right," I responded.

"Disgusting," Holly replied.

"I'm sure we will do better next time," I said.

"Next time?" Holly said, not unkindly. "Let me see if I can summarize your interview. You failed in spectacular fashion to get a job where you were the only viable candidate left."

"Now that you put it that way," I said, "bingo."

"You know what else?" she asked. "I'd bet good money that you did exactly the right thing."

"Huh? I'm not following this very well," I responded.

"Thirty years in business with a firm that did things the right way. Some sixth sense was telling you that something was rotten in Denmark," Holly said. "Further, my gut tells me that you haven't heard the last of Bob Santone and Food Basket."

"I've got Arnold Cable coming in tomorrow, and if I know him, he will have the lowdown on this opportunity," I said. "I know one thing that bothered me was the very elaborate directors' meeting room. The business is flat on its ass, and their workplace resembled the Taj Mahal. Makes me wonder what else I would have found if I had turned over a few more rocks."

"Think about it, Russ," Holly said. "This whole thing is riding on Bob Santone's shoulders. He came after you because, as Jim Sneed would say, you were translatable. You have been there and done that. Now we will see if he actually was convinced you were the answer or not."

"I think you are right. Bob is not going to get any help from the executive committee because it's a split vote. Joe Snyder, the CFO, is going to vote nay, and Garth Brewster is going to vote yea," I said.

"Juicy," Holly said. "If I were Santone, I'd turn to the executive search guy for an opinion. Where does he stand?"

"Not an easy decision for Jim Sneed. He told me in an earlier conversation that when you place people at this level, if that person fails, he owes the client another candidate for free," I said.

"Interesting," Holly said. "That certainly makes the cheese more binding!"

* * *

The next morning, Arnold Cable appeared in my office at the appointed time, and I was startled at his appearance. He was tan, had lost twenty pounds, and he was entirely too genial.

"Holy mackerel, Arnold, you look terrific! What fat farm did you go to?" I asked.

"And a hearty good morning to you, sir," Arnold replied.

"Man, you are way too jovial. How are we going to get you back in shape? I need that white pasty look that only a fluorescent light can paint. I need the grumpy, almost incoherent Cable who came in twenty pounds heavier and is as mean as a rattlesnake. I need the Arnold Cable who steals his mother-in-law's social security check out of the mailbox and spends it on the ponies."

In truth, Arnold was everyman. If he were wanted for a felony, he would not be captured by the description witnesses would render of him. He was of average height, average weight, somewhere between thirty-five to fifty years old with no visible scars or birthmarks.

"Of all people, you should know the world is spinning in a different direction now. There are more single people than married, the 1 percent crowd is taking a drubbing, Buffett pays less taxes than his secretary, Buddy Cianci is a radio megastar, Chinese financials are taking on water big time, and a New England Patriots tight end's actions put Whitey Bulger below the fold. Most importantly, it's amazing what a little exercise and vitamin D can do to change your appearance. But don't worry, Russ, that's all on the exterior. Inside I'm still the diabolic, idiot savant you used to know," Arnold concluded.

"Thank goodness," I said. "Let me get Hartman in here and talk some shop."

Hartman rumbled in, looked at Cable, and said, "Where did the other half of your body go? From Fatty Arbuckle to Slim Pickens. You make Al Roker look like Humphrey Pennyworth," Hartman said.

"I'm telling you guys, retirement is the ticket. Every day is Saturday," Cable said. "And frankly, both you guys look a little shopworn."

"Who wants to start?" Hartman said.

"I will," I said. "Early warning—this entire conversation could totally be academic. I'm pretty sure I talked my way out of the CEO job at Food Basket, even though I was the only viable candidate still standing."

"Jesus," Hartman said, "even the Great Wallendas can't match that feat."

"Let's put together what we have anyway," Cable said. "My friends say you two guys were the only people being considered for the job once the third candidate apparently self-destructed faster than a tape recording on the old *Mission Impossible* shows."

"Arnold, amazing. I know from talking to the horse's mouth that your information is 100 percent accurate. Carry on!" I said.

"This is from my Lawyers Weekly group, and they are generally on top of things. First, Food Basket is in worse financial shape than most people think. They may have to start selling off assets just to make payroll. Alex Santone was spending money like a drunken sailor, and the people looking after the books had to know about it," Cable said.

"Russ, that matches up with what I learned," Hartman agreed. "You asked me to check with my old company to see if Food Basket is paying their bills. They are paying but trying to extend the float. They are writing a check from Providence and sending it on a slow boat to China to a bank on the West Coast, hoping to get some float while it's traveling but at the same time using the date on the check to try to con the manufacturer into giving them the standard 2 percent discount for paying within ten days. Most manufacturers have told Food Basket that they no longer are eligible for the 2 percent discount because of tardy payments."

"That makes all the sense in the world," I said. "At my interview, Garth Brewster mentioned that the chain was no longer obtaining the bank's best rate."

"I can tell you," Hartman said, "word spreads fast in the manufacturing credit departments. It doesn't take long before the major players are aligned and preparing for the worst from a shaky customer."

"One other thing," Cable said. "This is a situation that organized crime loves. We have no indication, none whatsoever, that Food Basket has reached out to this element, but if they do, the vig will bury them."

"Vig?" I said.

"Vig," Cable said. "Where have you been? The interest charged by loan sharks is enormous."

"What else, Arnold?" I asked.

"This is on the down low," he said.

"Down low?" Hartman said.

"Were both you guys choirboys?" Arnold asked. "You know, the QT."

"Okay, Arnold," I said. "But how did you learn all this lingo?"

"I grew up in Providence. Grade school kids were collecting vig—usually it was my lunch money!" Arnold said.

"Got it," Hartman said. "But what was it you said was on the down low?"

"Lucy Santone and her lover are about to be indicted. That news is pretty widespread, but my question is, Does this start a run on the stock and send the whole organization to the crapper?"

"Any good news?" I asked.

"Sure. You didn't get the job!" Arnold replied.

CHAPTER 12

Putting the Heat On

Captain Cummings was walking down a long hallway in the federal building to assistant district attorney Donna Mitchner's office with his figurative fingers and toes crossed. He needed the wiretap warrant badly, or what looked like a case with a steel lock on it would disintegrate into a batch of "he said, she said" scenarios. That was never good business in his line of work, where fact was a necessity, and innuendo was a wind only a precious few could see.

As he turned the corner, he was greeted by ADA Mitchner, who said, "Here he comes now, Garbage Pail O'Brien looking for any scraps of evidence that will bring home the bacon!"

"I think I'm following your refuse to a prime porterhouse metaphor, but I'm counting on you, Ms. Mitchner, to be delivering the goods by sinking the eight ball in the corner pocket."

"This is your lucky day, Captain. I have your wiretap permits, and I am hopeful of finding our lost perpetrator. You've got two weeks, Captain. Make them count," she said.

"I don't want to seem ungrateful, but I need more time," he said.

"C'mon, man," she said somewhat exasperatedly. "Show me something compelling from these two weeks and I'll go to bat for you."

"Okay, Counselor," Cummings said. "I know you had a tough sell job on this one, and you came through like a champ."

"Wow, I never saw this side of you before, Captain," Donna Mitchner said. "I appreciate it, and further, if these wiretaps turn out to be critical to the case, I may have to take you out to dinner."

"Best offer I've had today, Donna," he said. "But it's early!"

"Hit the road, Cummings. You came so close to actually being gracious, and right at the last minute, you blew it."

"Story of my life. The taps will be installed by tonight, so tomorrow will be day 1," he said as he left her office.

Cummings had done his homework in advance. He called O'Malley and told him to call communications and fire up the wiretaps. O'Malley had three teams working around-the-clock ready to report any and all conversations germane to the case.

Just before he was to hang up, he said to O'Malley, "Pick up our suspect this afternoon and bring her in for questioning."

"Boss, you're going to blow the whole thing and put her on alert," O'Malley said.

"That's the idea, O'Malley," Cummings said patiently.

"I don't get it," O'Malley persisted.

"Unless we insert a little motivating panic, all we're going to get are conversations about the newest recipes," Cummings said.

＊　＊　＊

Lucy Santone appeared at Cummings's office at two o'clock accompanied by Detective O'Malley. She was stunningly beautiful, but Cummings felt she had a hard edge. She wasn't the slightest bit intimidated, and before the interview began, Cummings felt that he may have overplayed his hand. Her red hair was shoulder length, and her clothes fit impeccably on a slim but strong figure. She was not heavily made up, and her posture seemed more in line with a military background rather than a civilian pursuit. She towered over O'Malley, and when Cummings stood to greet her, she was looking him squarely in the eyes.

"Thank you for coming down this afternoon," Cummings said. "I want to first express my condolences for your loss."

"Thank you, Captain," she said. "But I don't understand why I am here, and why did Detective O'Malley have to Mirandize me?"

"It's only routine, Mrs. Santone," Cummings said. "You are not currently a suspect, but in all candor, you are a person of interest."

"Oh I see," Santone said. "Should I have my attorney present?"

"Entirely up to you," Cummings responded.

"Well, I'm here. So let's get started. If at any time I become uncomfortable, I'm assuming I'll be free to go."

"Absolutely," Cummings said. "My questions all revolve around a man named Bruno Jethroe."

Something in her body language made him think he'd struck a nerve.

"Who?" she asked.

"Bruno Jethroe," he said. "He's a bartender with a mostly petty crime rap sheet who we think may have been involved in your husband's death."

"Oh yes, I think I know who you mean. He's the bartender at a watering hole that my husband and I used to frequent," Lucy said.

"Well, don't take any chances with this man, Mrs. Santone," Cummings said. "We think he's armed, dangerous, and may be on the run. If he harmed your husband, you could be next. If he contacts you, I will expect you to notify me immediately."

"Of course, Captain Cummings," she said. "I don't expect this Jethroe person will contact me, but I will certainly let you know."

"Again, thank you for coming in," he said as he stood up, indicating that the interview was over.

O'Malley led her back out of the building, secured a ride for her, returned to Cummings's office, and asked, "How did it go?"

"I'm not sure. She doesn't scare easy. She's got a hard edge to those soft curves," Cummings said.

"Time will tell," O'Malley said.

"That's what we don't have a lot of," Cummings said. "Time is our enemy. I'm hopeful this little chat put her on the speed dial to Bruno."

CHAPTER 13

You Can't Be Serious!

A week had passed since I had my interview with the decision makers at Food Basket. Things were returning to normal at our food brokerage, and for the first time, I really appreciated how well things ran at our shop. The only person who seemed disappointed by the deafening silence was Holly. I think she thought I was growing a little complacent and that a good tug-of-war in the mud would stir up my creative juices. I was somehow ambivalent, but I think the enormity of the task was intimidating to me. I knew I'd have to go to Trip Galetti and beg him for help from Shirley Macober in his buying department and David Pondorf in distribution. I could lean on Holly for financials, but I needed Galetti's CFO, Dave Williams, to tell me about cash flow, internal costs, and, most particularly, if there were any games afoot that were siphoning off money that wasn't in the count.

In the middle of this daydream, my secretary buzzed me and told me that Jim Sneed was on the phone.

I picked up the phone and said, "Jim, my main man, I hope you are not hunting for other candidates gratis because one of your choices dropped a grenade on the conference table."

Sneed laughed and said, "It wasn't quite as loud as a grenade, but you sure made an impression. And I've got a new role for you."

"Have anything to do with driving a bulldozer through the interview process?" I asked.

"Indeed it does," Sneed responded. "If I think one of my clients is looking in the wrong place, I'm loading you up with ammo and sending you in to capture their attention."

"I can do that job!" I said.

"Believe me, I know. That was the goddamnest interview I have ever seen. It was classic role reversal. They became the interviewees, and you were running the show. Man, I wish I had it on tape."

"I think I learned that from Hartman," I said. "He's a bit more polite than I, but we are both at the point in our so-called careers that we are going to give our version of the truth with the bark off."

"Bark off, bark off!" Sneed snorted. "The bark was gone, the limbs were off, and the tree was being ground up for sawdust."

"Sorry about that. I blame it on Hartman, and the CFO, Joe Snyder, was irritating, to put it mildly. But that was counterbalanced by Garth Brewster. He was aces. Who is your next candidate?" I asked.

"You," said Sneed.

"Me?" I replied. "As Johnny McEnroe would proclaim, you can't be serious!"

"Dead serious," Sneed said.

"Those guys are really bright, or they are the dumbest people on earth," I said almost to myself.

"Some of each," Sneed said, not identifying who was which. "But all of them thought you were a man of conviction, a straight shooter, and have the experience to take them to their version of the promised land."

"Even my main man, Joe Snyder?" I asked.

"Even Snyder," said Sneed. "He joined the posse a little reluctantly, but frankly, Garth Brewster threatened to walk if you weren't offered the job, and that prompted Bob Santone to line up in your column."

"The terms?" I asked.

"Exactly what you asked for, except they sweetened the deal by offering you options at half of the stock price today, $5.50 per share, and doubled your potential take to $6,000,000."

"There doesn't look like any way I can squirm out of this one. When are they expecting an answer?" I asked.

"Yesterday," Sneed replied.

"Where do you line up on this move?" I asked.

"Right behind you," Sneed answered. "Part of the deal was that I would accept a role to bring best practices to management and undertake the dreaded R word: *restructure*."

I said, "Welcome aboard. We really need your help from the intelligence I have gathered."

"Thanks, Russ. I'm really looking forward to working with you. I think you might be just crazy enough to pull this off," Sneed said. "And I want to be along for the ride. If it's okay with you, we will meet at my office the day after tomorrow and finalize the terms of the contract. Who will be your representative to eyeball the legal mumbo jumbo?"

"Holly," I responded, "one of the few agents that gets 100 percent of her client's take."

"Amen to that," Sneed said. "My wife is the CFO of my company, and I'm on a very strict stipend."

"As it should be," I said. "Some would say the leash was a little tight, but speaking for myself, I really thrive under Holly's supervision, especially with the Food Basket job. That's going to take 100 percent of my focus and time for the next year."

"Good talking with you, Russ," Jim Sneed said. "I'll see you the day after tomorrow at my place, okay?"

"I'll be there," I said and hung up the phone.

*   *   *

Later in the day, I called Holly at work and asked her if she could meet me at Anthony's Pier 4 for dinner. It was one of our favorite places because we had our first date there, and I think we both knew at the time that we were going to forge a long-term relationship. I arrived five minutes before her and was at a table facing out toward the harbor. Suddenly she appeared, searched the rather sizeable room, and found me immediately.

I know that I'm somewhat prejudiced after almost twenty years of marriage to this woman, but I saw other heads turning to look at her as she moved toward our table. She was in a blue pinstriped skirt, vanilla blouse, and matching jacket beautifully tailored, and the only thing I could think of was that the manufacturer should be paying her big money for advertising its wares in such a spectacular fashion.

I stood up, kissed her, and said, "Hello, sailor, I've really been missing you!"

For some reason, this greeting really cracked her up.

"Nicest thing anyone has said to me all day by a long shot," Holly said. "What a great idea to have dinner together, especially here."

"I'm glad you like it. I just wanted to let you know that just about every customer in this room watched you walk over to this table."

Holly actually blushed.

"Why? Is my slip showing or what?" she asked.

"No," I said with a big smile, "it's because you are a striking woman with a presence, a buzz, if you will. Maybe like a movie star or a big-shot politico."

"Oh, Russ, I'm happy being your movie star."

The waiter delivered drinks that I had ordered prior to Holly's arrival, and we clinked glasses and took a quick peek at the menu.

"What's the occasion?" Holly asked. "I'm thinking Food Basket is the subject because it isn't our anniversary or one of our birthdays."

"Good guess. They are going to offer me the job at Jim's office day after tomorrow. They, in effect, doubled my asking price, so this time I need to leave the building with the job in hand," I said.

"How are you going to do that?" she asked with a huge smile on her face.

"I'm taking you with me!" I proclaimed.

"Brilliant stroke," Holly said. "Believe you me, you're leaving with that job, even if I have to convince Warren Buffet to buy Food Basket lock, stock, and barrel and fire the current management team."

"We are going to do that with or without Buffet," I said.

"Seriously?" Holly asked.

"Dead on the level. Sneed is researching best practices, but having the board sitting around while Alex Santone ran the place into the ground doesn't bode well for them," I said.

We ordered dinner and another drink and switched gears to Holly's work.

"I see a couple of lines in the forehead of that beautiful face," I said.

"Oh boy, the company gave me a good working over this time," she said. "They gave me a new fund to run."

"But that's good, right?" I asked.

"Well, kind of," she said. "I'd describe it as a fund for tree huggers, all things green, and lips that don't cotton to alcohol or smokes of any kind."

"What's left," I asked, "water?"

"Not if it's in plastic bottles."

"Sounds rough, but that's why they gave it to you," I said.

We then covered kids, parents, and animals and rounded back to the Food Basket issue.

"Have you got ideas forming in that pointed little head of yours?" Holly asked.

"It happens I do," I said. "But I'm going to have to be more clever by half now versus my job with Galetti. I don't have the muscle of, say, a chain like Wegmans."

"What do you mean?" Holly asked.

"Well, I saw Wegmans plunk down a store in the middle of their sharpest competitor, which has five stores within driving range."

"Sounds suicidal," Holly said. "Five against one. That doesn't seem like a fair fight."

"It wasn't fair…for the competitor," I said.

"I don't get it," Holly said.

"Well, the Wegmans store opened and did a fabulous business, and the net result was that the five profitable stores of the competitor began to lose money, Custer's Last Stand in reverse."

"Unbelievable. But you can't use this example for Food Basket because you said you didn't have the muscle to pull it off," Holly said.

"True," I continued, "unless I have a special circumstance or location. For instance, I recently read that Star Market and Shaws are closing down in New Bedford, Fall River, and Taunton. If I could find the right location, I might be able to build a megastore where competition may have gone to sleep.

"I'll need your help as well. Financially, what does our house need to look like to get banks to loan us money at a favorable rate? We need money to make money. We need to be aggressive in pricing, and it's going to be expensive. We are just not competitive."

"I'll get on it," Holly said. "Another good source of money would be Bob Santone. He's a money manager, and Cerberus Capital Management, a hedge fund, just purchased Albertsons, Jewel, Costco, Acme, Shaws, and Star Market from SuperValu."

"I knew I took you to dinner for a good reason," I said. "Great idea!"

"Next time you invite me to dinner, I'll book us a room at the Four Seasons," Holly said.

"I can't top that!"

CHAPTER 14

Law Enforcement Romance?

Cummings was in his office when Detective O'Malley burst in waving a disc. Beads of sweat were apparent on his forehead, and his face was so red that Captain Cummings thought O'Malley might have a seizure any minute.

"Grab a seat, O'Malley, and take a load off the floor. You look like you are going to have a stroke," Cummings said not unkindly.

"If I do, Chief, I'll go out a happy man," O'Malley said. "I've got a tape here you need to listen to from the afternoon of the second day of the wiretap."

"Has it got a good recipe for Indian pudding?" Cummings asked with a smile on his face.

"It's got a recipe for perjury and conspiracy to murder," O'Malley said.

"Let it rip," Cummings said.

O'Malley put the disc in the CD player, and they heard the following:

WOMAN'S VOICE. Baby, I miss you.

MAN'S VOICE. I had to hit the road. I came home, and there were three cops rifling through my apartment.

WOMAN'S VOICE. How did you know they were cops?

MAN'S VOICE. How does a fox know he's in a henhouse?

WOMAN'S VOICE. Right on with that, my little elusive chickadee. The police had me on the carpet the other day, and you were the person of interest they were looking for.

MAN'S VOICE. They think I killed your husband?

WOMAN'S VOICE. I think so. They said you were armed and dangerous and that you wanted to do me bodily harm.

MAN'S VOICE. They got that half right.

WOMAN'S VOICE. What do you mean "half right"?

MAN'S VOICE. I want your body badly, and I want to stick my tongue where it doesn't belong.

WOMAN'S VOICE. Oh, Bruno, cut it out. You know what happens when we have phone sex. We need to think about your continued freedom right now. Do you need money?

MAN'S VOICE. I do. Wire it to me in the next hour because I'm on the move.

WOMAN'S VOICE. Will do, sweet cheeks. Love you. Bye.

Cummings just sat for a minute, and then had O'Malley replay it for him from the beginning.

Then he said, "Good work, O'Malley. Keep me updated. I think we clearly have potential perjury here, but the conspiracy to murder is too thin. It almost sounded to me as if Bruno was surprised that we wanted him for murder."

"Yeah, but, Captain, if that was the case, why is he on the lam?"

"Because he is a lifetime chronic criminal. He obviously knows that his lover's husband has been murdered, and he knows we aren't tossing his place looking for stolen Girl Scout cookies," Cummings said.

"Okay, I guess," O'Malley said. "But I think you are seeing a suspect behind every tree. We got this guy stone-cold, hundred proof, for the murder of Alex Santone."

"Okay, let's say you are right, O'Malley. Where is our dead bang suspect? Do we have him in cuffs?"

"Ah, not exactly, Chief. We traced the call to the west coast of Florida, but by the time the local gendarmes arrived, Bruno was gone and so was his luggage."

"Damn. Okay, let's get to work on the money trail. Run down how Lucy Santone wired money and the whole nine yards. Also, get a picture of Bruno Jethroe to the closest airport and let's see if anybody recognizes him. I'll be with my favorite assistant district attorney."

Later that same day, Cummings was trudging down the long hallway to Donna Mitchner's office.

She greeted him by saying, "Hey, Alan, want to fight crime?"

"I'd rather take you out and dance the night away," Cummings responded.

"Shocker. Are you still on your meds?" she asked.

"No, do I have to be on my meds to ask a beautiful woman out?" Cummings asked.

"I guess not. But this is certainly a 180-degree turn from the hard-driving police captain that I've come to know," Donna said.

"I was just trying to make up for that faux pas when we last met where it seemed I wasn't grateful to be asked out for dinner," he said.

"Well, I need a little time to consider the new Alan Cummings. But I will say my initial impression is good," she said. "What have you got for me on the Santone case?"

"Some interesting stuff from the widow Santone."

Cummings played the conversation for Donna Mitchner in its entirety. Mitchner was rubbing her head just above her ears as if this process would reveal some profound truth.

Finally, she said, "It's a promising start. She's definitely heading for perjury, but we don't have much else. Let's keep digging. Have you picked up Bruno Jethroe?"

"No, we traced the call to Florida, called the local cops, but by the time they arrived at his motel, he was long gone," Cummings said.

"Okay, let's get this guy," she said.

Cummings rose to leave and had just reached her door when she said, "Alan, if you're not busy, be at my house at seven thirty on Saturday."

"Where do you live?" Cummings asked.

"You're a cop. You figure it out," she responded.

CHAPTER 15

Rock Bottom

We were cruising down Route 95 on the way to Jim Sneed's office in hopes of having an offer extended to become CEO of Food Basket Supermarkets. I'd had a dress rehearsal for this position and walked away without an offer in spite of being the only candidate left standing. But this was different. This time I had my agent, financial advisor, and oh, yes, the love of my life, Holly, sitting right next to me. She looked totally stunning in an off-green/celadon business suit, and only I in this group we were about to meet knew that she could be tougher than a saltwater crocodile at dinnertime.

I looked over at her and said, "I have to tell you that you look fabulous. Also, thank you for making this trip with me. I know things are hectic at work right now."

"You're welcome, Russ. By the way, you look pretty sharp yourself. What is the mood of this group?"

"According to our manager, Sneed, they have agreed, if not unanimously, that I'm their guy for the job. They are understandably jittery because everyone except the CFO knows that the clock is ticking and that their current downward trend needs to be reversed."

"Does the CFO have his head in the sand?" she asked.

"I think his head is somewhere else, but I can't mention where in front of mixed company," I said.

"Any other obstacles?" Holly asked.

"Not really, other than they need to climb off the mat and fight back. I quote Mike Tyson, who once said, 'Everybody has a plan until they get punched in the face.' We need to punch the competitors in the face."

"I was always a fan of Iron Mike," Holly said. "This could be a lot of fun."

With the aid of our GPS, we arrived at Sneed's office fifteen minutes ahead of time. We walked into one of the most elegant offices I'd ever been in—beautiful marble floors, antique touches everywhere, exquisite handmade furniture, and some of the most tasteful oriental rugs I had ever witnessed. To hell with the CEO job—I was going to ask Jim if I could have an office in his building!

At that point, Holly whispered to me, "Jesus, all of a sudden the stuff in our house looks like it came from Goodwill."

"Don't fall for it. The idea is to try to intimidate you before you even arrive at a conference room."

"Tell him it's working," Holly said.

Just at that moment, Jim Sneed rounded the corner and said to Holly, "What do you think of the joint?"

Holly responded by saying, "Good morning, Jim, very nice to meet you. To answer your question, I feel as if I've had a sneak preview of Buckingham Palace."

"We're delighted you are here. Not to denigrate Russ, but having you here is a huge benefit," Jim said.

"Why?" Holly asked, blushing ever so slightly.

"Well, you may know who Bob Santone is. He's in a related business to your profession, and he says you are one of the best and most respected portfolio managers in the business. Privately, he thinks he's getting a twofer with you in this equation."

"Should I just wait out in the lobby until this meeting is adjourned?" I asked in mock horror.

Jim and Holly laughed, and Jim steered us toward the conference room.

Holly whispered to Jim, "Is Lucy Santone going to make an appearance?"

"I really want to say no way, but her G-2 is really good, so I guess I'd say it's not on the schedule, but stranger things have happened."

The door to the conference room swung open, and the Food Basket group stood to welcome us.

Garth Brewster moved quickly to Holly to greet her as he said, "How did a big oaf like Russ land a beauty like you? I'm Garth Brewster, your friendly drug maven—er—drugstore maven."

"Charmed, I'm sure, Mr. Brewster. And I think my husband was quite off base in what he said about you," she said.

"Oh, and just what did the bohunk say about me?" Brewster asked.

"He said you were rude, crude, and socially unacceptable while at the same time feeling that you would be a major player in breathing air back into this corporation," she said.

"I hope I can live up to that reputation on both counts," Brewster said with a big smile.

Bob Santone made his way over to where Holly and Garth were standing and said, "Welcome, Mrs. Riley. We are pleased to have you here."

"Thanks, Bob. Please call me Holly. Actually, I'm excited to be here, and I know Russ is as well."

"I'm a real fan of yours. I heard you speak at a seminar on the subject of the supermarket industry. I thought it was special for two reasons: the first was you made the complex simple to understand, and secondly you told it to us straight up!" Santone said.

"What did I say that so impressed you?" she asked.

"Well, in an industry you were covering for your company, you told us there wasn't a single stock in the industry that you could recommend."

"In that case, I hope my boss wasn't there. I also know what you do generally, but I think you go to great lengths not to let portfolio managers know exactly what you are doing," Holly said. "A pleasure to meet you, Bob."

As the group milled around, Garth started the proceedings off by saying, "Let's sit in a mixed group, alternate feed, if you will, so one grenade can't take out all of one side or the other."

I thought that was a great opener, and I sat next to Joe Snyder, the CFO, with Garth Brewster on my other side.

Bob Santone opened the meeting officially when he said, "Welcome to the second try of offering Russell Riley the job of CEO of Food Basket. I think we should all consider the first attempt as a dress rehearsal."

A fun and informed comment. What tension was in the room dissipated, and we all felt ready to proceed.

"Besides Jim Sneed, who I think we all know, it's my pleasure and honor to introduce Holly Riley, Russ's wife, and a business-woman of distinction in her own right. She has managed one fund for almost twenty years, and it was the first fund to break a billion dollars at her company. Additionally, she is on the board of a savings bank in Sudbury, Massachusetts. I mention this because, not coinci-dentally, this bank has the best return rate of any bank in the state."

Spontaneous applause from the group made my bride blush ever so slightly as she said, "Of course I was only twelve years old when I started the aforementioned fund."

More applause and laughter as Bob quickly moved to the busi-ness of the day.

"Russ, we need you to take this job of CEO at Food Basket. Earnestly, we are heading in the wrong direction. We've taken to heart what you told us when we last met. We have looked at our needs, and we believe you are the person to fix them. Further, we know you are starting out in a deeper hole than when you took over Galetti during the court case. But I will tell you this, you have our commitment to turn this ship around. We know it won't be easy. Joe Snyder will tell you that this quarter's results could have a negative effect, but I'm of the mind that we should get all the bad news on the table instead of leaking it out one day at a time. Joe, what's it look like?"

Joe Snyder cleared his throat, stood up, and began to speak.

"It's a train wreck. The train hopped off the tracks and took a dirt road to the end of the line."

"Don't sugarcoat it, Joe," Garth said. "We can take it."

I laughed at Garth. I could tell this was the moment he was waiting for—rock bottom. Check the bullshit at the door because survival was a way better position than we were in now. But I think it was Garth's intent all along that we had to touch the bottom with a resounding thud to clear our heads and move Food Basket back to its status as a market leader.

As Joe continued to speak, I noticed that his voice started to move lower, almost to a whisper.

"We missed our volume target by 50 percent and our profit numbers by more than half. And more bad news—the next quarter may be the worst we have experienced in the last decade."

I almost felt sorry for Joe Snyder. He had a boss who was an absentee owner, and his bean-counting background didn't seem to offer up any leadership that would have pulled this operation out of the quagmire.

Just when I was feeling some empathy for this fellow, he said, "I just seem like a third wheel here. I think it would be appropriate for me to resign as CFO at this point. I'm greatly disappointed, frankly, that the corporation didn't look internally for a CEO. I think at the very least I warranted an interview for the position."

I looked at Sneed and Brewster as I thought to myself, "Holy shit, this guy is a disappointed office seeker for the CEO position!" I didn't see this one coming, but I didn't feel that badly as I could see by the expressions on the faces of Jim and Garth that they were caught flatfooted as well.

Bob and Holly seemed less surprised, and Bob addressed the issue immediately.

"Joe, I'm sorry you felt slighted. It certainly was not our intention. After this meeting, I will do my best to talk you out of resigning. But there's a chance I won't be able to do that, so I'm going to have to ask you to leave this meeting. I'll meet with you face-to-face tomorrow. Understood?"

Joe Snyder didn't say a word as he rose, gathered his briefcase and papers together, and left the room.

As the door closed, Bob Santone said, "Let's take a fifteen-minute break."

As we all exited the room to use the facilities and check phone messages, I couldn't help thinking that this session of "Russ tries to accept a job" was more bizarre than the first meeting. Having Lucy Santone come to the first one kept that meeting ahead in the bizarre circumstances category, but this meeting still wasn't over.

Holly sidled up to me and said, "That was entirely predictable. And it's my fondest hope that Mr. Snyder isn't leaving with a satchel of the company's money."

"Remind me not to try and hock any of the good silverware at home!" I said.

"Russ, you guys are always talking about plans leaking oil as they head to the stretch lap. This place is leaking money. Seriously, in the not-too-distant future, I'd have a big six—maybe it's big three now—accounting firm start counting the shekels."

Before I could respond, Garth joined us and said, "Snyder's resignation is not further bad news—it's good news. He couldn't find his ass in a sealed closet with both hands."

I laughed right out loud at Garth Brewster's comment and thought I should put Hartman with this guy and get out of the way. Finesse wasn't high on their report card, but straight-ahead reasoning, experience, and the ability to take a risk were way up near the top of their skill sets.

Jim Sneed came by, looked at me, and said, "Wherever you go, boy, you leave a trail of bodies!"

"Wait a minute, Jim. You can't blame me for this. I'm not on the payroll yet!"

We both laughed.

Bob Santone signaled for us to join him for a little chat.

"What do you guys think I should do about Joe Snyder?"

I looked to Jim, and he said, "It depends on how well you think he is doing at his job. He's put ten years in, so you must have some paper on him. Performance reviews should give you some data. But frankly, your job is compounded because he's an unhappy office seeker, and his attitude appears to be bad going to worse."

"Russ," Bob said, looking at me.

"I'd like to know if we have a candidate internally who we feel can take Joe's spot. If we do, I'd let him resign and give him a year's salary in severance."

"Okay. Thanks for the guidance," Bob said. "I'll take it under advisement. Let's get back to the meeting."

Bob introduced me as the new CEO and handed my contract to Holly. He followed that by telling us that Jim Sneed was officially on board to link us up with the best practices in the industry and to restructure the organization so that we could be competitive on a cost basis.

Finally Bob said, "I'd like to turn it over to Russ to hear his thoughts on the future of Food Basket."

"Thank you, Bob. I'm pleased, honored to be named the CEO of Food Basket, a company that has stood for delivering groceries to the consumer at a fair price. But for the last few years, we have been marching in place while others have made steady progress. Folks, we are not retro, we are old: old stores, old consumers, old employees, and most importantly, old ideas. And you think, 'What the hell, we will survive.' That's what Bohack thought. Zayre, Jordan Marsh, Filene's, Brigham's, Bank of Boston, W. T. Grant, Circuit City, First National Stores, and S. S. Pierce—all gone. This isn't Wall Street. There's no guarantee of 'too big to fail.'

"Have you been in the stores lately? The competitors' stores? I don't blame you if you haven't. It's not a pretty picture. Dating on milk in our stores averages about five to six days. The competitors', fifteen to seventeen days. Loyalty cards are not working. When you receive your register tape from a competitor, the bottom of it states, 'No card needed. You saved $10.74.' We have more class action suits by our employees than any other chain that we compete against. We have paid seven million dollars in settlements to workers who claimed they were underpaid, denied overtime, or discriminated against by management. We've been fined at twice the rate of our competitors for unsanitary conditions, rodents in the backrooms, and damaged merchandise not being properly disposed of by our employees.

"And that's the good news. The bad news is that our longtime competitors that are pounding us into the pavement are being annihilated by new competition. Being a standard grocery store is just not good enough anymore—sad but true. Walmart, Costco, BJ's, CVS, and on and on. We are not even standing still, we are retrogressing.

"Here are the initial steps I think we need to take to become not only competitive, but to just maybe make the consumer focus on our stores again. Hopefully, the competition won't be quite as alert. First, Bob, we need you to come up with 250 million dollars to get the stores back in shape in both pricing and renovation areas. Garth, Food Basket wants to immediately enter negotiations to buy your drugstore chain, and you will drive our plan to put a pharmacy in as many Food Baskets as possible.

"I will head up a group of operational people and some consultants I hope to hire to close the laggard stores and to build a monster store somewhere geographically that consumers from New Bedford, Fall River, and Taunton will think of as their store.

"Additionally, we are dropping loyalty cards and setting up a price structure that does not label us as the high-price spread among supermarkets. Jim Sneed will start his restructure program with his first priority being a top-rated CFO.

"Lastly, but importantly, Bob, Jim, Garth, and I are charged with getting the word to our store management personnel as soon as possible. My guess is that Jim is the best guy to prepare that presentation. Any questions?"

"Let's kick some ass!" Garth thundered. "Oops, sorry, Holly. Let's kick some butt!"

"Jesus, Russ, what did you have for breakfast?" Bob asked.

"The competition," I responded.

"I think we could all fall on our asses," said Jim Sneed. "But I'm going to love the ride!"

"Okay, let's get to work," Bob said. "Meeting adjourned."

CHAPTER 16

Butterflies for a Tough Guy

Alan Cummings had fought in a war, chased perps down dark alleys in the worst parts of Providence as a police patrolman, and outsmarted several felons who thought all cops couldn't walk and chew gum at the same time. He had risen quickly in the system, but it had extracted a price. His marriage had fallen apart faster than you could say "Through good times and bad," and he knew it was his fault. His real-life take was that if he couldn't make it work with her, then he wasn't meant to be married. She gave and gave and gave, and he took and took and took until she didn't have anything left to give. He still was filled with guilt like a good Irish Catholic boy was trained to be. In truth, he still loved her, but he would never be able to tell Patty Walsh that. She had remarried, had two children, and found what she was looking for the second time around. He was single, thirty-six years old, a college graduate with a good-paying, if slightly precarious, job, but he wasn't on a most-eligible bachelor list anywhere.

With his background, it was understandable that he was nervous as he approached Donna Mitchner's front door on Saturday at seven thirty. Just as he was about to push the doorbell, the door flew open, and Donna gave him a kiss on the cheek and said, "Check your sidearm in the pantry and come on in!"

Cummings laughed at Donna and handed her a bouquet of flowers and a bottle of wine.

"Donna, do you think I'm Matt Dillon? I don't have my weapon on me."

"Who is Matt Dillon?" Donna asked.

"Who is Matt Dillon?" he asked incredulously. "Am I going to get in trouble if I transport you over a state line?"

It was Donna's turn to laugh.

"Not by a long shot. Thirty has come and gone, but only recently."

As he wandered through the high-ceilinged foyer, he said almost to himself, "Hey, this place is amazing. For Christ's sake, Mitchner, you could put a full-sized bowling alley in here. Look at these ceilings. They have to be eighteen feet high."

"It's called a loft, Alan," Donna said. "Some really smart person took an old warehouse by the river and converted it into loft condominiums. So instead of a warehouse that is no longer viable, it's a place people want to live."

"You know, it's odd. When you are at work, you don't think about what people you work with do every day when they aren't working—where they live, what books they read, their politics. Part of it that blurs the line is that we don't live in an eight-to-five environment. You don't lay your shovel down at five o'clock and head for home," Cummings said. "Look at you—all business suits and briefs at work, and now I'm looking at this gorgeous woman in a most-becoming short ensemble that I couldn't describe if you paid me."

"You keep this kind of chatter up and you might see my briefs, Captain," Donna said. "And you're right. It's all about prosecution, and pretty soon, if you don't watch it, you can lose your identity. What is your story, Alan? Tell me."

"Really boring. One of five children, great family environment, probably just over the poverty level to lower middle class, both parents worked when that wasn't commonplace, but they always had time for their kids. Local Providence schools, went to Boston University on a hockey scholarship, ROTC, served in Iraq, came back, applied to go to the police academy, and have been in police work ever since. If I have any perspective at all, it's coming back from Iraq and feeling so fortunate, by the grace of God, that I was born in America."

"Great perspective, Alan. It's worth a lot to me. Women, mistresses, and secret international liaisons?"

"Jesus, Mitchner, didn't you just hear what I said about work and play blurring? Am I on the stand, Ms. Assistant District Attorney?" Cummings asked.

"No, no," Donna said. "Well, maybe you can't leave work entirely. But I was just trying to follow up on your thought of who are these people away from work: politics, books they read, other interests."

"Good response," Cummings said. "Okay, one failed marriage, no mistresses, and on the international front, I dream of an affair with Sophia Loren, even if she is a hundred! No current squeezes, to quote Whitey Bulger, and recreation is golf, favorite author, Lee Child, favorite book, *Truman*, favorite TV shows *Rizzoli and Isles* and *Homeland*."

"Hey, this is fun. I'm getting a really good picture of you. To add to your profile, I would say boyishly handsome and has stayed in shape in spite of being a desk jockey," Donna said.

"C'mon, Mitchner, don't make me get the rubber hose out. Start at the beginning," he said.

"Tell me more about the rubber hose! Only kidding," she said. "I'm an only child. It never occurred to me what my social status was—maybe near the top of middle class. Went to private school, was a bit of a geek, tall and thin, apparently not attractive to boys, but that all changed in college. The boys either got taller or I filled out more. Anyway, things changed. But I wasn't ready."

"Ready for what?" Cummings asked.

"As much as a guy tried to do to you in record time. I felt like a calf at roping time. I never met a guy in college that I really fell for, so my focus was on academics, not how many guys could get between my legs. So when it happened in law school, I was ready. You could say I was overrehearsed. It was intense. I gave myself to him completely, and he returned the passion in an equal amount. We were engaged to be married, and just before the wedding, he and his bachelor buddies went rafting, and he didn't come back. He drowned, and the social part of my life ended. It's that old lyric from Crystal Gayle when she sings, 'I can go to bed alone and never know his name.'"

"Terrible story," Cummings said softly. "I knew I was a train wreck, but it was self-inflicted."

Donna stood there with tears rolling down her face and said, "Believe it or not, I feel better having told you that story. Now I know how you got your nickname."

"Nickname?" Cummings said.

"Yeah, the guys at headquarters call you Father Confessor. They swear that there were perps who wouldn't talk to anyone, and you arrive, and in an hour you have them crying like a baby and pouring out their life stories to you," Donna said.

"It's that rubber hose we talked about earlier," he said with a smile. "Can I get you a refill? I saw where you made that first round."

"Ah, observant too," Donna said. "You'd make a good cop. Oops!"

"Seriously," Cummings said. "Two things—first, thanks for sharing that story with me, and second, I'm starved. You got anything around here to eat besides these paper-thin hors d'oeuvres?"

Mitchner laughed out loud.

"Let's handle the more important of these requests—the last one. I have a shepherd's pie bubbling in the oven, and it has your name on it."

"Oh, baby, I love it when you talk dirty," Cummings said. "It happens it's one of my favorite meals in the world!"

"You fix us that drink you were bragging about, and I'll put some dinner on the table," Donna said.

"Deal," said Cummings.

Donna noticed for a big man that he moved quickly and gracefully. It must have something to do with motivation.

Dinner was a delight. Donna had a table set up in an L-shaped room just off the living room. They talked and talked like old friends about any subject under the sun. Politics were predictable: she was left; he was hard right. Religion—they were both truants. Places to live—they both loved Chicago and the West Coast and gave New York City its due. But they felt fortunate to be in the Northeast, near the water, mountains, lakes, skiing—they loved New England. The only reversal of form was that she loved sports, and he loved art galleries and museums.

Finally, it was time for Cummings to hit the road.

He said, "Donna, I can't remember when I've had a more relaxed, better time. Thank you for your hospitality, charm, and open manner. I don't usually say anything nice about the DA's office, but for you I will make an exception."

"Cummings, you have been a delight to behold. Who knew? A homicide guy who knows the theater, arts, and museums. Better not let that leak out, Alan," she said.

She walked him to his car, kissed him with surprising passion, and sent him on his way.

CHAPTER 17

Macober, Pondorf, and Williams

Now the work was beginning. No more staring out of the penthouse windows and screaming at the masses, "Let them eat cake." Okay, they could eat cake if they bought it at the Food Basket bakery. It was confusing enough suddenly moving from the seller community of Food Brokers to the buyer side of a grocery chain headquarters. Complicating that crossover was that I wasn't even sitting in the grocery chain headquarters that was paying my salary; I was in the office of Trip Galetti, the CEO of Galetti Supermarkets. The only thing that sheltered me from collusion was not a single Galetti supermarket competed with a Food Basket store. Even so, I was pretty sure that Hartman would be dialing up the FTC and turning me over for aiding and abetting the enemy.

As background, Trip and I were very close. I was thirteen years old when I joined Galetti. We both lost our dads at that age, and I think I was able to help Trip through that trauma because I had had a similar experience. He worked for me the entire time I was employed at Galetti, and he and his mother, Maria, were responsible for seeing that I was able to cash in my stock after I had left the company. We were as close as people could be without actually being related. That is the major reason I felt secure enough to ask him for something that was high risk at best.

Trip was at his desk, drinking coffee, when he said, "Russ, I've seen that look before. You're about to ask me for something that is even off the wall for you!"

"You've always had good instincts. I'd consider this request a tad bizarre," I replied. "It's short and sweet. I need to borrow Shirley Macober, Dave Pondorf, and Dave Williams for three months as consultants to Food Basket."

"The only way I can see doing it is to cut them loose and have you pick up the tariff for that period," Trip said. "That would include benefits and a stipend at the close of their employment with Food Basket."

"Stipend?" I asked.

"Bonus, you cheap bastard," Trip said. "Hey, you are turning their lives upside down and adding a sizeable commute."

"Okay, you're right," I said. "I'll give them the equivalent of six week's salary as a bonus. How do we sell this to them?"

"I can't talk to them about it, but you can tell them that I have authorized this boondoggle," Trip said.

"Trip, I owe you big time for this. This job I have is daunting, to say the least, but this could be the key to winning the uphill battle."

"Consider it payment in full for all your contributions to Galetti over the years," Trip said. "I'll have Shirley and Dave in my conference room in thirty minutes. You'll have to journey down to the warehouse to talk to Pondorf."

"Thank you, Trip," I said. "I'm heading to the conference room to think about the pitch I want to give those guys."

Shirley Macober arrived first. She didn't knock; she came through the door like Alan Ameche without the ball.

She looked at me and said, "Oh fuck, nothing good is coming out of this!"

I laughed at her terse comment and wondered to myself how Galetti found people like Shirley. She was imposing physically: about six feet tall and somewhere around 190 pounds, and she was black.

Her husband was a long-distance freight hauler, and they had no children. He was a semipro linebacker, but in arm wrestling, Shirley wins three out of five. It's not to say she wasn't feminine because she was. She was well proportioned, funny, and very wise in the ways of the world.

Before I could gather my thoughts, she was saying, "From the look of you and where you are sitting, this could be déjà vu all over again, and I'm thinking I won't see you across from my desk next Tuesday trying to sell me on one of your new items. And if it is the former and you are back as president of Galetti again, I want to extend my sincere apologies for throwing you out of my office on numerous occasions, even though you demonstrated a need for that behavior."

I had to take out my hankie and blow my nose I was laughing so hard and so was Shirley.

Just at that moment, Dave Williams entered the conference room and said, "Oh shit, not you again," which set both Shirley and me off for a second time.

I used to meet with these people all of the time when I was employed by Galetti. Shirley was the head buyer, and David was in charge of pricing and profit. I often lost control of a meeting with them but never as quickly as this. This meeting hadn't even started, and I had lost complete control. I had forgotten how much fun and how good these people were at their respective jobs.

Dave Williams was a bargain. He had the same credentials as Joe Snyder, the CFO of Food Basket. The difference was that Joe was purely a bean counter—nothing wrong with that—but Dave, who could also count the beans, tried to find a way strategically or tactically to stretch his beans to the limit to provide competitive advantage. I think his driving mantra was interest avoidance. He frowned on items that were still sitting on the shelves after he had paid the bill. He was always talking mission, vision, and strategic planning rather than moving from brush fire to brush fire. Dave was in his early forties, small, a runner's body, married, four children, even split, two boys and two girls.

I led off by saying, "I'm here because I need your help. I've been asked and accepted the CEO job at Food Basket. You may have read that their CEO was gunned down in his house, and their board of directors has asked me to put their ship back in order."

"So," Dave Williams said, "we should probably investigate the competency of the board given that dubious decision."

Shirley smiled and said, "Don't those folks know that you ran such a great promotion here during the court fight it almost got all of us fired? In fact, you did get fired."

"You guys are right on both points. In fact, the CFO has resigned from the board, and that promotion you reference, Shirley, propelled me to the unemployment line," I said. "But let's talk about you guys and your role in the next ninety days. I've talked with Trip, and he has agreed to loan you guys to me and to Food Basket for ninety days. People employed by Food Basket won't know the length of your contract. All they will know is that fresh, experienced eyes are there to improve their departments."

"Is there a noncompete?" Williams asked.

"Any rewards for turning my life upside down?" Shirley asked. "Combat pay, as it were."

"Do we start ASAP?" Williams asked.

"Can we say no? We love you, man, but not enough to check our cars every day for ticking devices," she said.

"The answers to your questions are no, yes, yes, yes, but I hope you won't. Food Basket stores do not compete with Galetti stores, you will be given a substantial stipend for this ninety-day project, we start as soon as you tie up your current projects, and you can say no to the job and walk away."

Silence.

So unlike these two to be short of words or a thought or two.

Finally, Macober looked at me and said, "I know I'm going to kick my own ass later, but I'm in."

Williams looked at me and said, "Ditto for me. I'd make one suggestion, and that is I'd sure try and get Pondorf to join the party because when Shirley and I hatch a plan, we are going to need some-one in the warehouse to execute it."

"That's my next stop," I said as I stood to shake hands with them.

"I forgot what a smart honky you are," Shirley said as she departed the conference room as if the building were on fire.

I felt really good about having those two aboard. As Food Basket started descending in volume and profit, the stores became more independent and autonomous. A weak central headquarters was not a good thing, especially since the nose of the camel, Walmart, in this example, had somehow moved from under the flap of the tent to standing squarely in the middle of it. It might be analogous to a baseball team in an extended losing streak—each of the players hoping to pull his team out of the slump, trying to do things such as hit home runs that they are not capable of producing, thus extending the streak. We had to be smart, disciplined, and creative at headquarters and outwit competition at store level because we sure weren't going to outmuscle them.

As I arrived at the warehouse, I saw Pondorf right away. It was hard to miss him; he was six feet three inches tall and weighed a tad over three hundred pounds before that second foot took a firm hold on the scale. He saw me right away and lumbered toward me with a big smile on his face. I reached out my hand to shake his, but he stepped closer to me, picked me up, and gave me a bear hug that seemed to crush some unnamed internal organ in my body.

He said, "Russ, I'm glad to see you. I never thought I'd say this, but I miss all the harassment that you shoveled my way!"

"Well, David, you know I wasn't the smartest guy in the world," I said.

"No shit," Pondorf replied immediately. "You know, if I ordered a railcar of assholes and the car arrived at the siding and you were the only thing in it, I'd think that I wasn't short shipped."

"Yeah, well, if the roles were reversed, I would have known you were the only thing in the railcar because you're too fat for anything else to fit in there," I said.

"Now that's the old douche bag—all respect intended—that I met on my first day of work. What brings you here? I can't save your items if Macober discontinues them," Pondorf said.

"Actually, I have a new job, and I'm here to recruit you," I said.

"I know you aren't too observant, but I already have a job!" he said.

"I know. I just took the job as CEO of Food Basket, and I need you to come put their distribution system back in place. It's a ninety-day assignment, but nobody knows that but us. I've got Macober, Williams, and Cable signed up, but those guys say, and I agree, that they need a fourth for them to play bridge—you."

"Management okayed this nifty plan?"

"Yes, from a distance," I said.

"Now I know why your brokerage doesn't sell pet food," Pondorf said.

"Why?" I asked.

"Your guys would eat the samples."

"You in or out, big guy?" I asked.

"What's it pay?" he asked.

"Your salary plus 50 percent," I said.

"Sign me up," Pondorf said with a big smile.

"I owe you, David, and I really hate that," I said with a laugh.

"Don't think I don't know it," he said.

"Hey, I'm ordering a burger. Let me order you one. How do you like it?"

"Boil it. I'm Irish."

CHAPTER 18

Pounding the Old
Shoe Leather

C aptain Cummings had made considerable progress on the case since last visiting Assistant District Attorney Donna Mitchner. The wiretapped phones helped trace Bruno Jethroe to Brazil, where he was captured and eventually extradited to the state of Rhode Island's judiciary system. Additionally, several calls between Lucy Santone and Jethroe had established a strong link between them.

Alan Cummings was of the "three yards and a cloud of dust" school of prosecution, and he was urging Mitchner to charge them both with murder and be done with it. But Donna Mitchner was hesitating and wanted to proceed with caution, and she was convinced that prosecuting Jethroe for the murder was a lay down, but obtaining a "guilty as charged" for Santone was not a solid bet by any means.

"Look, Alan, you're the cop, and you have gathered some excellent evidence, but we really don't have enough evidence to convict Lucy Santone of a similar charge."

"Why not?" Cummings asked somewhat exasperatedly.

"Because you have done too good of a job of proving Bruno Jethroe did it. You've got his gun as the murder weapon, he has no alibi, and he has this obvious connection to the victim's wife. As you would say, Little Bo Peep could prosecute this one."

"Okay, but you feel the evidence against Lucy Santone isn't a lock?" he asked.

"Murder is one thing, but conspiracy to murder is another. I want to set Lucy Santone up in case I'm right about her wiggling off the hook for conspiracy to murder," she said.

"Care to share?" Cummings asked.

"Sure, and I've done it before, so I feel pretty good about it working. We try Bruno Jethroe first by establishing probable cause with the judge. Then as a part of his trial, we call Lucy Santone as a witness," Donna explained.

"She's not going to testify against him," Alan said.

"That's the point, my handsome keeper of law and order. I anticipate she will lie through her teeth about her relationship with Bruno Jethroe," she said.

"All of a sudden, the light is cascading through the darkened channels of what I call my mind," he said. "Then you separately try her for conspiracy, and even if she is found not guilty of conspiracy, she has committed perjury."

"You got it," she said.

"Brilliant," he said.

"Thank you, sir," she said. "It's nothing. All in a day's work."

"You know what I like about it the most?" he said.

"What?" she responded.

"It's dirty pool, diabolical, bordering on schizophrenic behavior," Cummings said with obvious admiration. "And the irony—this devious plot is delivered by a gorgeous woman who one would think only had beautiful thoughts."

"Let that be a lesson to you," Donna said with a laugh.

"It's weighed heavily on me. Believe me, I was hoping to fool around with you this weekend, but those plans just went in the crapper."

"Pity," Mitchner said. "Story of my life. I drive away the good ones. Would you reconsider if I promise not to bring some diabolical plot down on you?"

"Your place or mine?" he asked.

"Yours," she said. "What's the address?"

"You're a lawyer who digs out the facts. I'll leave that question for your stellar and bizarre mind to solve," Cummings said.

*   *   *

Miles away from Mitchner's office, Detective O'Malley was canvassing Bruno Jethroe's neighborhood to see what he could learn about him. His immediate search for tidbits turned up some surprising evidence. A neighbor in the next building talked with Bruno fairly frequently, mainly because they both worked the same odd hours. He had told this man, Howard Anderson, that he had "popped a big-time executive from Providence." Another regular at the bar where Jethroe worked was told by Bruno that the victim's wife "better keep her mouth shut," or he would kill her. A third witness, also a regular at the bar, told O'Malley that Bruno "was about to come into some serious insurance money" and his days working at the bar were numbered.

O'Malley made arrangements for all three witnesses to sign affidavits, but it was the third witness's story that intrigued him. He called Captain Cummings and said, "I think I have a new angle—big-time insurance payout to the widow."

"Way to dig around in the muck, O'Malley. That's some good police work. Nothing like pounding the old shoe leather," Cummings said with enthusiasm. "I'm on it."

CHAPTER 19

Turning It Around Slowly

I was at home, sitting on the family room floor, playing with our lab, Mr. Jinx and Ms. Lucy. At first we thought Mr. Jinx was a boy, but it didn't take us too long to discover that he was a girl, and thus the Ms. Lucy was added. When she was in trouble, which was often, Holly called her by her formal name, but somehow the two names morphed into Juicy. Juicy was two years old, one hundred pounds, her teeth were no longer the pinpricks of a pup, she loved jumping and swimming, and she was entering what I thought was her second puppyhood. We took her to a trainer, and she performed with perfection, but when she came home, all that training rolled off her like water off a duck. But right now, she was lying right next to me in a very unladylike posture. She was lying on her back with her paws up in the air, and she was snoring loudly. I had taken her for a run and a swim, and she was just plain tuckered out. I sometimes lie on my back and snore loudly—sometimes loud enough to wake myself up. I was hoping Juicy wouldn't follow suit and wake herself up. So far, so good. I moved slowly away from her as I heard a car crunch into the gravel driveway. I was expecting Arnold Cable. I'd dragged him out of retirement to help me with this new venture at Food Basket.

We'd been on the job for slightly more than thirty days, and several things were beginning to emerge. First, I was surprised how comfortable I felt doing a job for an entity that I knew so little about. But the basics were the same: grocery stores, a warehouse, management, worker bees, and the daily battle to win the consumer. What also helped was that decision making wasn't difficult for me. That does not imply that all of my decisions were good, but I didn't labor over them. The very first was that I accepted Joe Snyder's resignation, even though he was making hand and arm signals that he might have been a little hasty in resigning. One-armed push-ups somewhere, but not here, Joe.

Next, I obtained feedback that Shirley Macober, Dave Pondorf, and Dave Williams were being received positively by the Food Basket team at headquarters and the warehouse. One of the most important pieces was delivered by Jim Sneed. He had put together a presentation that demonstrated our only chance to climb out of the hole we were in was to centralize our power at headquarters and not have our eighty stores going off to execute eighty different merchandising plans. I loved Sneed's approach, which was we're not too big to fail and that we were precariously close to becoming another forgotten entity on the way to broken dreams. Being a mile marker on a deserted highway of Chapter XI grocery outlets translated directly to our workers as unemployment.

Arnold approached the door wide-eyed and said, "Where is the monster dog?"

"Sleeping like a baby," I said to Arnold. "You know that tan of yours I saw a couple of months ago is starting to fade."

"Oh yeah, even as we speak, I can feel the ulcer starting to kick up. Some people I know are carriers," he said.

"I'll ignore that remark," I said with a laugh. "Arnold, you know I count on you to look at the big picture internally and tell me if we're overextended, on schedule, or half-stepping. What are you thinking, and what's your sense of how we are doing?"

"Overall, the meter has hardly moved, but it has moved upward. So we're going in the right direction. In no particular order, dumping Snyder was right. He not only seemed like an ordinary CFO, but his people despised him. His number two, Larry Baldwin, is doing a bang-up job as the new CFO, and Dave Williams has his complete confidence. They've found something that I'll round back to—remind me at the end.

"Garth Brewster could be the find of the decade. He is pushing all the right buttons, and our stores are constructing in-store pharmacies with good speed. Importantly, store personnel are excited about it.

"Bob Santone has secured a 250-million-dollar loan for us at a favorable rate, and the renovation of stores has begun. I've been to every store, and I think there are five that need to be closed. These five are in worse shape than any A&P that I supervised back in the day.

"Here are things we are thinking about, but we really haven't started yet: We want to put a superstore in a location equidistant from New Bedford, Fall River, and Taunton. Other stores are fleeing this area because these towns are beat down, and the shrink factor is twice what it is in other cities that have a better economy. It's perfect. They actually have a couple of industries to include the fishing industry and health care. But they are on the forefront of a potential gambling location, and they could grab a piece of the deepwater windmill business just nine miles offshore. But we are lacking one thing," Cable said.

"What?" I asked.

"A fixer, an influence peddler," Arnold said. "Someone who can deal with the local power brokers, line up politicians, excite the unions, show up at all the local get-togethers, and schmooze. Also, he needs to have some pull on State Street with the state pols right up to the governor."

"I'm sorry, Arnold. I don't know anybody like that," I said.

"Yes, you do," Arnold said. "You know him intimately."

"I give up," I said totally exasperated that I didn't have a clue who Arnold was talking about.

"Joe Galetti," Arnold said.

"Are you kidding me?" I responded. "Arnold, for Christ's sake, he fired me from Galetti!"

"Yes, he did," Arnold agreed. "But when the court ruling went against him, he tried to hire you as CEO."

"Desperation move by a guy who was holding the short end of the stick," I said.

"How many years did you work for him?" Arnold asked.

"Thirty years if you include the time I worked for his dad," I answered.

"Did he not put you through college and hire you full time when you graduated?" Arnold asked, pressing his case.

"Okay already, I'll think about it," I said.

"Another area we haven't tapped into but think could be a boost for us—we are searching for an image, but I know one thing I want to do at store level. I want our store personnel to know our customers, not just the demographics, but their names. When customers ask where something is, I don't want our employees talking out of the sides of their mouths over their shoulders. I want them taking those consumers to the spot where those items can be found. Also, I have started eliminating all of those cardboard displays and stacks of cases in the aisles. Unless it's something that is supplementing an item on the shelf that we can't keep on the shelf, like skinny popcorn, they are history. I'm having professional cleaning agencies come in for the more rundown stores that haven't seen a coat of wax since Paul Whatshisname rode his horse through Boston."

"Paul Whatshisname?" I asked.

"You know, the silversmith," Arnold replied. "Look, Russell, it's baby steps, but it's all about pride and wanting to win. Save the social media crap for guys a lot smarter than me. We need to know what the opportunities are here for our consumer. When people flash around health care as an industry, are they talking about medical technicians or menial minimum-wage earners for over fifty-five prisoners of hip replacement surgery?"

"Jesus, Arnold," I said, "let's not advertise for menial minimum-wage earners on Facebook, okay?"

Arnold broke into a doubled-over laugh and said, "So you think I'm a little too intense, Russ? Remember, you were the guy that told me I'd grown soft in my old age with the advent of retirement."

"I love it, Arnold. You are all the way back, my man," I said. "Better than ever, and this idea of pride, winning, and baby steps is right on target. Maybe it's *Pride and Prejudice*. Only kidding, but let's get the agency to light it up. They haven't come up with much to date."

Arnold looked tentatively in the direction of Juicy to see if he could make his getaway before Juicy licked him to death.

I shook his hand, opened the door for him, and said, "Thanks, Arnold. I know it's uphill, but I feel like the wheels are moving, even if I can still count the lug nuts as they are turning."

Arnold's last words now that he was safely outside were, "Russ, call Joe Galetti. We need an influence peddler with his kind of clout. So what if he fired you…twice? I'm betting he was right at least one of those times."

I said nothing but gave Arnold a hand signal sometimes known as the fickle finger of fate.

CHAPTER 20

Face-to-Face

Cummings was deep in thought as he perused the documents that Sergeant O'Malley had provided for him on the financial condition of the widow, Lucy Santone. Alex Santone's will was a bit of a surprise. He had left 75 percent of his estate to his three children, 15 percent to his first wife, and the remaining 10 percent to Lucy Santone. Even though it was a reasonably large estate, Lucy would be left with about $200,000 after taxes, and Alan Cummings was guessing Lucy thought that this amount was fairly meager for seven years of marriage. It didn't take long to confirm that suspicion when O'Malley uncovered an insurance policy for $2,500,000 naming Lucy as the beneficiary. Interestingly, the amount had been increased by a million dollars six months ago.

He had a strange reaction to this evidence. His gut told him that Lucy Santone wasn't that obvious. In the area of circumstantial evidence, things were piling up against her in record fashion. They could now trace $20,000 that she sent to Jethroe in Florida, and through an attorney she had posted $50,000 bail for him. Clearly their relationship was more than a bartender whom she and her husband hardly knew.

Cummings left his office and went directly to Donna Mitchner's office to discuss his findings with her.

When he arrived, she looked up from her desk and said, "Do you have an appointment, Mr...."

"Yocnevich," he said.

"Mr. Yocnevich," she said, but she couldn't carry it off with a straight face and broke into a huge grin. "What can I do for you, good-looking?"

"I want to chat a little about our case," he said.

"Okay," she said, "your face is telling me that something isn't kosher."

"Not really. Between phone calls, the letter we already have from the crime scene, and financial records, Santone and Jethroe are closer than two hogs in mating season. The evidence against Jethroe is substantial, and from listening to him for two hours on the wiretap, if he were a homing pigeon, he might not be able to find it," he said.

"What's the problem?" Mitchner asked.

"She's way smarter than this. It's like she's leading us along through the forest with a trail of breadcrumbs. Forget the fact that she could do so much better than this guy. Maybe it's just me, but evidence is piling up faster than I ever expected."

"Listen, Alan, it could be purely physical. I don't mean to be crass, but maybe he throws it in the pool and jumps after it, if you follow my drift."

"I follow you," Cummings said. "The other piece is that Bruno Jethroe, at least on the phone, has never said he actually killed our victim."

"Relax, Alan," Donna said. "This indictment is coming from the grand jury, so the evidence is pretty strong."

"What do you mean?" Alan asked.

"Well, if you go before a judge for probable cause, it translates to the event was more likely than not. If it comes out of the grand jury, it means guilty beyond a reasonable doubt," Donna explained.

"I didn't know that, and I've hung around a lot of courtrooms," Alan said.

"That's not written in stone, but that is my interpretation. On to more important stuff—are you still on for Saturday?"

"Depends," Alan said.

"Depends on what?" Donna asked.

"We're on if you can navigate to my place," Cummings said.

"Count on it," came the reply.

* * *

Just miles away, Lucy Santone was making ready to storm the fortress again. She was on her way unannounced to try to talk to the new CEO, Russell Riley, and she wasn't in a mind to be deterred. She might only have 10 percent of the action right now, but she hired a small roomful of lawyers to make the case that the minimum share she should have was 50 percent of the family stock. But in her own mind, she would settle for a third of the action.

She was dressed in an elegant pair of dress slacks and a blouse that was just this side of immodest. She always liked to see how long it took the male population to become mesmerized by cleavage—not long usually.

She entered Riley's suite and started to charge by the secretary to the closed door of Riley's office.

"Whoa, whoa there," a woman said as she left her seat with relative ease and blocked Lucy's forward progress. "Can I help you, Mrs. Santone?"

"I want to see Russell Riley. It's urgent," Lucy said, not at all discouraged by this temporary roadblock.

"Not on my watch. You are going to have to make an appointment, which includes what you want to talk about," the secretary said.

"This is preposterous. Up until three months ago, my husband was the CEO of this pop stand," Lucy said in an exasperated tone.

"I'm sorry, Mrs. Santone, but that and $2.43 will get you an extra-large hot decaf coffee at Dunkin' Donuts," the secretary responded.

"I will report you for insubordination, young lady," Lucy said.

"So be it. But no appointment, no access to this office," the secretary said evenly.

* * *

At that very moment, Shirley Macober sailed out of my office under a full head of steam, followed by a three-hundred-pound giant, Dave Pondorf, and then I appeared like a scatback looking for a hole to run through. I was startled to see Lucy Santone standing in harm's way as the two behemoths exited my office.

I was surprised to see her outside my office at all, but I recovered in time to say, "Lucy, are you gate-crashing again?"

She threw her mane of red hair back and really had a good laugh.

"I am, but so far not successfully."

I looked at my secretary and said, "Okay, Melissa, let's have Mrs. Santone come into my office, and would you please call Dave Williams and push our appointment back fifteen minutes."

"Will do," Melissa said as she stood aside to allow Lucy to enter my office.

Lucy started toward my desk, but I motioned her to another part of the suite, where there were two comfortable chairs and a coffee table.

"May I get you something to drink, Lucy?" I asked.

"No, thank you, Russ. I won't be long. I've been checking up on you," she said.

"As I have on you," I responded.

"The only thing you were checking out the last time we met was my ass," she said with a smirk.

"Guilty as charged," I said. "But on the other hand, if you want people to actually listen to you, you might think about minimizing the physical distractions."

Surprisingly, Lucy's neck colored slightly, and I really couldn't tell if it was her natural coloring or that she might actually have blushed.

"Touché, Russell, but remember, all is fair in love and war."

"Which one is this?" I asked.

"It's war right now, but things could change," she said coolly.

Now it was my turn to fumble around a little.

"Lucy, if you have checked me out, then you know I'm not very subtle. What is the purpose of this visit to my little fiefdom?" I asked.

"I'm a widow now, so I have to watch out for my financial interest. Your job and how you perform it have a lot to do with that eventual outcome," she said. "I went to the archives of the Boston Globe—what a rip-off, by the way. As soon as you bring up an article and read a paragraph, they want you to drop a nickel in their pocket, or an annoying pop-up appears asking you to subscribe to the *Globe*. That's how I got to the archives in the first place. I'm a subscriber. But I digress. I read everything I could about the Galetti trial, including you being questioned by Joe Galetti's lawyers regarding an affair with Maria Galetti."

"So?" I asked.

"Sew buttons," she replied. "I wanted to feel secure that we don't have a skirt-chasing CEO not buckling down to fixing this sorry-ass, crap-handle grocery chain. The previous CEO did enough womanizing for three people."

"And how are you feeling now that we have had this little chat?" I asked.

"Better. I'm just not sure that if you give it all you've got, you can save this dump. I don't shop at Food Basket," she added.

"Pity," I said. "We really need every consumer we can garner. Here's what I know about you: born in New England, lost your dad at an early age, persevered in school as a good student and an extraordinary athlete, scholarship in basketball at an excellent university, dropped out after a year, pregnant, married the father, had another child not by the same man, divorced your husband, survived as a secretary/administrative assistant until you ran just slowly enough to have Alex Santone catch you and marry you."

"So?" she asked.

"I'm the least of your worries. Researching a trial from another decade and grasping at an affair that never happened isn't in your financial interest or any interest, frankly. You don't have a skill set that will help me turn this chain around for you, and, by charging in here, all you have done is put me behind schedule in cranking up this chain as it once was. All you need to know is that I am going to succeed here or die trying. I would think you have bigger fish to fry. The newspapers are filled with Alex's murder, and your name pops up enough to make me think that the authorities think you are in the mix. So if you'll excuse me, Lucy, I really have work to do."

Lucy stood up, picked up her pocketbook, reached out to shake my hand, and said, "There, that wasn't so hard, was it? This conversation has been very educational, and as a result, I feel that Bob and his executive committee picked the right guy!"

CHAPTER 21

Videos in Your Microwave

I was sitting with Hartman, Sneed, Cable, and Brewster on Craigville Beach in West Hyannis Port. We were in swimsuits with a medium-sized cooler of cold beer, huddled around one of the weirdest-looking cookers on Earth. It looked like a wastebasket, and rust was slowly eating away at its bottom. The cooking grill was about three inches below the surface of the wastebasket. I'd learned over the years that this was a key facet of this Rube Goldberg looka-like because no matter how hard the wind blew, it never interfered with the cooking process.

But I was worried.

"We need to get this cooker into the shop. The fenders are showing extraordinary wear and tear."

Hartman took a close, long look at it and said, "I think I can patch it with some tin and superglue."

"I just ate the best burger I've ever eaten in my life. I vote that we do nothing to disturb the essence of this miracle machine. All in favor," Garth Brewster said.

Hartman, Cable, and Sneed all voted for it, and I abstained, knowing my case was lost.

"The motion is carried," I said, "by a group with almost as much brain candlepower as Thomas Jefferson when he dined alone in the presidential dining room."

"What are our girls doing?" Sneed asked.

"Dropping our plastic all over Hyannis," Hartman said.

"Let's hope that's all they are dropping," Brewster remarked.

"Whoa," I said, "let's take that one off the tape before we all are sleeping in the Volvo Motel. On to more mundane subjects. First, a follow-up. Arnold, when you were at my house last month, you were going to circle back to something, but instead you ran out of the house, hoping the dog wouldn't intercept you. What was it you wanted to tell me?"

"Right, it's important, but it's only a feeling based on no data, okay?" Arnold said.

"What's new?" Hartman said. "Since when did you let lack of data get in your way?"

"Jesus, are you guys always busting balls, or do you want something to chew on?" Cable asked.

"Okay, Arnold, go," Brewster said. "I'll try and hold off Hartman."

"Okay, before I was so rudely interrupted, Dave Williams is a numbers guy, but he's not a geek in a white lab coat. He's in the stores on a frequent basis. He did some math to include a store's volume, share of market, cash through the register, and average dollar transaction," Cable said.

"He used to do that all the time when I was at Galetti," I added.

"He feels the cash receipts are light, that more money should have been generated. Not much, but more," Arnold said.

"Holy shit," Brewster said.

"What are we doing about it?" Sneed asked.

"Dave is working it, and he'll report back to us when he has something more definitive," Cable responded.

"Bill, has the agency come up with a campaign for us? I'm okay spending some dough, and I think with Macober, Pondorf, and Williams, we can coordinate a hell of a promotion to coincide with it," I said.

"Russ, sometimes it's better to be lucky than good. If we had done anything earlier, it would have been premature. But now, thanks to Arnold and his band of merry workers, the stores really look good. They are sparkling clean, the aisles are clear, the endcaps now have products on them that people actually want to buy, and we have people in the aisles that the consumer can approach if they are lost. Small stuff, but the windows sparkle, and the flower department is actually seasonal. Up 'til now, for instance, we've had mums in the department in June and July. I think they came from Brazil, but no self-respecting flower shopper who knows anything is going to buy mums in July," Hartman said.

"Who knew?" Brewster said.

"Knew what?" Arnold asked.

"That Hartman would know a mum from a second-base bag. Extraordinary!" I said.

"The agency is working on a bizarre theme that could be an all-time bust. But frankly, given our position in the marketplace, we can't afford to come out with some mundane theme like a 'bucket full of savings,'" Hartman concluded.

"Drumroll, please. With that introduction, this theme has to be way out there!" Arnold said.

"It's total Hollywood!" Hartman exclaimed. "You may not have noticed, but all the films now have special effects—aliens, matrix people, blood-drinking neighbors, Cruise living in a pod nine hundred feet above the ground. Big Brother is watching. Homeland cameras and videos in your microwave watching your every move."

"Oh shit, I don't have to dress up as an alien, do I?" I asked.

"Maybe," Hartman said. "But for now, no. We have not ordered you any special uniforms. It would be something like, 'We don't want to read your e-mails, and we won't be sending any domestic drones to hover over your house, but we do know what you buy in your grocery store, and we're using all means of communication and social networking to bring you into our store. Come to Food Basket for an out-of-this-world experience.'"

"Have we tested it?" I asked.

"Happening right now in Newport," Hartman said. "Should have an early reading in ten days."

"Jim, any best practices we can incorporate that you have picked up from the myriad of boards you sit on?" I asked.

"Yes, indeed," Jim responded. "But to do it, we need to bring our IT skills into this century. Let's use Amazon as an example. If you buy a Graham Greene novel, you will receive an e-mail from them saying if you like Graham Greene, you may want to read books by John le Carré and Daniel Silva."

"Okay, with you so far," I said.

"We need to do a better job of reading our cash register tapes. For instance, if somebody is ordering two dozen eggs, there is software now that may reveal that someone in that family is on a high-protein diet. So Food Basket starts sending her coupons and reduced pricing on those high-protein items. We view prices for her by algorithms on items she buys frequently, and we send her digital coupons. This is all done by an app on her phone. In effect, she's shopping with an electronic list that she can add to if she forgets some items."

All of a sudden, the light went on in Garth Brewster's head.

"Hey, wait a minute. If we do this well, we grow a loyal customer, everyday shelf prices become less important, and our competitors can't open up our ad every week to see what we are really up to."

"But, Jimmy," Hartman said, "what kind of volume bump do we get if we do this?"

"The stuff I've read says between 1 and 1.5 percent," Jim responded.

"Okay, but have we the capability to pull it off?" I asked.

"Yes, we do," Arnold said. "Give the project to Larry Baldwin, and he, with the aid of his platoon of geeks, will do a bang-up job."

"Other subjects, issues, or unfinished business?" I asked.

"Yes," Arnold said. "Have you given any more thought to hiring an influence peddler?"

"What's this all about?" Hartman asked.

"Arnold thinks it would be a good idea to hire Joe Galetti to grease the skids for the Fall River–New Bedford–Taunton megaplex store we want to build," I said.

"Wow, he was one of the best, no doubt about it," Hartman agreed. "But is he still relevant? His crowd was Teddy, Tip, Volpe, Kevin White, Brooke, and Billy Bulger. Separately, I don't trust the son of a bitch."

"The key is that Joe Galetti is the godfather of influence peddlers in the state. He knew all of the families, including his son's generation, which is currently in the statehouse in big numbers. But the kicker is—and don't ask me how I know this—his political contributions get him invited to every head table at every big-time political event that means anything. If you don't have his support, even a democrat would have a tough time getting elected. Ask Martha Coakley when she ran against Scott Brown a few years back," Arnold Cable said.

"I thought he was dead," Garth said.

"Isn't that the guy who divorced his wife and ran around with this high-powered lawyer?" Sneed asked.

"He's not dead, and yes, he did date and marry Diane Dunbar, who is a senior partner in a law firm."

"You know her name?" Garth asked.

"I dated her in high school and college," I said.

"Jesus, does Holly know about your checkered past?" Jim Sneed asked.

"She does," I responded.

"I think it's a great idea if he has any juice left," Garth said.

"I like it too," Jim said. "But isn't this the guy who canned you?"

"The very same," I said.

"Talk about turning the other cheek," Garth said.

"And he must have had good personnel skills," Sneed said.

We all laughed at Jim's comment. It certainly seemed on the surface like a strange bedfellow relationship.

"Okay, gentlemen, thanks for the partial vote of confidence on the hiring of Joe Galetti. What about in-house politics?" I asked. "How are we going to approach Trip and Maria and the other members of the family?"

"I don't think it would be a problem if you got out in front of it," Hartman said. "I think Trip and Maria would be okay with it, but if they aren't okay with it, I wouldn't do it. They, particularly Trip, have gone the extra mile in loaning us resources that we vitally need."

"I agree," Cable said.

"Let's head back to my place and find the girls," I said.

CHAPTER 22

All Night Long

Donna Mitchner was surprised again. She was sure when she ran down Alan Cummings's address that it would be a duplex in the back of a strip mall and the other resident would be a kindly Italian man who used lots of garlic to cook. She imagined the smell of the garlic permeating the entire house and that Alan's furniture would be covered in various-colored cloths because stuffing was leaking out everywhere. In contrast to all the clutter and early Morgan Memorial furniture would be wonderful artwork everywhere.

"Oh my, oh my, very wrong again," she thought as she prepared to ring the doorbell of a fashionable condo in the North End of Boston. She had this crazy thought just before the door opened that she was at the address of another man named Alan Cummings. But when the door swung open, it was her Alan Cummings, and he had a big smile on his face.

"First things first, you look absolutely beautiful. But you have that look on your face that you are at the wrong address and that you should be on your way to a five-story walk-up in Mattapan," Cummings said as he took her hand and gave her a hug.

"So much for my poker face!" Donna said with a hearty laugh. "I hope the defendants won't find me that easy to read. And thank you for the compliment. By the way, you are the best-looking police captain I know."

"How many do you know?" Alan asked.

"You're it," Donna said with a big smile.

"It's a bit of a shallow victory, but I won't turn it down. Any trouble finding this place?"

"No, the wonders of GPS and MapQuest," she replied.

"Come on in. I want to show you the place. Did I tell you that I'm really glad you are here? No kidding. I've been humming a tune all day while I labored over a hot cookstove," Cummings said.

"An elegant condo and he cooks, this is a little overwhelming," Donna said.

"Okay, I better fess up. My ex picked this place, and I cheated on the meal by walking two blocks to my favorite Italian restaurant and picking up our food."

Mitchner couldn't help but laugh out loud.

"Jesus, Alan, one twist of the dial and you blurt out the truth. That's what I love about you. You honestly can't fabricate anything. A straight arrow with integrity, not bad."

"Well, I'll tell you one thing: I want to keep doing things you love about me because, Mitchner, you are special," he said.

"Knock it off, Cummings. You are embarrassing me!" Donna said.

"Sorry," Alan said. "How about a drink? I made some vodka martinis and then put them in the freezer. Guaranteed to satisfy, and I really did make them myself."

"Great. This place is absolutely spectacular. *Elegant* is the word that I'm thinking of at the moment. This is the farthest from a man cave as I've ever seen. But why Boston? You're a born and bred Providence–Rhode Island guy."

"That's probably the reason. I went to school here, and I think it's a great town to be a part of, and rush-hour traffic really doesn't play a role with my hours," Cummings said.

They talked about everything but work, and Alan was just getting up to check on dinner when Donna said, "Alan, I've got a wonderful suggestion for a first course."

"Oh," said Alan.

"Me," Donna said.

Cummings held out his hand and led her to the bedroom, where they undressed each other and lay in the bed. They made love and then lay in each other's arms for about ten minutes without saying a word.

Finally, Donna kissed him and said, "You are a puzzle. A hockey-playing police captain who favors art, museums, an elegant condo, and silk sheets, go figure. But I own you now, Cummings. If I spill the beans at work, you're finished." She kissed him again.

"Not so fast, Ms. District Attorney. What if I leave the video of this encounter in the courthouse running over and over again? Enticing a police captain to falsify evidence by granting sexual favors," Cummings said.

"Video?" Donna asked, quite startled.

"Only kidding," Cummings replied. "How about a little dinner?"

"Great idea, you smooth talker, you," Donna said as they both headed for the shower.

"Smooth talker?" Alan said. "I was heading into the kitchen to check on dinner."

"How'd that work out?" Donna asked.

"Like a dream come true," Alan responded.

CHAPTER 23

Promoting from Within

I was home and happy in spite of the fact that Juicy had eaten my left slipper to a point that it was almost unrecognizable. The right slipper was unscathed. What was this dog thinking? Was I going to hop around on my right foot for the rest of my life? I really didn't understand the "human being and pet" relationship or psychology. She was my pal, but she was a pain in the ass. She was always glad to see me, and I'm not sure that I could say that about everyone else. If somebody tried to rob the house, the would-be culprit would be licked to death, and it was more than abundantly clear that you left nothing on a table that could break when it hit the floor and nothing on a kitchen counter that had any relationship to food, including flour or a two-pound bag of coffee beans. Nothing survived the nose and jaw of Juicy.

I was moving around the aforementioned kitchen, keeping a wary eye on Juicy, while I was preparing dinner for Holly. She was returning from a very infrequent business trip, and the kids were at Grandma's because they knew they'd be fed better over there. Claire, my mother, loved those children, and they, in turn, adored her. Holly would give me some grief when she arrived home, and I knew the word *abandonment* would be in the mix somewhere. But I had her favorite drink, a Manhattan, chilling in the refrigerator, and I was making my one and only "smashed" potatoes, fresh peas, a wedge salad smothered in bleu cheese, and a porterhouse steak ready to meet its maker on the grill. Do you have any idea how many pea pods have to be shelled to come up with a decent portion for two people? Hundreds of pods went to their graves, sacrificed for the sake of this meal. I know it sounds a little juvenile, but I love to mix the peas into the mashed potatoes before consuming them.

Just then, the door burst open, and Holly said, "How you call your lover girl, Mickey?"

"Oh, Sylvia, oh, baby, oh, Sylvia," I said.

"Hey, lover boy, grab the suitcase for me, will you? Let's see, the kids are at Claire's, and you're making me dinner. I think I'll go away more often," she said as she headed upstairs to get out of her business garb.

When Holly returned to the kitchen, I served her a chilled Manhattan, and she said it was smacking-lip delicious.

Then she looked at me with a wary eye and said, "All this wonderful greeting means you have a problem you want to talk over, no?"

"Oh yeah, it's a dandy requiring finesse and a very light touch," I responded. "But that can wait. Enjoy your drink, relax, and tell me about your day."

"It was fun. I went out to try and learn how a company ticks, what separates it from its competitors, and to talk personnel decisions at the very top. It was a seminar and a workshop, and the instructors were top-notch. One of the case studies I'm sure was P&G. In the past twenty years, this much-admired firm has actually canned two CEOs."

"What was the problem?" I asked.

"Well, I don't know if we uncovered the answer, but the discussion became very lively when we looked at the management strategy of promoting from within and not going to the outside to consider candidates."

"Wait a minute. Isn't that what your company does?" I asked.

"Very good, Russ. Between now and next Monday, I have to report to the CEO on my findings from this session," Holly said.

"Well, if your company changes its policy, I might become your CEO," I said.

"Don't hold your breath," she said. "Seems like you have your hands full with the two full-time jobs you have now!"

"Point well taken. I'll be back in twelve minutes with a medium-rare porterhouse, and you get all the fillet," I said.

As we were sitting at the table, Holly said, "Russ, you can bypass jail and collect two hundred dollars because this meal is delicious. You may have a limited number of dishes that you can cook, but there is something to be said for specialization. I'm trying to figure out which of these four things is my favorite, and I can't do it. Great job!"

"I'm tickled that I make the love of my life this ecstatic," I said. "Are you too worn out to help with a situation that isn't nearly as egregious as promoting from within?"

"I'd rather have a cup of coffee, a cognac, and go upstairs and whisper sweet nothings in your ear," she said.

"Are these two tasks mutually exclusive?" I asked.

"Absolutely not," Holly said. "But you have to throw a little more into the bargain. Your end is a little light."

"Fair enough. Okay, I'll add to my end a Ted Lepcio autograph, a used second-base bag, and tidbits from my interview with Lucy Santone."

"Sold. Forget Lepcio and the second-base bag and skip to Ms. Santone," she said.

"All in good time," I promised.

"Okay, let's start with your problem," Holly said.

"I want to hire Joseph Galetti as an influence peddler with local pols, planning boards, and town managers," I said. "How would you go about doing that?"

"First of all, I love the idea," Holly said. "It's so far from anything I would think of doing. It's crazy, bizarre, and right on the money. Who came up with this beauty?"

"Cable," I responded.

"What are you guys calling a bonus now? I forget," Holly said.

"A stipend," I responded.

"With all haste, get Mr. Cable a stipend for sheer creativity. Okay, first things first. Clear it with Maria and Trip," Holly said.

"I did, and they are okay. In fact, Maria thought it would be the best thing in the world for the old man. He's busy, but not in a business sense."

"With those roadblocks removed, it's time to plan an approach. Just off the top of my head, definitely not on the phone. The offer has to be made at a place of Joe's choosing and not that disgusting place where you and Trip meet. Joe likes the perks. Definitely a car and driver."

"Car and driver, no way. I'm the CEO, and I don't have a car and driver," I said.

"You want to land this guy, or do you want to whistle by the graveyard?" she asked.

"I need him badly. There's nobody short of Buddy Cianci who can schmooze like this guy. And he's got his hand in every pol's pocket in the state."

"Okay, a car, driver, put him on the board, and make him a title that only Jim Sneed could dream up. But for all of this, Russ, you milk this cagey old bastard. I know you need him to look at the operation too. Don't forget the Galetti board disagreed with Joe fairly often, but when it came to the numbers, he was right nine out of ten times. He wasn't pretty, but he ran circles around his competition."

"Amen," I responded. "Thanks to you, I have a game plan. It's ironic that Joe will learn almost immediately that our financials are still pretty shaky, but he won't relate that to the fact that he has a car and a driver."

"Now, about Lucy Santone," Holly said.

"Oh no, no, no," I said. "It's time to go upstairs and whisper in my ear."

Holly smiled at me and said, "You drive a hard bargain, Russell Riley, but you know I'm putty in your hands. Give me one tidbit about your interview with Lucy Santone."

"Okay. She wanted to know, and I quote, how I was going to fix this sorry-ass, crap-handle grocery chain."

"Wow," Holly said. "Tell me more, Mickey."

CHAPTER 24

The Influence Peddler

I dialed his number with some trepidation as things really did not end well between us. In a sentence, he fired me; he lost a court case, 750 million dollars, and his job as CEO of Galetti after being one of the primary forces in building the chain from one store to sixty stores. Hell of a sentence, don't you agree? He was Joe Galetti, now almost eighty years old and not looking for any handouts. Joe was a multimillionaire, still very active in politics and community affairs, and like the old days, I was hoping to ride on his coattails to turn Food Basket around.

He answered the phone with a terse hello, perhaps halfway thinking it was some sales guy telling him that his "I've fallen and I can't get up" gizmo was ready to be shipped to him from a phantom warehouse.

"Joe, it's Russell Riley. How are you?" I asked.

"Russell, it's nice to hear your voice. It's been quite a while, but I've been keeping an eye on you. I know you're currently the CEO of Food Basket," Joe said.

"As His Honor Eddie Koch would say, how am I doing?" I asked.

"The truth or do you want me to leave the bark on?" Joe asked with a chuckle.

"Bark off, Joe. For Christ's sake, when did you ever sugarcoat anything?" I asked.

"Never. You are doing way better than anybody thought possible. So good that your competitors are planning a little surprise party for you. They are worried about Food Basket again as a competitor. They've seen what you have done to the stores, the ad campaign, and the clear difference in pricing. The biggest single improvement is that your out-of-stock rate has been cut in half, and that means the worker bees are kicking butt and morale is improving. That's the good news."

"And the bad news?" I asked.

"You're still odds-on not to make it because your competitors no longer think you are a sleeping dog," Joe responded.

"Joe, I thought you were retired. How could you possibly know all this stuff?" I asked.

"It's a gift, kid, and sprinkling some incentive around here and there doesn't hurt either. But you didn't call to talk shop. What can I do for you?"

"I have a proposition for you," I said. "How about lunch or dinner in the near future?"

"Tomorrow night, Barker Tavern in Scituate at five. Ask for my private dining room."

"Will do," I said, but Joe had already hung up.

That went way better than I could have expected on several levels. First, I didn't expect him to be that cordial, but what really blew me away was his knowledge of our current position in the marketplace and what our competitors were saying and thinking about us. If, in the back of my mind, I thought Joe was beginning to gum his oatmeal, I quickly dismissed that notion. I may have taken his genius for granted, but for the thirty years I worked for him, he outsmarted and was quicker and more creative than his much larger competitors. It was a classic case of the big guys overlooking a much smaller competitor until one magic day he had sixty stores and had taken two to three billion dollars of grocery money out of their hip pockets.

Back in my office the next day, looking at the sales numbers for the week, the door flew open, and Melissa rushed in with the latest copy of the local grocery weekly followed closely by Garth Brewster and Jim Sneed. The front page of this edition in bold letters read, WATCH OUT, YOU CATEGORY KILLERS, FOOD BASKET HAS WOKEN UP AFTER A TWENTY-YEAR SNOOZE. Under the headline, it read, "New CEO did it once, and he can do it again." We were all leaning over the conference table, gawking at the front page. It was a rehash of the murder, but surprisingly the article had good information on our move to pharmacies, current price changes, and the new media campaign. The concluding paragraph, although gratifying, served as a road sign for our competitors to try to place some heat on us before we could get off the mat.

"In less than three months, the new management team has reminded this reporter what a Food Basket store used to stand for in the neighborhood. They are one of the few organizations who try to learn your name. The staff seems glad to see you, the store is easy to shop, and the place sparkles. I'm not kidding—you can see your image in the shiny floors. It's not a megaplex with the back wall of the store so far away that it looks like a fog bank has formed between you and it. I can wheel around a Food Basket in twenty-five minutes, gather everything I need, and head for home. My time is worth something, and I don't want to spend it in a supermarket. Welcome back to the neighborhood, Food Basket."

This last paragraph garnered two hoorays and a "Fuck." Jim Sneed and I cheered, and Garth Brewster was decidedly unhappy as he said, "Crap handle, there goes the element of surprise and my stock options. I was hoping we could sneak up on these guys a little bit longer so we could rabbit-punch the snot out of them."

Jim Sneed jumped in and said, "Garth, you are absolutely right about the element of surprise, but, man, this is survival time. Just imagine what kind of fix we'd be in if we were still sliding backwards. Your stock options wouldn't be worth the powder to blow them up, and we'd be trying to worm ourselves out of Chapter XI proceedings."

"Jim, that reminds me that the script you prepared with the 'We aren't too big to fail' theme was huge. I get more feedback at store level about what an eye-opener that was and how it translates to an immediate need to take our game to another level," I said.

"I agree," Garth volunteered. "It wasn't a scare tactic. It was the truth for everyone to see in the cold light of day."

"Thank you, gentlemen," Sneed said. "While I've got you guys, I wanted to let you know that we are well on our way to rightsizing the organization. It looks as if 10 percent of the organization has responded to our retirement package, and under ordinary circumstances that would turn up twenty to twenty-five million dollars."

"I hate 'Under ordinary circumstances,'" Garth said.

"It's akin' to 'I brung home the saddle, the hoss is dead.'"

"I hear you, Garth, but if we didn't have an incentive, these people might work until they expire," Sneed said. "Importantly, from what I can gather from performance reviews, over 70 percent of them are ranked in the bottom 25 percent of their peer groups. The package includes six months' salary, benefits under COBRA, and ninety days of a placement firm helping them to find another job."

"Jim, that is good work. I think restructure work is some of the most difficult work we do, and you have led the way in directing our human resources department," I said.

"Garth, give us the lowdown on the pharmacy project."

"Like shit through a tin horn," Garth replied.

"Is that good or bad?" Jim asked.

"Really good. Things are moving so well, I can't get the glove up before the ball zips by. The powers that be actually like what we are doing. They think we are the little guy fighting the behemoth. We are the last vestige of the old independent pharmacists who know the whole family and who will keep them from taking something that could be potentially harmful."

"I don't get it," I said. "You are a pretty big drug chain in your own right."

"But they have known me since I had one store," Garth said.

"But CVS started here, didn't it?" Jim asked.

"Oh yeah, but that's the point. They are the biggest, and these folks don't want to see me squashed like a bug. We have pharmacies up and running in thirty-seven of the seventy-five stores. Recall, Arnold has closed five stores. We have plans for thirty more, bringing the total to sixty-seven of the seventy-five stores. Eight stores just can't handle a pharmacy. By the way, I am by far the most popular guy at the local pharmacy schools as I am employing a goodly number of their recent graduates."

"Wait a minute," I said. "Have we got all rookies in these new store pharmacies?"

"C'mon, Russ, I didn't just jump out of a dustbin. I've mixed and matched from my current stores, and I have hired some experienced ones as well that my store personnel have vouched for. Here's another idea for another day. If certain competitors are driving you crazy for one reason or another, check out my store locations, and if I have one near one of their outlets, let me run some items that will drive them crazy. We could hit them high and low. We could run a Pampers item at an insane price to draw our target consumer, or we could switch it up and run shingles shots for free because currently they aren't covered by Medicare. Russ, eight thousand people a day are turning sixty-five years old."

"That is absolutely brilliant, Garth, but can I ask you a non-related question?" Sneed asked.

"Sure," Garth said.

"What the hell is a dustbin?" Jim asked.

Everybody was laughing, but I didn't want to forget to tell Garth something important.

"Garth, man, you are our secret weapon. I know you don't like us to talk about the stuff you accomplish, but you have done one hell of a job. I really appreciate it, and the store personnel love your approach of nothing is impossible if you do it as a team."

"Actually, I really appreciate the comment, especially coming from you guys, who are no bullshit and just plain fun. And oh yeah, I'll be especially happy if the stock goes to forty and I become a multimillionaire."

"What else," I asked, "before our little impromptu meeting breaks up?"

"One thing," Jim Sneed said. "We have less than thirty days left on the contracts of Shirley Macober, Dave Pondorf, and Dave Williams. Any chance of getting an extension from Trip for them?"

"Yes, we have an agreement on an additional sixty days, but that's it. They need them back, and I can't blame them," I said.

"Russ, we need to talk to those folks before they go and get an assessment of who they think should run those departments when they are gone," Jim said.

"Great idea," I responded. "Would you please set that up with Melissa?"

"Will do," Jim replied.

* * *

Early that same evening, I arrived at the Barker Tavern to meet with Joseph Galetti. This was the perfect place, it seemed to me, to talk about the economy of influence. The inn was established in 1640, and I'm guessing more than a few feathered quills had to sign off on the Barker Tavern before it became a reality. Coins had to change hands to ensure that the main roads passed by the inn and that the stagecoach stopped at the Barker Tavern rather than a competitor. Some civil-minded citizen took on the task of purchasing the land, convincing the sawmill up the river to deliver those extra-wide pine boards, contacting the chimney masons to make the Barker Tavern their number one priority, and producing a product that made the rich, powerful, and politically savvy rainmakers call the Barker Tavern their place to do business. In my mind, Joe Galetti, influence peddler, bon vivant, sage, confidant of the decision makers, was one of many in a 400-year span who had perfected the economy of influence.

I had eaten at the tavern on a number of occasions, and I thought the food was excellent, although I don't pretend to know the finer points of dining. I can tell you that Cathy, the bartender, makes the best Bloody Mary I have ever tasted.

I was running on Lombardi time, so I was fifteen minutes early when I asked to be shown to Mr. Galetti's private dining room. I had expected to be the only one there, but when I opened up the door, Joe was sitting at a table with a huge red wine, and at the adjoining seat was a Bloody Mary that had to have my name on it.

I shook Joe's hand, and we gave each other a hug. We had worked together for a long time; his family put me through college and hired me full time after I graduated. Truthfully, I loved working there until the very end, when the family food fight split them in half and sent me on my way to becoming a food broker. Joe looked older, but don't we all. He was pencil thin, tall, gangly, and his hair looked like it had been combed by the leg of a chair. To me, he looked like a retired schoolteacher or a CPA, but not like one of the ten most influential people in the state.

He started in on me right away.

"Do you remember when I told you Comet would never outsell Bab-O?"

"Oh yeah, and within a year, Comet was selling triple what Bab-O was moving," I replied. I picked up my Bloody Mary and made a toast. "To old times, old memories, and old friends."

"Old friends," Joe said as we tapped glasses and had a drink.

"How did you know to order me a Bloody?" I asked.

"Cathy told me when I mentioned I was having dinner with you," Joe said.

"Catch me up with you. I see your name in the paper, but that's about it," I said.

"I still have an office in the building, but I have nothing to do with the business. I can tell you from my stock holdings that they are making a lot of money and that the wounds inflicted in the court battle have never healed. I'm still doing a considerable amount of philanthropy, and I've become a silent partner in Joey's computer business."

"I know he sold one of his companies to Microsoft for millions," I said.

"The count is three now. They finally got smart and put him on exclusive retainer for seven figures annually," he said.

"To think I used to threaten him when he was a young guy that if he didn't shape up, I would leave him permanently in Dairy," I said.

"Believe me, he remembers, and he wanted to be remembered to you when I told him I was going to be seeing you," Joe said.

"Personal life doing okay?" I asked.

"Well, Diane and I divorced after almost two years of marriage. We really didn't fight much. We just didn't have anything in common besides you," Joe said. "You know me, I'm an introvert really. Give me a good book or a problem that is difficult to solve, and I'll work on it for days. Tell me about you."

"Took this job at Food Basket. Couldn't help myself. The chain was on the brink, but as you said, we are making baby steps in forward momentum," I said.

"No, no, the important stuff—family," Joe said.

"Very fortunate in that regard. I can't even begin to tell you what a difference Holly's made in my life. The kids are turning out pretty well, and if I didn't have a dog that has a thing for eating my shoes, I'd be darn near perfect."

"That's great to hear," Joe said. "You know, you were a big part of the success of Galetti. Both Maria and Trip think so, and I do too. In retrospect, you did a great job managing the chain during the court fight, and I should have given you a bonus, but instead I fired you. I'm afraid that may have been a time when my personal life interfered with my business decisions."

"That's nice of you to say, Joe. I really appreciate that. There were plenty of good times to offset that circumstance," I said.

We were just starting on bowls of clam chowder that had magically appeared without our ordering them when I said, "Is it a little too early to talk some shop?"

"You're kidding, Russ," Joe said with a smile. "When was it ever too early to talk shop?"

"You make a good point. I would like to have you represent Food Basket as a consultant to the CEO," I said.

"Oh Christ," Joe said in mock alarm, "let me guess. You need a fixer, a good old-fashioned influence peddler."

"Shit, who's been blabbing their face off to you?" I asked.

"Hell, Russ, if I told you that, I wouldn't be a good fixer. The definition of a fixer is highly secretive, backslapping, with pictures of every important person in bed with a giraffe. But for you, so you don't think you have a leak, it was Trip," Joe said.

"Okay, at least it's still in the family," I said. "I want to build a megaplex store equidistant from New Bedford, Fall River, and Taunton with easy access to it from all three cities. Shaw's and others are closing stores in this geography because the economy is so bad."

"That means the shrink is bad too," Joe reminded me. "People are filling their pockets with stuff two to three times as much as locations that are more affluent."

"Yeah, I know, Joe, but I think the economy will bounce back, and I'm willing to make the prices such that people will get off their asses and drive. And service, meat, and fresh produce are going to be at a standard that equals your dad's store in Newton Center," I said.

"It's a dry cleaners now," Joe said. "I love your contrarian approach of marching into a place that everybody else is running from, but besides pure bravado, what are you basing the volume of store on?" Joe asked.

"Lots of things. You've got the fifth, sixth, and eleventh biggest cities in the state. Although it's not in cement, deepwater windmills are planning a major job just nine miles off of New Bedford. Gambling has a big interest in placing more than one casino here. The medical industry, including elderly care, is a good-sized factor. And we need to bring business on down here like the one Curt Schilling started up in Rhode Island. Not a good example, I know because it went belly-up. We need to improve air and boat service to Martha's Vineyard and Nantucket, not just for vacationers, but primarily for skilled workers who can't afford to live there but who need to travel there for employment. Why is Boston getting all the film business? Somebody is filling those movie companies' pockets with money and tax incentives. Where are the architects to take some of these old shoe factories and turn them into sought-after lofts? Seriously, Joe, I don't need some local pol who didn't make it out of fifth grade doing the strategic thinking for what this area could be. We need a Buddy Cianci. Say what you will about the guy—he turned Providence from a pot full of piss to the envy of almost every midsized city in the United States."

"Things didn't go so well for him in the end," Joe said. "He landed in an eight-by-ten room with a toilet and a roommate."

"No argument there," I said. "But he had a vision, and he knew how to make it happen. You have that same gift, Joe, and I want you to apply those skills here. As you would say to me often, *capisce?*"

"*Capisce*, absolutely," Joe said, laughing.

As we were drinking coffee and working on a B and B, he talked about what he needed.

"Russ, I'll need a car and driver. I don't see as well as I used to. I want to sit on the board so I get a feel for the personnel. I don't want a salary, but stock would be a powerful incentive for me to produce at a high rate."

"Done. But let me tell you a little secret, Joe. You don't know how to produce at anything but a very high rate, incentive or no incentive."

"Anything else?" he asked as he was about to pay the bill.

"Two things. First, I'd like to pay this bill. It's been a delightful meal with a very important mentor. And the first business I want down in this neck of the woods is Joey's computer business."

"Great. You can pick up the check, but the one guy I have no influence over is my son."

"I hear you, Joe," I said. "Tell Joey for me if he doesn't move here, it's back to Dairy for him!"

Joe laughed. "Great to see you, Russ. Thanks for the opportunity. I'll be on the case this Monday."

CHAPTER 25

May They Burn in Hell

I was on my way to work on Monday, and my mind was a blank slate. Usually things were brewing and churning up there, but after a relaxing weekend at home, my motor just hadn't cranked up yet. I was half listening to WBZ, and the deep-voiced newsman was saying, "This is what we are following: wife and heir of the Food Basket fortune and her paramour, an itinerant worker from Pawtucket, indicted by a grand jury in the murder of her husband, Alex Santone."

If I wasn't focused before, I was now. We all knew that something was going to break surrounding this heinous crime, but frankly, I didn't expect it to be *the* story. This wasn't like my previous experience at Galetti Supermarkets with the press. In that instance, all the participants and action centered the headquarters building, and the TV trucks and various equipment had actually blocked access to the warehouse as our suppliers tried to deliver goods. In this case, Lucy Santone really had no affiliation with the everyday business, so we would be spared that inconvenience. My immediate thought went to our stock price. We had been making steady, if not spectacular, progress, and the stock was reflecting that as we slowly edged upward. Holly, who followed the industry for her company, told me that some of the people in the industry likened us to the little engine that could.

I knew that this was going to be a "no comment" day at Food Basket headquarters. I called Arnold Cable because I knew he and his Lawyers Weekly gang would know what was going on. Arnold had actually graduated from law school but had never taken the boards, and he was fascinated by the ACLU, RICO, and a whole bunch of acronyms I knew nothing about.

"Arnold, what's the skinny on the indictment?"

"Not a big surprise. I told you a month ago that they were in session. The scuttlebutt here was that Bruno Jethroe was a dead-bang lock for murder one, but Lucy Santone on the same charge is a surprise. What effect do you think it will have on the stock?" Arnold asked.

"I haven't a clue. I'm sure I'll be talking to Bob and Garth later on today, and they will have a better fix on it than I do," I replied.

"Timing is everything in life," Arnold said. "Just when things seem a little desperate is the time to come out and kick some butt."

"Don't make me drag it out of you, Arnold," I said.

"Do you remember why you ran that huge sale at Galetti that ended in your termination?" he asked. "The competition felt that Galetti was vulnerable and that they might be able to pick up some cheap share points."

"Okay," I said, not really following Arnold's train of thought.

"A distraction by any other name is a distraction—court case over family stock or murder in the living room. The trade is seeing the progress that Food Basket has made over the last four months, and this is their window to take it all back."

"I'm all over it, Arnold. Would you mind telling Shirley and Dave to be in my office at 10:00 a.m.?"

"Done. What about Williams?"

"I've got him working on a special project with Joe Galetti, so I'm going to leave him alone. What is the data saying on our media test in Newport?" I asked.

"Very strong recall, mostly because it's so far out there. The agency thinks it's a winner."

"When did an agency ever say their copy sucked?"

"Never. But I like these young guys. They remind me of the *Saturday Night Live* writers before they became famous," Arnold said.

"You watch *Saturday Night Live?*" I asked.

"Never miss it," Arnold said.

"Arnold, the more I learn about you, the more I think you are the renaissance man of the grocery aisle. Can you sit in with Shirley and Pondorf?" I asked.

"Can do," Arnold replied.

"Great. Bye."

My phone was ringing, and when I picked up, it was Garth Brewster, who said, "Man, I feel like we're in the middle of a Mickey Spillane thriller."

"Who is Mickey Spillane?" I asked.

"You're kidding. You can't be that young!"

"Kidding. My favorite was Shell Scott," I said. "Just the man I want to talk to. I'm meeting with Macober and Pondorf at ten, and we are going to run a balls-out promotion."

"You know what?" Brewster said. "I think we can pull it off, and I didn't think so four months ago. I've got another idea. Let's break advertising that gives the consumer 4 percent off her bill every week through the end of the year. Two messages, one to the consumer—we are not the high-priced spread anymore. And the second to our competitors, 'Up yours!'" Garth said.

"Great idea. Maybe all of our competitors will team up to bury us at sea," I said.

"Jesus, Russ, I'm telling you this is the most fun you can have with your clothes on," Garth said as he hung up.

Next call was to Bob Santone, and he said, "Want to go back to the food brokerage business, Russ? It's not too late to walk away!"

"No way. First, that business is booming, so you were right after all. It's running better with Hartman than it ever ran with me there," I said.

"I told you, man. You were the eye candy," Bob replied.

"Second reason is we are just now hatching a plot that could send you to the street with your tin cup and pencils to supplement the 250 mil you have already secured."

"That's easy, Russ," he said. "But I need some collateral because I've already pledged your house."

"Holy shit," I said. "Talk about the definition of giving at the office and giving at home!"

"Listen, Russ, just don't tell me what you are doing. It's not that I don't want to know, but I don't want to be accused of inside trading because of the family connection," Bob said.

"Quick question," I said. "What do these headlines mean to our stock price?"

"Not a clue," he answered.

"What?" I said. "Isn't that your business to know?"

"Guilty as charged. But you guys are screwing those industry gurus up. You've got a buzz going. They are beginning to think that you are going to make it where they thought you had no chance. Honestly, it's fifty-fifty that the stock goes up, riding a contrarian wave of negative vibes. Russ, I don't know how to tell you this, but you have the foremost industry guru living in your house," Bob said.

"Well, kick me in the ass and call me Lash LaRue," I said.

"Lash LaRue?" Bob said. "Who the hell is Lash LaRue?"

"Sorry, I was playing old detective names with Garth earlier. Bye, Bob," I said as I hung up.

I was in the building, and I had forty-five minutes before Shirley and company arrived. I took my shoes off, put my feet up on the desk, placed my hands behind my head, and just stared at the ceiling for five minutes.

The thought that kept creeping through my head was the customer, the customer, our consumer, our consumer. We still had a way to go before we convinced her that we were her place to buy her groceries. For Christ's sake, Lucy Santone's fortune was riding on Food Basket, and she shopped elsewhere.

At the appointed hour, the door opened and Shirley Macober and Dave Pondorf appeared, filling the doorway. Macober turned toward the giant Pondorf, assumed a dance position, and Pondorf whirled Shirley around the room in what I thought was a bit of an accelerated foxtrot. Then they separated and did a very deep bow. I jumped to my feet and gave them a standing ovation as did Arnold Cable, who was standing behind them.

"To what do we owe that fabulous show?" I asked. "Honestly, Pondorf, you reminded me of Ron McDole, the defensive lineman for the Washington Redskins who was aptly nicknamed the Dancing Bear. And, Shirley, who knew?"

"You should have known. All honkies think we black folks have rhythm, and Pondorf was a star athlete back in the day," Shirley said. "It's our way of saying thanks for putting us on this special assignment. We have learned a ton, met some terrific folks, and we only have thirty days left to labor on your behalf. Thank God."

Pondorf chimed in and said, "Not to be disrespectful, Mr. Chairman, but we think you are the same old no-talent guy who fooled Galetti for thirty years. But we thank you for the excellent bonus and the opportunity to work and fix some stuff in the Food Basket distribution system. It was very fulfilling and rewarding."

"Well, I want you guys to go out on a high note," I said.

"Oh, fuck, Dave, a high note my ass. This means we'll be working weekends until the warden lets us go," Shirley said.

"You were expecting a gold watch?" Pondorf said with massive hands pointing toward the sky.

"I was expecting a pat on the back and a shot of whatever fine whiskey is lurking in the chief honky's credenza," Shirley replied.

Cable had lost it completely when he saw their dance number, but now he had his hankie out, and tears were rolling down his face when he said, "Never have so few people won such a lopsided verbal skirmish in so little time. The team of Macober-Pondorf, 10 and Riley, 0."

"I told you, Arnold, it's unmitigated abuse and harassment hardly seen this side of Gitmo," I said.

"Okay, here's the game plan. We take the fifty best-selling items, lower the prices below our competition, ship massive quantities to the stores, and break the advertising a week from Wednesday. Arnold, we'll need to start up the new media advertising ASAP."

Pondorf piped up and said, "This is going to be easier than you think from a warehouse standpoint. Food Basket has a drop-ship, direct-to-store capability that we don't have at Galetti. Basically, we can load up three stores' merchandise on a truck and drop it directly to the stores, bypassing the warehouse."

"I love it when you talk dirty," Shirley said to the group.

"Sexual harassment!" Pondorf yelled. "You all heard it."

Cable lost it again; out came the hankie as he choked out, "Inmates, 1! Ha, ha! Management, 0."

"Seriously, Russ," Shirley said, "what makes you think that Food Basket can stand up to the competition? Honestly, there's not much muscle here."

"Location, location, location," I said, "and execution, execution, execution. We've got seventy-five prime locations, we're supplemented by a forty-five-drugstore chain, and we can execute, especially if we have the element of surprise. This chain is starting to adopt an attitude, and when we pull this off, our folks are going to know that our competition is in for a tussle. Look at Barilla, for instance. They were a bunch of no-name pasta producers in Italy who banned together and formed a worldwide dominant company. That's the way we have to think. This is only one event, but this could be the one that takes us to the winner's circle.

"Just for your ears only, and Larry Baldwin will have to see how it affects the bottom line, but right after you pull off this aggressive pricing promotion, we will follow that with advertising that tells the consumer we are going to give them 4 percent off their Food Basket receipt from now until the end of the year."

"Everything?" said Pondorf. "I'll be driving back here to shop every week."

"Not everything, Dave," I said. "Beer, wine, cigarettes, milk, lottery, stamps, and bottle deposits will be excluded."

"That's going to give competitors some sleepless nights. Maybe they will head to Garth's pharmacies for a remedy," Shirley said.

"I'll say this," Arnold said reflectively, "I've been in this business for over forty years, but this one-two punch is some crazy shit! Man, if we are going down, we are going out in style!"

"I can tell you one thing: We are six weeks into a quarter that our former CFO said would be the worst in history, we are going to blow away the number from the same quarter a year ago, and we have just begun a path of solid traction. And one other thing, Arnold, when our circular comes out for this promotion, I want you to grab that business writer you've been playing footsies with all these years and compare our prices to the leading competitor's," I said.

"You'd plant a story like that?" Pondorf asked.

"In a New York minute," I said.

"My hat is off to you. What do you think, Shirley? And you thought he was a choirboy."

"I did. I also thought he was a cute little honky!" she said with an evil smile.

I could actually feel myself blush a little when I said, "Shirley Macober, I'm telling your husband on you!"

We all laughed as we went to work pricing the items we were going to feature, and if we disappeared in a sea of red ink, we would all point our fingers at Garth Brewster. We spent the next two hours pricing the items, checking the reliability of the vendors to deliver, and locking in the advertising agency to our media needs, frequency, and approximate gross rating points.

When that work was completed, I took four glasses down from the cabinet and poured everyone a neat glass of single malt scotch.

Shirley made the toast: "To the competition, big and small, may they burn in hell."

And we all tapped glasses and said, "May they burn in hell."

CHAPTER 26

Double Indemnity

She dialed his number and waited impatiently for him to pick up. She was highly agitated and wishing she had a cigarette. Suddenly a voice came on the phone and said, "Hello."

"It's me and I'm sinking fast," she said.

"I specifically told you not to call me."

"I'm on a burner. It can't be traced."

"That's fine, but what if they are tapping my phone? You don't think that they already have you on voice recognition?" he asked.

"So what if they do? They have nothing on you. Unlike you, I'll soon be sharing a cell with a Bella Abzug lookalike," she said.

"What are you worried about? This thing is working just as we planned. Don't fold on me now," he said.

"Listen, Sunshine, I'm thinking you're a better salesperson than Ross Perot and his flipcharts. Let me see if I can count the ways: You're watching the Red Sox from a luxury box, and I'm eating chop suey off a tin tray. What's wrong with this picture?"

"Look, I can't hold your hand twenty-four hours a day. Shape up and stick with the plan. The DA has walked right into our trap. They have a bunch of circumstantial evidence, and they got greedy. No way they are going to hang murder one on you," he said.

"What about Bruno?" she asked.

"He'll do the time for the crime," he said.

"If I'm found not guilty for murder one, do they get another crack at me for conspiracy?" she asked.

"No way. It's clear—it's double indemnity. Now listen to me. I'm not going to say this again. Stick to your knitting, and this time next year we'll be on a tropical island sucking on something with a tiny bamboo umbrella in it," he said.

"I'm hanging on by my fingernails. But if you don't line up the right lawyers and I'm found guilty, I'm going to sing long and loud. Count on it," she said.

"You keep that talk up and you might not make it to the trial," he said.

"Jesus, what happened to the bamboo umbrellas?" she asked.

"Dead people can't drink," he said.

"Easy, big fella," she said. "Any chance we can rendezvous at some remote location?"

"No way. Now get hold of yourself and let's get through this. Listen, I've been skimming off the top, and all that money is going into our account in the Caymans, so if you get depressed, think about a large floor safe stacked with thousand-dollar bills. Stick to your knitting. Things are on course."

He hung up. She threw her burner in the trash and turned on the TV.

CHAPTER 27

Joe Friday Lives

Bruno Jethroe's trial was over so quickly that with the press of the everyday business, I didn't see any of it firsthand. In five days, he was found guilty of murder in the first degree, and by all reports the evidence was overwhelming, but at the same time, the public defender representing Bruno either could not or would not offer much evidence to exonerate Mr. Jethroe.

Maybe it was morbid curiosity that drew me to the trial of Lucy Santone, but I was in the second row. It wasn't her pure beauty that made me side with her. And maybe it was self-inflicted, but she was resilient, smart, and one of those people who, when given a path to take, picked the wrong one. I didn't particularly like her, but I admired her spunk.

A police officer dressed in civilian clothes was on the stand. A very attractive woman lawyer was questioning him, and he answered the questions with a minimum number of words. I wondered to myself if they had a Jack Webb school of "yes, sir, no, sir" for court proceedings. I hear people in my mind's eye saying, "Who is Jack Webb?"

"Now, Captain Cummings, did you ask Mrs. Santone if she knew Bruno Jethroe?"

"I did," responded Cummings.

Cummings was an impressive-looking fellow—black hair, handsome with the map of Ireland etched in his face, definitely a former athlete with large hands, and he wore a charcoal gray suit, which I estimated cost pretty close to a grand. What do these public servants make nowadays?

"What was her response?" the woman lawyer asked.

"Who?" he responded.

"Her response was 'Who'?" repeated the attorney with the great legs.

"What was your immediate thought?"

"I thought I saw her flinch when I mentioned Mr. Jethroe's name," Cummings responded.

One of Lucy Santone's battery of lawyers jumped to his feet and said, "Objection, Your Honor. This isn't a face-reading process. This is total speculation."

The prosecution's lawyer, Assistant District Attorney Donna Mitchner, responded by saying, "Police Captain Alan Cummings has done hundreds of these types of interviews, and he's trained to watch these kinds of tells from a suspect."

"Tells," said the judge. "Ms. Mitchner, I'll presume that you are a poker player, but in this instance, Attorney Rosenbloom for the defense has the winning hand. I'll sustain the objection."

Mitchner turned back to the witness and said, "What did she say next?"

"I tried to jog her memory by telling her that he was a bartender with a pretty extensive rap sheet," Cummings said.

"Did she respond to that description of Mr. Jethroe?" Mitchner asked.

"She did," said Cummings. "She told me that he was a bartender at a watering hole that her husband and she used to frequent."

"Now, Captain, during the course of your investigation, did you uncover any evidence that made you suspect that their relationship was a good deal closer than she was intimating?"

"I did," replied Cummings.

I was getting really irritated with this police guy. It was like leading a blind person through a patch of poison ivy, carefully, so carefully. I wanted to scream out, "What the hell did you uncover?"

"Tell the court specifically what you found at the crime scene, Captain," Mitchner said.

"A love letter from Lucy Santone to Bruno Jethroe with very specific references to her love for him and her complete disdain for her husband," Cummings said.

This turned the courtroom into complete disorder. Several people, I assumed reporters, left the room, and the judge hit her gavel three times, calling for order. When she threatened to clear the courtroom, order was restored, and she wisely called for a twenty-minute break.

I turned to walk outside when I ran into Arnold Cable.

"Arnold, you just missed a dandy—a love letter that links Lucy Santone very closely to Bruno Jethroe."

"I'm guessing Santone's battery of lawyers aren't going to make that disappear," Arnold said. "Word is that this group makes a lot of things disappear."

"I don't know. The guy is a police captain, and I don't think I'd want to meet him in a dark alley!" I said.

When court resumed, ADA Donna Mitchner brought the letter forward to the judge and said, "I'd be happy to read the letter if the defense would like to hear it in its entirety."

Rosenbloom leaped to his feet and said, "It's not necessary, Judge, we have a copy of the letter as a part of discovery."

I was beginning to warm up to Donna Mitchner. She might be beautiful, but she could put the knife in and twist it. Cummings was still on the stand, and Mitchner looked at the captain and said, "Do you have any other evidence concerning this relationship?"

"We have interviews from Mr. Jethroe's neighbors as sworn affidavits, and we have a series of recorded phone calls between the defendants."

"Okay, let's hold the interviews since they were done by Detective O'Malley and go to the phone calls. What was your impression after listening to them?"

"That they were intimate. They carried on a good deal of phone sex, and in the interim, she wired him some $70,000 while he was on the run from the law, which includes the bail money that allowed him to be on the street."

"Objection," screamed Rosenbloom. "This is speculation smearing my client without due process."

"Judge, I'd be happy to play these phone conversations for the court, and I will submit as evidence the bank records that will show Ms. Santone wiring money to Mr. Jethroe."

Rosenbloom reversed field very quickly and said, "We will stipulate to the content of the phone conversations being as Captain Cummings described them in his testimony, Your Honor."

Donna Mitchner wheeled away from the judge, looked at the somewhat flustered Rosenbloom, and said, "Your witness."

Rosenbloom moved quickly to a position directly in front of Captain Alan Cummings and asked, "Are you and the assistant district attorney intimate?"

Mitchner was on her feet and said, "Objection, Your Honor. What possible relevance could this have to a court case where neither one of us are the defendants?"

The judge looked at Mr. Rosenbloom and said, "I have a tendency to agree with Ms. Mitchner unless you have anything else to say."

"Your Honor," Rosenbloom said, "I mean no disrespect to my worthy adversary, but this type of cozy relationship puts my client at a hefty disadvantage. This tag team's focus on my client seems extreme when she is fighting for her very life."

"I'll overrule this objection, but I feel this is mighty thin gruel, Mr. Rosenbloom," said the judge.

"Well, Captain?" Rosenbloom said.

"What was the question again, Mr. Rosenbloom?" asked Captain Cummings.

This caused a big laugh from the crowd, but Rosenbloom kept his cool. Now I admired Cummings. Rosenbloom had to know that he wasn't questioning a rookie.

"Are you and Ms. Mitchner intimate?"

"We are," Cummings admitted.

"Now Mr. Cummings," Rosenbloom said, "according to my records, you found the letter at the crime scene on April 12 but did not interview Ms. Santone until May 2."

Cummings took his notebook out of his pocket, flipped through a few pages, looked up at Rosenbloom, and said, "That's correct."

"Then you already knew Ms. Santone's relationship with Bruno Jethroe before you interviewed her," Rosenbloom said.

"Yes, I had read the letter," Cummings said.

"But in your interview with Ms. Santone three weeks later, you asked her if she knew Bruno Jethroe, right?" he asked.

"Yes, sir," Cummings responded.

"So, Captain, this is a clear case of entrapment. You led this poor unsuspecting citizen along a path of deceit, trying to make her seem like an outright liar."

Rosenbloom looked at Captain Cummings for a response.

"Is there a question buried in that little diatribe, Mr. Rosenbloom?" the captain asked. "For the record, she was lying."

The courtroom exploded into laughter, and this time Rosenbloom didn't keep his cool. He said, "Judge, I believe you should declare a mistrial. This so-called police officer trapped my client into making false statements on the record."

"Absolutely not," said the judge with some vehemence. "It's called good police work. You need to take your defense up a level, Mr. Rosenbloom. Do you understand, Mr. Rosenbloom?"

"Yes, Your Honor, I do," Rosenbloom said.

The judge called a one-hour recess for lunch.

Fourteen Is the New Thirteen

I'd left the murder trial at lunch on the first day, but at least from the newspaper reports, it looked as if the prosecution had a pretty solid case. I had learned from Arnold Cable and his Lawyers Weekly group that Bruno Jethroe would take the stand for the defense, and I wanted to see a part of that proceeding. I'd been a witness in the Galetti debacle, and it was no picnic. Assistant District Attorney Donna Mitchner was smart, experienced, and beautiful, but she had that killer look of a hungry hired assassin, and I wanted to see that gunfight.

I could no longer see the lugs on the wheel of our momentum as it moved. Speed had increased perceptively, and gross sales, profits, appearance of the stores, and good advertising carried us into our major effort to show the consumer that their neighborhood super-market chain was priced competitively and, like Norm on *Cheers*, we knew their names. It started out badly—like a well-meaning person trying to push a peanut up a hill with his nose. It kept rolling back down the hill. But Arnold Cable at store level and Shirley Macober, Dave Pondorf, and Dave Williams worked miracles in their respective departments, avoided resentment, and to some degree, actually bonded with the Food Basket employees. Garth Brewster joined forces with Bill Hartman, and they became a major pain in the side to our competition by running one or two well-known items at insane prices in what were now the Food Basket drugstores. Additionally, Brewster had single-handedly provided prescription availability in a majority of our stores. Hey, what am I trying to say here? We were having fun, and a leg was moving toward kicking a little butt!

Two people I have failed to mention had made contributions, but more in the periphery than the mainstream, everyday business. Bob Santone secured the loan that allowed us to operate, and Holly spotlighted us in her industry as a possible turnaround success story. Our stock was ticking ever so slowly upward as we had moved from five and a half dollars a share to just under eight dollars. To my surprise, the current trial had absolutely no effect at all.

And so it was with great sadness and some trepidation that I met with Macober, Pondorf, and Dave Williams for the last time.

Pondorf, the gentle giant, led off with his usual commentary.

"I'm going to miss you, Russ, like I'm going to miss a canker sore."

"Yeah, it's going to be tough giving up that 140-mile commute every day," said Dave Williams.

"Well, actually, I'd like to stay a little longer so I could pat that cute little tush of yours, Russ," Shirley Macober said. "But I think we've done all we can do here to make you look good. And believe me, that takes more makeup than Oprah has on the covers of her magazine."

"I expected a good deal more fawning on your part as I extended your stay here for sixty more days than the original contracts and compensated you handsomely for it," I said with a straight face.

"What?" said Pondorf. "We would have run faster than a turkey at Thanksgiving time if you'd let us go after the first ninety days."

Williams and Macober laughed. They knew I was just pulling their legs.

"Tell me how you view your departments now versus when you first arrived," I asked.

"Same people, but now they give a shit," said Shirley. "They are seeing the positive sales figures, withdrawals, and the supervisors in the field are giving them positive feedback on eliminating out-of-stocks."

"Similar story in forecasting and profit," Williams said. "The difference is just when we think we have a feel for forecasting, Shirley and Dave crank it up, and we are too slow to adjust. We need to get ahead of the increased withdrawals, and we're doing it."

"Like they said," Pondorf said, "the distribution folks have a lot of pride. I'd hire any one of them to work with me at Galetti. Additionally, Russ, we are leaving you on a high note. This big bomber of a sale has been a smash, and the Food Basket share of market will be up more than 10 percent if I don't miss my guess."

"I'm really looking forward to that," I said. "It's been a while in coming, and I'm sure Walmart won't be affected at all, but our grocery brethren are going to take it in the shorts."

"I don't know if you guys saw it yet," Arnold Cable, who had been silent to this point, said, "but the Providence Journal is running a story comparing our prices to others in the marketplace, and it gives us some severely good press."

"Arnold, you did it!" I exclaimed. "You planted that story, didn't you?"

"Well...er...I may have supplied some data for it," Arnold said with a sly smile.

"My thanks to all of you, especially Shirley and David Pondorf," I said. "Maybe you'll get me fired again."

"One can only hope," Pondorf added.

As those two got up to leave, I shook their hands and received hugs from both of them. Shirley's parting comment was, "Russ, I wish you the best. Hurry up and solve this dilemma so you can come back to your old job, and I get to kick you out of my office every other Tuesday!"

"Will do, Shirley," I said. "I miss taking my lumps from you, even though I was responsible for your training."

Pondorf piped in one final comment as he headed down the hallway, "Hey, Russ, after Shirley throws you out of her office, come on down to the warehouse. Some of the guys and I will box you up, staple you, and ship you to a store."

I looked at the two behemoths heading down the hallway and said, "With friends like you, who needs enemies?"

I went back in the office, sat down at the table with Dave Williams and Arnold Cable, and said, "What do we know about the short on total revenues?"

"We know how it's being skimmed, but we don't know who," Williams said.

"I have a theory," Arnold said.

I cut Arnold off and said, "Let's have the facts first, David."

"Okay, it's actually pretty ingenious. We traced it to one store in Warren, Rhode Island. There are fourteen registers in that store, and we are only getting receipts from thirteen of them."

"I'll be damned," I said. "How can you not report a register?"

"Because it's a phantom," Williams said. "I was in the store with the paperwork, and I kept counting fourteen registers when the paperwork I had said there were thirteen registers."

"Well, if it isn't supposed to be there, how did we know we're light any revenue?" I asked.

"Simple," Arnold said. "The warehouse withdrawals were too high to the store volume."

"Not so simple," I said. "Who figured it out?"

"I did," Williams said. "We run these kinds of inventory withdrawals versus sales all the time at Galetti."

"Dave, you are the bean counter supreme for busting this one. Talk about a needle in a haystack. You had to run down thirty stores to find this," I said with a good deal of wonder in my voice.

"Yeah, and the truth is I'd made my way through most of them before I stumbled on to this little beauty."

"Where's the money going?" I asked.

"Right to the basement into a secured room that is padlocked and marked off as a restricted area."

"How much are they getting?"

"Between fifteen and eighteen million a year," Dave responded.

"Holy shit," I said, "that's a lot of money."

"It would be a nice retirement nest egg, but in a three-billion-dollar company, it's a fly on an elephant's ass."

"How long have we been watching?" I asked.

"About a week. We have a camera on it 24-7," Williams said. "Nobody's showed yet."

"Okay, Arnold," I said, "what's your theory?"

"Guess who lives in Warren?" he asked.

"I give up."

"Your erstwhile CFO," Arnold said.

"Joe Snyder?" I asked.

"The very same," Arnold responded.

"Arnold, can you find someone among your acquaintances in Providence who can get a financial status on Snyder?"

"Can do, boss," Arnold said.

I turned to Dave Williams and said, "I knew you were good, but this was really great work on your part to uncover this plot. You are headed back to Galetti, but I'll personally keep you up to date on this one."

"Thanks, Chief," Williams said. "Two things—first, I'd bring Joe Galetti in on this because his connections could help us to determine how deep this goes."

"What's the second thing?" I asked.

"Hurry back home and play golf with me. I need some easy money."

CHAPTER 29

It Just Didn't Add Up

It had come down to Bruno Jethroe. The prosecution had done its job and locked and loaded Bruno for a lifetime in an eight-by-ten room. They had motive and the murder weapon belonging to Mr. Jethroe, and the defense put him on the stand hoping he could provide evidence that Lucy Santone was not involved.

Bruno was about five feet nine inches tall, and I was guessing he weighed 220 pounds. He had oversized arms and a large chest that made his head look smaller than it actually was. He was dark complexioned, slightly balding, and his face just to the right of his lips had a twitch. We all knew Bruno. The newspapers had profiled him thoroughly to include an interview with his third-grade teacher who remarked that in music class "Bruno sang very low and sometimes not at all."

He was to stay in school for three more years and then leave to become an errand boy for a drug czar in the local region. Bruno bounced around on the fringe of the crime element, spent time in juvie, and in so doing, made the wrong kinds of friends. For today's session, he was dressed in a pair of light-brown-covered cloth pants and a blue button-down shirt.

After he was sworn in, Lucy's attorney began by asking him a bit of a leading question: "Mr. Jethroe, having been found guilty of murder in the first degree, do you understand the allegation against Ms. Santone?"

"I do," said Bruno. "It don't get more serious than murder one. But this case against her is totally circumstances."

"Do you mean 'circumstantial'?" her attorney asked.

"Whatever. In plain language, it's bullshit," Bruno said.

"Mr. Jethroe," the judge said, "I'm going to ask you to refrain from swearing while on the stand."

"Sorry, Judge," Bruno said.

"Now, Mr. Jethroe, what is your relationship with Lucy Santone?"

"Very close," replied Bruno.

"What do you mean?"

"We met five years ago. I did odd jobs for the Santones, including driving them to airports and other destinations. Over time, we became lovers," observed Bruno.

"And were you in this relationship right up to the time you were extradited back to Rhode Island?"

"Did you not listen to the phone calls between me and Lucy? I'm beginning to wonder about her representation," Bruno said.

This brought a titter from the crowd, but Lucy's lawyer was unfazed as he said, "Just setting that straight for the record, Bruno, and yes, we listened to and we have been over the evidence with a fine-tooth comb.

"Last question and important question. Mr. Jethroe, was Mrs. Santone in any way connected to these events that led to the murder of Mr. Santone?"

"How could that be?" Bruno asked. "I didn't murder Alex Santone, so how could Lucy be connected to it as an accomplice on some kind of cahoots to take him out?"

"Thank you, Mr. Jethroe. Your witness," the lawyer said as he turned to Donna Mitchner.

"No questions, Your Honor," Mitchner said.

It was nagging at me. I don't know what Lucy Santone's defense strategy was, but I couldn't help feeling what an odd couple Bruno

Jethroe and Lucy Santone were. Everything pointed to Bruno Jethroe as the killer, but it was too neat, too pat, a breadcrumb trail to his door. I believed him when he said Lucy wasn't involved in the murder of Alex Santone, but the reason I believed him was that by association, I didn't think he had killed Alex Santone. He was small potatoes; he could steal your credit card and run up a bill at Target, but he just wasn't up to this task.

Suddenly I snapped out of it. I had a business on the brink, I hadn't contributed to my food brokerage business in six months, and my kids were calling me Uncle Dad because I was away from home so much.

CHAPTER 30

Progress by the Inch

I was excited, but I didn't know why. Bill Hartman and Garth Brewster, smart and smarter, had asked me to come to the Woonsocket store to look at something they had been cooking up. As I walked into the store (wash my mouth out with soap), I thought I was in a Whole Foods or a Trader Joe's. Employees were in chef's hats attending shiny glass counters that had exotic cheese wheels, homemade breads and pies, a sandwich and hoagie bar, a sushi section, and six sets of steaming containers of various comfort foods to fix homemade meals. It was so unlike any Food Basket store I'd ever seen, I actually felt a little disoriented. Standing at the end of this montage of delectables in complete uniform, including chef's hats, were Hartman and Brewster with big smiles on their faces.

"I absolutely love this. Jesus, I thought just for a second that I walked into the wrong store," I said.

We all shook hands, and I wanted to give these guys a hug for their creativity. Hartman had an article in his hand from the local newspaper that praised the efforts made in this store, but it concluded that Food Basket had been uncompetitive for so long on price that "only a miracle would cause Food Basket to regain a foothold in the industry."

"He's right," I said as Hartman and Brewster looked somewhat surprised. "He's right, but he didn't look deep enough. We've been putting one foot in front of the other, cleaning up stores, remodeling, lowering pricing, running a megapromotion, changing our media approach, and collecting new consumers like pennies in a wishing well. But the difference with your idea is that it's exciting to the consumer, and our competition is going to have to work to emulate it. Our other advantage is that we have almost 7 percent of the grocery stores, second only to Stop and Shop, so we can spread it to more consumers more quickly than most."

"Maybe we can do what John Catsimatidis did in New York," Hartman said with a smile.

"Who the hell is John Catsimatidis?" Garth asked.

"He is a billionaire who owns Gristedes Supermarkets and who was making a run for mayor in New York City," Hartman said. "His chain has been losing share in New York for years, so he decided to remodel one of his supermarkets and called it Trader John's."

"What happened?" I asked.

"They were hit with a cease-and-desist order from Trader Joe's," Hartman said. "They went to court, and his defense was, and I quote, 'My name is John, and I'm a trader. I don't know what their problem is.'"

"Okay then, I'm presuming that this little plan you have hatched won't be called Trader Garth's," I said.

"It is tempting," Garth said. "But no, we do plan to try and convert 8 to 10 percent of the stores in the right locations to this format."

"Excellent work. I'm really proud to know you guys. We have our first six-month shares coming out next week, so cross your fingers and toes," I said. "See you later. I'm off to see Joe Galetti."

As I drove back to headquarters to meet with Joe Galetti, I needed to switch gears to a whole new topic. Driving time had always been thinking time for me, but with the advent of cell phones, texting, tweeting, and other social media devices, I found that my thinking time was severely reduced. I know some of my friends would immediately think that was a negative as I wasn't the quickest mind out of the blocks to begin with. I solved the problem quite simply by shutting everything down at drive time. I've had texters coming right at me before they regained control of their steering wheels. Put me in the camp of the nonmultitasker. I'm a "one thing at a time" type of guy.

Just as I was laying out my theory on working efficiently, my cell phone rang. I had forgotten to turn it off.

I picked it up, and on the other end was Arnold Cable, who said, "Hey, boss, news from the security camera in the basement of the Warren store."

"Fire away," I said.

"The money was picked up yesterday," Arnold said. "It was a longtime employee of the store, and I thought you'd be interested in his next stop."

"Joe Snyder's house?" I asked.

"Right on the money, not meaning to make a pun here, Russ."

"What about his financials?" I asked.

"Still working on it, but nothing looks out of order so far," Arnold said. "What do you want to do next?"

"Nothing," I said. "Let's let it ride. This is bigger than both of us. I need to have a sit-down with Bob Santone. He doesn't want to know the everyday stuff, but this is major embezzlement."

"Okay. How do you like the Woonsocket store?" Arnold asked.

"Fabulous," I said and hung up and turned the infernal machine off.

Joe Galetti was waiting for me in my office. I could tell he felt right at home when I walked through the door. Joe was casually dressed in a golf shirt; he had a cup of coffee in his hand and was leaning over the *Wall Street Journal* with his shoes off.

I laughed at how he had turned my office into his living room as I said, "I never came into your office with my shoes off."

"You could have. Kick yours off, relax those bunions. Mine were really barking today," he said.

"How are you?" I asked. "Other than very comfortable."

"I'll tell you the truth. I'm terrific, and I'm happy to report that most of the power structures that I knew intimately are still in place or it's a next-generation relative who is now carrying the baton."

"Is that good?" I asked.

"In one way that I was not expecting, yes. I thought some of these new faces would treat me as a relic, but a lot of them treat me as some kind of godlike icon," he said with a big smile.

"How about our store location for Fall River, New Bedford, and Taunton?"

"Good news and bad news," he said.

"Bad news first," I said.

"Shaw's and Star have leased the area that you want to build on."

"Crap," I said almost to myself. "Good news."

"You are the proud new owner of all the land that surrounds their site," Joe said.

"What the hell! I said.

"Wait. Did you just do what I think you did?"

"I did," Joe said.

"Let me see if I have it right. They have this great plot of land to build a store, but they have no access to it," I said.

"You were always a smart kid," Joe said. "I'd be expecting a call from their real estate folks any day now. And, Russ, my scouts are telling me that they really don't intend on building a store there and that they could use the money by selling it. They lost a cool 1.5 billion last year, and the new management is anxious, to say the least."

"Okay, Joe, I forgot what a brain beats between those ears of yours. I'll look forward to their call. In the meantime, I need to run another scenario by you that will require some digging on your part," I said.

It took me about three to four minutes to explain to Joe what was happening with the cash register that was firing money into the basement and Joe Snyder's involvement. He listened very carefully and then asked, "Who is your accounting firm?"

"Deloitte and Touche," I replied.

"All right, call Toilet and Douche and tell them to get out here and get to the bottom of this like they should have whenever this started. And by the way, give Dave Williams the equivalent of what you usually pay those guys and stiff them."

"Okay, what else?" I asked.

"Nothing else. Let me nose around and find out if this is an isolated incident or if it's connected to other illegal activities."

"Got it," I said. "Glad to have you on board, Joe."

After Joe had departed, I checked my messages and dialed the one number that always makes my heart skip a beat.

"Holly Riley."

"Russell Riley," I responded.

"I was just day dreaming about you," she said.

"I like the sound of that," I responded.

"Yeah, we were in the middle of some unnatural sex act, and your mother walked in," Holly said.

"Sounds more like a nightmare," I said. "But that's why I called."

"Unnatural sex?" she asked.

"I was thinking I'd give my mom a call and see if she'd stay over with the kids and we might repeat our dinner out. You could throw in that luxury hotel you are always bragging about."

"That's such a good idea that I'll arrange everything, including calling Claire. We're really tight, you know," Holly said.

"I know. Mom brags about you all the time. She says your financial advice has made her a woman of means!" I said.

"Okay, it's settled. I'll pick you up at your building at four o'clock."

"Four? That's pretty early," I said.

"I thought we'd see if the hotel accommodations are up to snuff," she said.

"I love you," I said.

"I love you," she said, and she hung up.

* * *

After lunch, I made the call that I really didn't want to make because it involved some serious bad news. I asked to speak to him after I had identified myself to his secretary. The next thing I heard was Bob Santone.

"Bob, it's Russ. How are you?"

"A lot better than I was six months ago, thanks to you and your Les Brown Band of Renown."

"Things are looking up. I won't spoil the fun for you, but if you get a chance, drive on down to the Woonsocket store and walk inside."

"What's up?" Bob asked.

"Just do it. It'll make your day," I said.

"So are you on schedule? One year to turn us around and you turn back into a pumpkin?" he asked.

"You may have to put up with me a little longer. But I can tell you this thing is starting to turn around," I said. "We owe Trip Galetti plenty for his contribution, so if you can think of some way to express our appreciation, that would be helpful."

"I can't believe you have his uncle working for you," Bob said.

"He's a schmoozer, a fixer, and an influence peddler, and he's making a difference for us," I said. "On the financial front, we have a major hiccup that you need to know about. Our gross receipts were coming up short by fifteen to eighteen million a year. I put Dave Williams on it, and we found that in the Warren store, the cash from one of the registers was, in effect, going to someone's account in the Caymans."

"Jesus on a piece of melba toast," Bob said.

"I'd prefer a little three-bean salad," I said. Bob laughed.

"Jesus, Russ, you are good. You can make me laugh when eighteen million is flying out the window in a parcel post container. What do we know? No, wait. Who found this?"

"Dave Williams, CFO of Galetti," I said.

"Russ, I don't mean to be a geek, but he literally found a needle in a haystack. We have over two thousand registers in those eighty stores," Bob said with a slight tone of amazement.

"Now what do we know?"

"The security team put a 24-7 camera on where the proceeds were going and recorded a longtime employee of the store gathering the money. His next stop was Joe Snyder's house," I said.

"What are we doing about it?" he asked.

"Nothing until we talked to you," I responded.

"What should we do?" Bob asked.

"I'd start by taking the security footage to the police, arresting the employee, and see how long it takes him to sing," I responded.

"I'll handle it," Bob said. "And I'll give Trip a call to thank him. Russ, this is pretty characteristic of what your team has done for the last six months. We are very lucky to have you on board."

"Thanks, Bob. Keep me in the loop on this embezzlement thing, okay?"

"Will do. See you," Bob said.

CHAPTER 31

A Shadow of Reasonable Doubt

I knew that I should be hard at work at my desk, but the six-month shares weren't due until noon, so I snuck off to court to hear the final arguments in the Bruno Jethroe and Lucy Santone murder trial. The prosecution was up first, and Donna Mitchner just looked well prepared. In fact, she looked sensational in a blue linen suit with subtle white piping at the wrists of the jacket and around the bottom of the skirt. If I were the judge, I would have to admonish the male members of the jury to pay attention to the content of the words, not the looks of the person delivering them.

But as soon as she spoke, all visual distractions receded into the background. Her voice was strong and sure, and those green eyes were focused on the objective: sending two people to prison for life.

"Ladies and gentlemen of the jury," she began, "I think that we have proven without a shadow of a doubt that Lucy Santone and Bruno Jethroe conspired to kill her husband so they could reap the benefits from his will and a two-and-a-half-million-dollar insurance policy on the victim's life. Let me remind you that sixty days before Mr. Alex Santone was gunned down in his own living room, his wife,

Lucy Santone, increased the insurance policy from $1.4 million to $2.5 million, and that Mrs. Santone hand-carried the premium payment to her insurance agent.

"Additionally, we have the love letter from Lucy Santone to Bruno Jethroe found at the murder scene which states her unequivocal love for Bruno, her disdain for her husband, and I quote, 'Soon he'll be gone and we will be able to make a life of our own.'

"As for Mr. Jethroe, we have him as a guest of the state for the foreseeable future. Recall, we have sworn affidavits from Mr. Jethroe claiming that he would live out his life on his, and I quote, 'mistress's insurance money.' He also told a neighbor, and I quote again, 'If my bitch doesn't keep her mouth shut, I'll pop her too.'

"Ladies and gentlemen, I believe in due process, but I'm a little embarrassed to be taking up your time with this case. These two people, Lucy Santone and Bruno Jethroe, murdered Alex Santone without a pang of conscience. I'm asking you to come back with a guilty verdict for Ms. Lucy Santone, and then I will push to ensure that she receives the maximum penalty under the law. Thank you."

The lawyers for the defense were a little slow to move when one of the three stood with some three-inch-by-five-inch cards in his hand. He was almost perfectly round. If you laid him on his side, he could roll all the way down a bowling alley and guarantee you a strike.

"Esteemed members of the jury, what we have here is a kerfuffle. The able prosecutor in this case has confused circumstantial evidence and the mutterings of a man to his neighbors as actual facts. Just a few examples.

"They say that Ms. Santone should be convicted of murder when they already have the shooter—and he has been found guilty.

"They claim that Lucy Santone planned and conspired with Mr. Jethroe to kill her husband, but there is not one conversation in the hours of conversation that the wiretaps provided to substantiate that allegation, nothing.

"They foist on you a love letter from Mrs. Santone to Mr. Jethroe that is evidence that they killed the victim. It says, and I quote, 'I can't wait until we are together on a more permanent basis.'

This is reasonable evidence to put two people away for life? Could they have been talking divorce or just leaving an abusive husband? Oh, did the prosecution forget to tell you that Lucy Santone's husband was a drunk and a wastrel who was driving an eighty-store grocery chain into the ground with his excesses?

"This case by the prosecution is a clever display of partial facts. It's like a display in a store—if you pull a key can out of the middle of it, it will collapse under its own weight.

"In summary, ladies and gentlemen, all they have is a weapon with no fingerprints on it. That's their key piece in the middle of the display. If you start to ask questions about it, the rest of the scenario falls apart. Perhaps Ms. Santone may be guilty of perjury by not admitting her relationship with Mr. Jethroe, but her involvement in the murder is both ludicrous and circumstantial.

"We are counting on you to provide the due diligence to see if the facts hold up or are just part of a clever patchwork to make you think you've heard an open-and-shut case when there are more gaps in it than two acres of gopher holes.

"Thank you for your time and consideration, ladies and gentlemen of the jury."

All during the summations, Lucy Santone sat in an elegant light pink suit with a white blouse, and she seemed not to move at all. It appeared that she didn't even blink. But to me, she looked like a slightly vulnerable, very attractive neighbor who had to be in the wrong place. Somebody had made a mistake. She should have been at a soccer practice with one of her kids instead of being on trial for murder.

I thought the lawyer for the defense did just what he had accused the prosecution of doing. He had introduced the confusion, to use his word, kerfuffle. His sole mission was to place that shadow of a doubt in the jurors' minds. Would they come back and say there was a reasonable doubt that Lucy killed Alex Santone? I really didn't know, but the world would know when the jury came back with a verdict.

Me, I had more mundane things to think about, to include our six-month shares. They were important to me, but I couldn't help think that Lucy Santone had much more serious consequences to ponder.

CHAPTER 32

The Common Denominator Is

The shares were in, and we couldn't hoist some French champagne, but we could take a couple of drags off a bottle of prosecco! We had gained a half point of share to 6.8 percent, and the market leader had stayed even at 11.3 percent. Surprisingly, we had taken share, it appeared, from some of the nontraditional food outlets such as BJ's Wholesale Club and Target. I wouldn't have guessed that, and I was hoping that those outlets thought of it as an aberration as well. I felt that we would have taken it from more traditional competitors, but beggars can't be choosers. According to The Griffin Report, it was the first gain of market share for Food Basket since the July–December period of 2007, a long time between drinks of colored water.

That same day, the local rag came out with a price comparison of six traditional grocery competitors, and our total for the chosen fifteen items was $36.15, second to the big guy's total of $34.06. That's why he is the big guy! I had this feeling that Arnold Cable might have done something to speed this pricing survey to publication. The phones were ringing off the wall. People actually wanted to talk to us. The first call I made was to Holly. She was pleased, not surprised, and told me that our stock had touched ten dollars midday but had since fallen back from that high.

Next call should have been to Bob Santone, but instead I called Shirley Macober and Dave Pondorf on a conference line and said, "Sweetheart, we're up half a point, and the latest published pricing analysis has us second to the big guy."

"Who you calling sweetheart?" Pondorf grumbled.

"You guys were great. Take a bow," I said and hung up.

Next call to Bob Santone turned an unexpected corner after I delivered the good news on pricing and share.

Bob said, "Great job, Russ. Who would have thunk it? I'm afraid I have some more somber news, however. Joe Snyder was found this morning hanging in his garage."

"Jesus" was all I could muster.

"I am guessing the police will want to talk to you," Bob said.

"Why?" I asked.

"Being let go at Food Basket, depression, any enemies, etcetera," Bob said.

"That sounds like they don't think it's a suicide," I said.

"I don't know, Russ," Bob said. "I'm a little out of my depth. On a happier note, I stopped at the Woonsocket store, and I was totally shocked. Great merchandising, great attitude by the employees. I'm not kidding, Russ, they are actually having some fun in that store. Tell Garth and Hartman that my hat's off to them!" Bob said.

"Will do," I responded and hung up.

I put my feet up on the desk and stared straight up at the ceiling. What turned out to be a fairly straight-up project—bringing an eighty-store food chain back to life—was growing more complex by the minute. On the periphery, we had a murderer about to come to justice, and another potential one looming ever closer. I really didn't want to be involved with the city police concerning Joe Snyder's death. We had bought land to encompass the piece we really wanted, I had two of my executives slicing cheese with chef's hats on, a cash register that delivered directly to the basement, and competition that wanted revenge for the most recent share numbers. I kept thinking about what Dr. Phil says to the troubled visitors on his show: "The common denominator is you!"

CHAPTER 33

Missing Natalie Jacobson

I started to move into a positive gear as I perused the daily rag. I thought I was in a tough spot. How about this PFC who released all those secret documents, received a thirty-five-year prison term, and he now wanted to be known as Valerie! Two questions kept running through my mind: Who was going to pay for his/her change of sex operation? And why did a PFC have access to those documents in the first place?

But what was really making my day was that Holly and I were on the way to our cottage on Craigville Beach to visit with Jenny and Bill Hartman and to eat some delicious food cooked on the infamous wastebasket cooker that Hartman has perfected. It occurred to me that we might do a side business at the brokerage selling this type of machine to the public and/or using it for an in-store display piece.

"A buck three eighty for your thoughts," Holly said.

"Thinking about how I'm looking forward to this rendezvous and if it would be a viable idea to manufacture and sell Hartman's wastebasket cooker," I said. "How about you?"

"I was thinking you need to be careful about what you wish for," Holly said. "I really wanted you to take this job. I thought it would be stimulating. You seemed a little bored lately, but I don't know if I didn't overdo it a little. You've got a tiger by the tail. What are you thinking?"

"I'm loving it, but you are right. At times, I've felt that I'm over my head and yearn for the days when the worst thing that could happen was that Shirley would toss me out of her office," I said.

"Have you and Bill talked about your future employment?" Holly asked.

The woman is uncanny. She knows where I'm going before I get there. For future reference, I better not even form the word *affair* in my mind because before I know it, I'll be spending my nights in a cardboard box in a hobo camp.

"I've been thinking about it. I really like the food brokerage business, and I love the idea that Hartman and I have built a business from scratch. I'm not sure I have a closer friend in the world."

"Besides me," Holly interjected.

"Besides you," I said. "But I love the interaction of the store and the consumer. I love walking down aisles, seeing great meat departments, and the thrill of trying to outthink and outplan the competition. But fortunately for me, I don't have to make a choice because I've already put the gears in motion with Jim Sneed to find my successor."

"Oh does Bob Santone know this little tidbit?" Holly asked.

"Well, not directly. But when I first talked to him, he told me the job was for about a year."

"But things have changed," Holly said.

"How?" I asked, not understanding where Holly was going.

"Sometimes you are a little naïve," Holly said. "And I love you for it. But step back for a minute. We have this guy. We'll call him Russ in this story. In his first job a feuding family goes to court, and on the first day of the trial, first cousins with the same first and last names get in a fistfight. But Russ pays no attention to this distraction, other than fantasizing about a TV reporter named Natalie Jacobson, and actually builds the chain's volume while the family continues to lob grenades at close range."

"Natalie who?" I asked.

"Don't interrupt, I'm rolling. Then after that sleight of hand, he's asked to become the CEO of a chain where the CEO is murdered and the CFO is pumping money into a basement. He has now started to move the speedometer forward on this chain, which most people had already placed in the graveyard. It's working on about six and a half of eight cylinders, and the forward momentum is palatable. The stock is 25¢ a share from doubling to $11 a share since he took over.

"Here's the question, Russ: Why in the world would Bob Santone ever look for a successor?"

I rolled it over in my mind, looked at Holly, and said, "God, you're even more gorgeous when you get all fired up. Here's the question for you."

"Okay," Holly said, looking at me with a very skeptical eye.

"It's rumored that Hartman has gone Chef Boyardee on us. He's fixing things like shrimp kabobs. How do we get him back to hamburgers and hot dogs on the waste/paper basket cooker?"

"Russ!" Holly said.

"You're probably right. One thing this conversation has shown me is that I need to huddle with Hartman on this very question," I said.

"Right answer," Holly said. "It's easy to take credit for the turnaround, but in truth, your management team is kick-ass."

We pulled into our place near Craigville Beach and stood outside to admire it. It's called a cottage, but that covers a lot of ground on Cape Cod. A cottage can be anything from a five-hundred-square-foot, one-bedroom place to a ten-thousand-square-foot house with a free standing garage apartment, a swimming pool, and a dock with a one-hundred-foot schooner tied up to it with a crew of five. A cottage is a cottage is a cottage.

Ours is near the low end, built in the early 1920s; it is a converted barn. The key feature is a master bedroom that leads to an open porch with a view of the ocean that is exquisite. We didn't know anything about the area, but Bill Hartman made it his mission to convince us that we needed a place down here fairly near his cottage. The boy can sell!

As we looked down at the beach, we saw two people sitting between a curious ring of smoke and knew immediately that Jenny and Bill Hartman had fired up the cooker and were probably wondering where we were. We hustled inside, changed to bathing suits, grabbed two towels and two beach chairs, and headed to the beach. As we moved closer to the beach, we saw that there were some pretty good-sized breakers and a nice little ten-knot wind, the kind of day when one could be burned by the sun and not feel it because the breeze kept it cool and comfortable.

Jenny greeted us with a hug, and Hartman allayed my fears of him going upscale gourmet as I saw burgers and dogs ready to be cooked.

I said, "Thank God for burgers and dogs. The rumor was that you'd gone all scallops wrapped in bacon and oysters on the half shell."

"Oh we have," Jenny said. "But that kind of effort is for our more elite company. The ones, you know, Russ, who keep the food brokerage solvent."

"Ouch," I said, "I expected that kind of response from Bill, but *et tu*, Brute?"

"Hey, I've got an idea," Holly said. "After a year in the job, let's have Jim Sneed go to the board and offer Bill up as CEO of Food Basket, and Russ will take over at the brokerage."

Bill was standing amongst us, towering over us, in fact, listening to us, and laughing when he said, "Hell, yeah, and we will make Jenny, Holly, and Lucy Santone, if she dodges the hangman's noose, board members. How about that?"

And so it went most of the afternoon as we stuffed our faces and drank cold beer. All of the tidbits discussed were bizarre, but the weirdest story I heard was that a group or neighborhood was taking the DNA of all the dogs in the area. Then if a neighbor found dog droppings in his yard, he could have them analyzed to find the guilty party. I was quite relieved that it wasn't my neighborhood because with my luck I would have been assigned the task of delivering the various samples to the lab.

Much later, the four of us met at our house for cocktails and dinner. Holly had prepared and served clam chowder, turkey tetrazzini, a chopped salad, and two bottles of white wine.

Bill and I were sitting outside after dinner when he said, "Russ, we really need to talk your future plans, but I think it's a little early at this point. Now that you're well past the sixth month as CEO, I have another suggestion. Let's take yet another page out of the Galetti handbook and throw a night for the Food Basket suppliers. The timing is perfect. The manufacturer and broker organizations can't believe that Food Basket is on the move. They like our attitude, the relationships we have built with them, and they are looking for ways to make Food Basket a market leader. They think the new regime is fair-minded yet hard as a woodpecker's lips. They think you are trying to catch people doing things right—a very odd circumstance for two groups that are naturally adversarial. Let's throw them a shindig they won't forget. No burgers or dogs— top of the line all the way."

"I think you are right on the button, as usual, Bill," I said. "And don't feel badly about stealing this idea from Galetti because I thought it up when I worked for them. I also agree with you about future roles and the timing. But here's my question: Are you coming as a Food Basket consultant or as a supplier?"

After thinking about it for a minute, Hartman said, "A supplier. I want to be eligible for the door prizes."

CHAPTER 34

Stick a Feather in My Cap

I know, I know. I should be hard at work, but I couldn't help it. I had a ringside seat to hear the jury's verdict in the Alex Santone murder case. I was surprised at Lucy Santone's appearance; I thought she'd be wearing something staid, conservative. But no, she was in a tight skirt, and she was nearly falling out of a pale yellow blouse. I thought—and maybe she did too—that if she was going to be wearing correctional house orange for the foreseeable future, then she was going to go out in a blaze of glory.

We were all standing as the judge walked briskly to her desk, banged her gavel twice, and said, "Mr. Foreman, has the jury arrived at a verdict?"

"Yes, we have, Your Honor," the foreman said.

The judge leaned forward and asked the defendant and the officers of the court to remain standing and nodded at the foreman without saying another word.

"We, the jury, in the case of Mrs. Lucille J. Santone, find her on the charge of murder in the first degree, not guilty."

The courtroom exploded, and a number of people left the room quickly. In spite of the judge's efforts, it took a good five minutes for order to be restored, and it only quieted down when she threatened to clear the courtroom.

The judge looked at the foreman, asking if the jury had any further business.

The foreman said, "Yes, Judge, in the case of Mrs. Santone, we recommend that she be bound over to face two counts of perjury."

The reaction to this verdict was strange. The court was almost totally still as people tried to comprehend what just had happened. Lucy Santone's smile faded quickly as she seemed to understand immediately.

She walked over to where Donna Mitchner was standing and said, "You fucking bitch, you couldn't get me on the murder one indictment, so you added this spurious piece-of-shit charge."

Donna looked at Lucy Santone with those green piercing eyes and said, "The DA's office, in your case in particular, is glad to be of service."

"You'll get yours," Lucy said as she saw Alan Cummings moving toward her. "I'm sure you'll be humping your boyfriend here in celebration tonight. Enjoy it while you can."

Cummings closed the distance between Lucy and himself very quickly and said, "Let's not add threatening an officer of the court to your charges. Please return to your seat."

Oh, that exchange was worth the price of admission! Lucy and Donna squaring off—that was a six to five pick 'em for sure, and I wanted a ringside seat. The judge had one more piece of business to complete.

She said, "Mrs. Santone, you are free to go with the existing bail, and your sentencing will be one month from today. This court is adjourned."

I wanted to contact Arnold Cable and see if he and his Lawyers Weekly guys could tell me what was going to happen to Lucy Santone.

* * *

Donna Mitchner and Alan Cummings made the prediction by Lucy Santone more accurate than one could believe. They both left work early and went to Cummings's place in the North End. They had a couple of drinks, and Alan actually made a dinner of pasta and meatballs. However, what really set off the meal was a red sauce that they both voted a twelve on a ten scale. After dinner, they celebrated by stripping down to the bare essentials and pouring champagne over each other. It was a little over the top, but they both thought they had to blow off a little steam, and they succeeded in that endeavor in grand style.

After showering and cleaning up, they patted up some pillows on Cummings's king-sized bed and talked, not like fellow workers, but like friends and lovers.

"Nice job, Ms. District Attorney," Cummings said. "You nailed Jethroe and you got Santone with a classic backdoor maneuver."

"Thank you so much, Captain," Donna said. "But I think you just promoted me beyond my station."

"Soon enough it will come," Cummings said. "But I wouldn't feel right if I didn't warn you to be careful. I've had dealings with Mrs. Santone, and she doesn't make idle threats."

"I will keep a lookout, for sure," Donna said. "But you know there is a related case coming up."

"Do you mean the Joe Snyder hanging?" Alan asked.

"Yes, and the common thread is Food Basket and the Santones," she said.

"I know. In fact, I'm about to call and interview Russell Riley, the CEO of Food Basket," Cummings said.

"Oh I know who he is," Mitchner said. "I've read about him. He was in charge of a chain north of here while the family that owned it was in court vying for control of it."

"Galetti Supermarkets, I remember reading about it because after doing what was reported as a good job of operating it during this crisis, he was fired!" Cummings said.

"Yeah, that's the guy." Mitchner nodded in agreement. "And I'm pretty sure I saw him in the courtroom during this trial. It seems to me that he'd be the perfect guy to run Food Basket after Alex Santone was murdered."

"I've already run a check on him, and he sure doesn't need the money," Cummings said.

"Family money?" Donna asked.

"Not really. He received just over twenty-five million for the private stock he owned in Galetti when he left. Additionally, his wife, Holly Lansing, is a very successful portfolio manager for a large mutual fund here in Boston," Cummings said.

"Holly Lansing, not Holly Riley?" Donna asked.

"She's just Holly Lansing in business, Holly Riley to the rest of the world," he responded.

"What would you think if I were married to you and I was Donna Mitchner and not Donna Cummings?" she asked.

"Are you proposing?" Cummings asked.

"What if I am?" asked Mitchner.

"I'd say stick a feather in my cap and call it macaroni," Cummings responded.

"You can call yourself anything you want to—I'd marry you in a New York minute." With that, Donna rolled off the bed onto her knees and. "Alan Cummings, will you marry me?"

Cummings rolled over to her side of the bed, kissed her, and said, "Yes, I'd be honored to do so. Now come to bed, wench."

* * *

Miles away in another state, an entirely different conversation was taking place in a king-sized bed in the penthouse of a building that overlooked the city of Providence.

She said, "This isn't working out like we expected. I walked on the big one, but that legal beagle dyke nailed me on a bullshit charge."

"Yes, she did. And she ain't no dyke. I think we did too good a job of salting the mine," he said.

"What do you mean?" she asked.

"That letter we left at the scene was too obvious. It took Bruno to the cleaners, but it was the main support for the perjury charge."

"Can you do anything about it with the judge?" she asked.

"I'm trying, but it's uphill for sure," he replied.

"What is the maximum sentence?" she asked.

"Six years for each occurrence, so twelve years," he responded.

"What do you think I will get?" she asked.

"It depends. If you get the maximum, I'd read that as the judge throwing the book at you because she thinks you are guilty of the murder charge. In that case, I'd have our team appeal."

"What do I serve in that case, good behavior included, if the appeal fails?"

"Five years," he said.

"Jesus, I can't do that," she said.

"Let's wait and see," he responded. "In the meantime, let's do what you do best—climb on and ride this pony."

CHAPTER 35

Dames and Door Prizes

I was in the office looking at an idea that Bill Hartman had come up with that would limit our liability when we double coupon but that would still satisfy the consumer. As I was trying to punch holes in it, my secretary told me that Sam Sasso from Shaw's was on the phone.

I picked up the phone.

"Greetings, Mr. Sam Sasso from Shaw's. What can I do for you this morning?" I asked in my most sincere voice.

I was pretty sure he was on the wrong end of Joe Galetti's skull-duggery regarding a rather sizeable plot of land in the Fall River vicinity. For some reason, one of my dad's favorite tunes was coming to mind, entitled "Don't Fence Me In."

"Mr. Riley," he said, but I interrupted him.

"Call me Russ," I said.

"Russ," he said, "I'd like to talk to you about a land transaction. I am the vice president in charge of real estate for Shaw's."

"Sam," I said.

He interrupted me and said, "Call me Mr. Sasso."

I laughed out loud, and I knew instinctively that I was going to like this guy.

"You're messing up a good alliteration," I said, "Sam Sasso of Star/Shaw's."

"Point taken. Call me Sam," he said. "I'm taking a chance here because he's probably your godfather, but in plain English, Joe Galetti has fucked me again!"

"Again?" I asked.

"Yeah, twenty years ago when I was with First National, he pulled a lease on some property on which I had a handshake agreement. When I went to the town and county folks to complain, I didn't get the time of day," Sam said.

"That sounds like my boy," I said. "What's he done this time?"

"Oh this is truly Machiavellian, even for Joe. He bought all the land around a site we were considering for a store so that the only access we have to the land is through a swamp," Sam said.

"Okay, got it. Let's skip all the posturing and BS, Sam. How do you come out whole on this transaction?" I asked.

"I've been around long enough that I don't give a damn about looking good. I'm a couple of years at the max of joining up with Arnold Cable and his gang," Sam said.

"You know Arnold?" I asked.

"I do. He's the best. And by the way, in spite of all his bellyaching, he's having a blast working for you again," Sam said.

"Nice to hear," I said. "Frankly, Arnold has been a godsend. He's saved our bacon more times than I care to remember. Here's what I'm thinking about this land gridlock situation. Rumor has it you want to sell it and that you weren't going to build on it. True?"

"True," Sam responded.

"You paid five hundred thousand dollars for it according to Town Hall property records. We pay you six hundred thousand dollars and you're out from under with a nice profit."

"Seven hundred thousand," Sam responded.

"Six hundred and fifty thousand," I countered.

"Done," he said.

"Even though I think you took me to the cleaners. I know Joe would have offered no more than four hundred thousand," I said.

"And I would have taken it," Sam said.

"You're kidding," I said.

"I'm kidding," Sam said. "But tell that old fart for me that I owe you a beverage of your choice, something that I would never offer him."

"Will do," I said. "Sam, a pleasure, I mean it, doing business with you."

"Same here. So long," Sam said.

I rarely analyze phone calls, but in my mind that deal got done so quickly because of his line "Call me Mr. Sasso." I liked him and trusted him because he didn't come on like a steamroller. He had a good sense of humor. There is something to be said for finesse and experience. It cost me at least fifty thousand dollars more than I should have paid for that land, but I really wanted it.

*　*　*

Later that day, I had picked up Holly at work, and we were on our way to Food Basket's First Annual Suppliers' Night. Arnold Cable had arranged it at an upscale country club on the Massachusetts–Rhode Island border, making travel to the festivities as convenient as possible. It was a nightmare of logistics, with over 350 people and their spouses, mistresses, partners, or company associates. What I liked about this type of event was that we had a chance to leave our weapons at the door and socialize with people whom we ordinarily only saw in business dealings. It was particularly weird for me because I had spent the preponderance of my time on the grocery side, but I also had spent a reasonable amount of time on the supplier side.

I probably shouldn't have been surprised, but Holly excelled at these types of events. She had a natural curiosity about the people her husband hung out with, and she made a strong effort to communicate with this group. She looked very elegant in a shoulder-to-floor gold lamé evening dress.

I said to her as we entered an enormous room with a bar set up in each corner, "You are really enjoying yourself, aren't you?"

"Yeah, why not? I'm with my favorite guy, mixing it up with the people he deals with every day. Believe me, this group is more fun than my fellow employees at the mutual fund," she said.

Waiters were at the ready in large numbers, serving delicious goodies, and the activity was halted only once when Arnold announced the lucky winners of a trip to Hawaii. Several other folks laid claim to some other door prizes, such as wide-screen TVs and some digital equipment that was well beyond anything I knew about.

As the lights were blinking and we were being herded into an elegant dining room, a small commotion broke out in the far corner of the room, and I could see the fiery red hair of Lucy Santone.

For once in his life, Arnold Cable looked panic-stricken as I said to him, "Was she on the invite list?"

"Absolutely not," Arnold responded.

"Don't panic, guys. I've got this one," Holly said, and she was on her way over to intercept Lucy Santone.

I have to say that this was quite an entrance. As we were about to settle into our seats at a table, Holly and Lucy, each with a wine-glass in their hands, slowly strolled over to our table and sat down. They were gabbing as if they were old friends, and quite frankly, the two women added a special feeling of beauty and mystery, a buzz, if you will, to the entire proceeding.

I heard Lucy say, "It was so nice of you to come over and rescue me and make me feel so at home, Holly."

"My distinct pleasure, Lucy," Holly said. "I have great empathy for your position with this organization, and at least from a woman's point of view, I know what it's like to be considered a pariah to the establishment."

Holly then introduced Lucy to the remainder of the people at our table, which included Garth Brewster and his bride, Arnold Cable and his wife, and Bill and Jenny Hartman, who joined in talking and working over a first course. A number of suppliers stopped by our table to say hello and to thank us for throwing this shindig.

Just as Arnold was making his way to the podium, one of the larger manufacturer's representatives stopped by, and it was evident that he'd had too much to drink. He started in on me, but in truth, it could have been anyone at the table.

"Hey, big guy, I see you are surrounded by all your minions, and you've got a convicted felon to boot."

"Nice opener," I said. "And you are?"

"Artie Brown, sales manager of Colgate."

"Remind me to review your company's SKUs in the morning, Artie," I said.

"Oh great, maybe you could discontinue the whole line. I am interested in how you acquired all these door prizes tonight," he said.

"What's it to you?" Garth Brewster asked. "You working a night gig with the IRS?"

"I am guessing the money came from questionable charges to the manufacturers, such as slotting allowances," Artie said in an accusing manner.

All of a sudden, out of the corner of my eye, I saw Pondorf, the giant, lurching toward Artie Brown. Pondorf was reaching for Artie's neck when Hartman stood, redirected Pondorf to the left, and Shirley Macober, like a tugboat to an ocean liner, led him away, but not before Pondorf yelled, "You think it doesn't cost anything to handle your items, you little pint of piss? Come on down to the warehouse and I'll shove your ass into one of your miserable cases and FedEx you to your house!"

"Food Basket, the genial host of a suppliers' night, all of which was paid for by the suppliers," Artie said.

This situation was starting to escalate in an ugly manner and would soon be out of control when Lucy Santone glided out of her seat, took Artie by the elbow, and said, "Let's go get some coffee. I admire a guy who states his opinion, even if it isn't very popular."

"Thank you very much," Artie said, obviously quite charmed by the beautiful woman on his arm. "And you are?"

"I'm the convicted felon you mentioned earlier," she replied.

Score one for Lucy Santone. I looked at Holly, and she clapped her hands and smiled as if to say, "Lucy just saved your bacon, big boy."

Arnold continued his march to the podium and opened the proceedings by saying, "One of our major suppliers just stopped by our table to tell us he was a little honked off that he didn't get a door prize. So if any of you want to bring yours up here, we will award it to the disgruntled customer."

It was just the right note on which to open. Brewster and I gave out awards that were met with great enthusiasm. Everybody was waiting for the last presentation, which was named the No Is Just a Request for More Information Award. It went to a broker who was trying to sell a line of dishware. He made eleven separate presentations, mailed letters weekly to key store personnel, and kept us apprised of a media campaign that was pretty much nonexistent. Finally, Garth informed the broker that he would do a test market of the item in three stores. Incredibly, the stuff sold out in record time. It made us all laugh because most of us remembered that thirty or forty years ago, dishware was a big item, but somehow, over the years, it had sunk into oblivion. It was a good lesson to all of us to take off the blinders.

The broker rushed up to the podium, took the trophy, which looked like the Wimbledon award, raised it over his head, and used the old Ted Baxter line from *The Mary Tyler Moore Show*, "It all started in a five-thousand-watt radio station…"

The crowd jumped to its feet and gave him a standing ovation.

As we exited the dining room, I saw Holly grab Arnold and give him a big hug. He had pulled it off, and it had been a top-notch banquet from beginning to end. Holly and I drove home almost without a word between us.

If I had to participate in one of those dog-and-pony shows more than once a year, I'd have to reserve a place on a funny farm.

The next day was almost worth the effort, however, as people who had attended called in to thank us and tell us what a good time they had. I called Arnold in and told him that I'd instructed our comptroller to cut him a check for $5,000. He told me it was totally unnecessary but that he could find a use for it.

While I had him, I said, "Arnold, do me a favor and review the Colgate-Palmolive distribution."

"Want to chop a few items?" Arnold asked.

"You know, my thought is a wee bit contrarian. I know Artie made an ass out of himself, but the purpose of this event was to build relationships with our suppliers, not to have a fistfight," I said.

"Okay," Arnold said.

"So look at his line and find an item we should carry and buy it," I said. "At the very least, Artie will be surprised and confused."

"I'll do it, boss, but for the record, I'd like to give that guy a kick in the balls," Arnold said.

"What fun would that be?" I asked. "Let's see how Artie Brown handles it."

CHAPTER 36

Food Basket on a Roll

I was on the phone with one of my favorite people in the world, Hartman. Uncharacteristically, he was moaning and feeling sorry for himself.

"So what's your problem?" I asked.

"I was at our largest customer, pitching a new line of salsa, and I told their vice president of sales that I had eight trucks hovering outside of his warehouse so he could be the first in the marketplace to promote it. He looks at me and says, 'That's great, Bill, but don't send those trucks here.'"

"Why not?" I asked.

"Because the number one selling salsa competitor has dropped his price 20¢ a unit below our introductory deal, so the customer can run our competitor at $1.99 per unit while our best price would be $2.19 per unit."

"Bill, that's easy. You're not competitive. You need to go back to the manufacturer and get him to match the number one salsa's deal," I said. "He's below the decile at $1.99, and your $2.19 price is as exciting as kissing your sister."

"Can't squeeze blood out of a rock. We already committed the rest of our introductory money to advertising and couponing," Bill responded.

"Two things to think about—when I was at Galetti, the number one salsa guy was known to give sweeter allowances to the larger accounts. We discontinued their entire line when we found he gave the big guy a better allowance than he gave us," I said.

"Jesus, you were a mean bastard back in the day," Hartman said, somewhat in awe.

"Yeah, well, that's what I liked about P&G. Your allowances might have been crappy, but you knew there were no games," I said.

"What's the second thing?" Hartman asked.

"Go to the brand people and see if you can rustle a free coupon out of them. I remember that P&G or KC ran a free coupon on White Cloud as an introductory merchandising tool. I liked the idea but realized at the same time that I had to support it big time—no choice—or my consumer would slaughter me. Displays in every store and it was a gigantic success."

"I'm on it," Hartman said. "And, Russ…"

"Yes," I replied with some trepidation.

"You just earned your keep at this brokerage house," Hartman said.

"Glad to be of service," I said.

My line buzzed, and when I picked it up, Melissa, my secretary, said in a very formal voice, "There is a Captain Alan Cummings here to see you."

"Really," I said. "Have him come right in."

The door opened, and Captain Cummings walked in.

As I stood to greet him, he shook my hand, smiled, and said, "I hope this isn't a bad time for me to bust in on you."

"Not at all, have a seat. Coffee?" I asked.

"Yes, please, black."

I stepped over to the silver pot in the corner and poured us both a cup of coffee. I liked Cummings, even though his minimal responsive answers to questions in court at the Alex Santone trial drove me wacky.

"What can I do for you, Captain?"

"I'm here concerning the death of your controller, Joe Snyder."

"He was our CFO, but I'm not sure that matters," I said.

"I don't think it does," Cummings said evenly. "But the fact that our medical examiner has declared his death a homicide probably does."

"That surprises me. I thought he hung himself," I said.

"In the interim, your folks have reported the money-laundering scheme and Snyder's involvement in it. What do you know about it?"

"Why am I being asked?"

"Because you are the CEO of the organization. You are not a suspect or a person of interest," Cummings said. "That's not to say you aren't interesting."

"You have checked me out?" I asked.

"No, but my fiancée knew who you were from a previous life," Cummings said with a smile.

"Would that be the charismatic and quite beautiful Donna Mitchner?" I asked.

"Very good. No flies growing on you, Mr. Riley!" Cummings said with a hearty laugh. "She's a fan of the work you did for Galetti Supermarkets. She saw you at the Santone trial."

"Oh yeah, I was there, and that exchange between your bride-to-be and Lucy Santone at the prosecution table was worth the price of admission. Then you arrived and broke it up," I said.

"Let's see if I can get back on track. This is purely a fishing expedition, but I was hoping you might give me a lead. So far we've got bupkis," Cummings said.

"I haven't a clue. May I call you Alan? Captain Cummings is a little awkward."

"Absolutely," he said.

"In truth, he was the only guy of the company officers that I took an instant dislike to."

"Just food for thought," Cummings said. "You and your organization should start to prepare to face a pretty substantial suit from the IRS. They are going to want to collect taxes on every nickel that flowed to the basement in the store in Warren."

"You are so right," I responded. "Thank you for the heads-up. I'm looking into some aspects of Snyder's work here, and if I find anything interesting, I will get in touch."

Cummings stood up, smiled, and said, "It's been a pleasure," as he headed for the door.

I just had time to sneak out for lunch before meeting with Garth, Joe Galetti, Arnold, Hartman, and Jim Sneed to catch up on current events and future plans. Lunch was at a little out-of-the-way diner that was actually a converted railcar. They had a pastrami sandwich on a kaiser roll accompanied by one of the world's greatest potato pancakes.

We usually held these meetings in remote places like Craigville Beach, but I thought Joe Galetti would be more comfortable in something a little more familiar, so we were holding it in a conference room near my office.

When I entered the conference room about ten minutes ahead of time, Joe Galetti was there doing the Jumble.

He looked up at me and said, "What's the matter, you afraid I'd get sand in my shoes?"

"You know about those meetings? They are supposed to be hush-hush," I said with a smile.

"I have my sources," he said. "I understand you had a good discussion with my friend Sam Sasso of Shaw's."

"He's no friend of yours, Joe," I said. "He still remembers when you stiffed him twenty years ago when he was with First National Stores."

"Sticks and stones," Joe said. "Did he like the deal you offered him?"

"He did," I responded, "because you gave me the right intel. His company wanted to unload it, and they made a nice buck on it."

Just at that moment, Hartman, Cable, and Brewster arrived, which short-circuited our conversation. They each had greeted Joe Galetti when Jim Sneed entered. Jim made a point to go over to meet Joe because they did not know each other.

Shortly after that, Garth rapped his hand on the conference table three times and said, "You're probably wondering why I called this meeting."

We all smiled at this slightly bizarre man, and I said, "For the record, Joe said he wouldn't mind a bit meeting on Craigville Beach if, and only if, Hartman provides the food from his wastebasket cooker. Who wants the floor?"

"I'd like to mention something for us to ponder. We don't need an answer right now, but this group needs to be thinking about it," Jim Sneed said.

"Go, Jim," I said.

"This group has done what very few thought could be done. You have turned Food Basket on its ear, and in all modesty, it could be a comeback-of-the-year candidate. But we are in the beginning of month 9 of a one-year contract. My job is to find a successor for Russ, but I wanted this group to at least have it consciously on your minds," Jim said.

"I second that," Hartman said. "I truly would like to get my partner back at our company. How about Artie Brown from Colgate to replace Russ?"

There was great laughter from the group.

"I'll support this successor option," Arnold said, "because I can get back to retirement, which at this point is a faint memory."

"Wait a minute," Brewster said. "Jim, who are you performing this task for?"

"Bob Santone," Jim responded.

"Have you talked to him since Russell took over here?" he asked.

"No, I haven't. I needed to get a grip on the board's views before going to Bob," Sneed said.

Joe Galetti spoke up and said, "Another key question is what is Russell's thought process, stay or leave? If it's leave, then it's decided unless Bob sweet-talks him into staying."

I had to cut this one off because I had no idea what the answer to Joe's question was, "Let's table that so I can bring up one issue that you need to know about now. Captain Alan Cummings was in my office this morning to tell me that the medical examiner's office has declared that Joe Snyder's death was a homicide."

There was silence from a group that wasn't usually the quiet, unobtrusive type.

"I know that back in the sixties and seventies, the city of Providence led the country in murders per capita, but I don't want to be the supermarket chain known for this kind of statistic. Arnold, anything new on any irregularities financially with Joe Snyder?" I asked.

"None," Arnold responded.

Joe Galetti said, "Let me get with Arnold on this. I'd look to put my son, Joey, on this one. His expertise in scratching up data is well documented."

"Moving right along, while we are right here, let's have a round of applause for Joe and his work to secure the land we need for our megaplex store. We have broken ground on this project," I said.

A standing ovation followed for Mr. G. from his fellow conference-room participants.

"An update on our 4 percent caper developed in a shadowy recess of Garth's brain. Larry Baldwin, our young financial maven, has given us the go-ahead with this project," I said.

"What does it mean to the consumer?" Jim Sneed asked.

"Here's the math," Garth said. "According to official Department of Agriculture figures, the average family spends $190 weekly, so the approximate savings annually of our 4 percent merchandising vehicle would be $400. Another way to think of it is two weeks of free groceries for that family."

"Garth, did any of your fingers leave your hand while you were putting that equation together?" Hartman asked before he burst out laughing.

"Well, maybe one, but only briefly," Garth said with a smile. "But, man, if I'm a competitor reading 'Food Basket offers 4 percent off your purchases now through December 31,' I'd be looking to take a permanent hike."

I closed the meeting with the latest numbers for the quarter, which beat the estimates of the experts handily. The stock was just a tick over twelve dollars a share, and when the numbers hit the street on Tuesday, I expected a bump up. Would fifteen be too much to hope for? Probably.

CHAPTER 37

Take It to the Limit

Lucy Santone wasn't ready for incarceration as a guest of the state of Rhode Island for the next five to ten years. She was beginning to think that she, as well as Bruno, were the foils in this drama, and the closest she'd ever come to an exotic island would be the sand in the bottom of the metal containers used to put out cigarettes in state facilities. She didn't have anybody to blame but herself; she fell for his line because she had wanted to. After months of sexual abstention from her drunken husband, she had become heavily involved with Bruno, eventually setting him up for murder, and continued with him on this reckless journey because he was simply the best she had ever had. She hadn't wanted to think about the future or if the scheme had made any sense. She had been into the moment, right now, not for tomorrow or next month.

Not now. The focus had changed. But what were her options? She needed insurance. But whom could she call? There was really only one person, but she wasn't thrilled with his friends—Detective O'Malley, the kindly homicide detective she had at first believed. But O'Malley had ended up providing the evidence that was a major factor in sending Bruno up for life. And his girlfriend, Donna Mitchner, Jesus, what a barracuda.

But she dialed his number, and he picked up on the second ring and said, "Captain Cummings."

"Captain, this is Lucy Santone."

"Yes, ma'am, what can I do for you?"

"If I told you that, Ms. Mitchner would be terribly upset," Lucy said.

After a brief silence, Cummings said, "Okay, Mrs. Santone, how can I help you?"

"We need to talk. I think my life is in danger," she said.

*　*　*

At about the same time, just miles away, Arnold Cable was put through to Russ at Food Basket. Arnold was sitting in the Merrill Lynch office, where he had done business for years.

"Russ, news and I don't know what to make of it."

"Blurt it out, Arnold," I said. "Enlighten me."

"Food Basket results are out, and we're currently selling at $18.00 per share," Arnold said.

"Jesus!" I replied.

"Not a shareholder to my knowledge, Chief," Arnold said with a malicious chuckle.

"What are your Merrill Lynch folks saying?" I asked.

"They like Food Basket. They call it the Little Engine That Could, but they don't love us up 50 percent," Arnold responded. "The reason I'm calling is that I thought you should give Jim Sneed a call. He is on several boards, and he might have picked something up."

"Screw that," I said. "I'm hot footing it over to Bob Santone and cashing in my options."

"You're kidding!" Arnold exclaimed.

"I'm kidding," I said. "I'll get right on it."

"And, Russ," Arnold said, "next time you take one of these gigs and you pull me out of a well-deserved retirement, get me some options, okay?" Arnold said.

"Arnold, I'm getting one dollar for salary, and you are getting two hundred and fifty grand. You sure you want to make that trade?" I asked.

"Only with the aid of hindsight, Chief. See you later," Arnold said as he concluded the call.

I buzzed Melissa, and when she came on the line, I said, "Melissa, see if you can find Sneed for me. It won't be easy!"

"Will do, Russ," she said.

While I was waiting for Melissa to perform the impossible, I started counting with fingers and toes, figuratively speaking. If I were doing the math right, and I probably wasn't, I could walk away with more than I did from Galetti Supermarkets. It's just another lesson in life's path of illogical conclusions. You don't have to be smart, good-looking, hardworking, or have a high acumen to live a nice life. You just have to be lucky and have a brilliant and beautiful wife.

Several minutes had passed when Melissa buzzed me and told me that Jim Sneed was on the line. I picked up the phone and said, "Hey, Jim, how are you?"

"I'm well. Sitting on a raft in a lake with my beautiful bride, eating a turkey and Swiss cheese on a kaiser, and drinking an ice-cold Corona."

"Wow, you're doing a whole lot better than me! I'll be brief because you are obviously on vacation or your office environment is quite extraordinary," I said.

"It's the former," he replied.

"Here's the deal. Our numbers came out, and we are up 50 percent. The stock guys really like us, but they don't love us up 50 percent. Something is going on, perhaps a takeover," I said.

"What do you care? You're a short-timer," Sneed said.

"Maybe so, but I don't want any surprises on my shift. Nose around with your boards, will you?" I asked.

"I will, Russ. See you later," Jim said.

How times change. Nine months ago, anybody and his brother could buy Food Basket for $5.50 a share—as much as you want for as long as you want. Now we were looking over our shoulders if a sizeable chunk were purchased. The next logical person to call would be Bob Santone. Who knew what was going on under the cover of darkness in the merger and acquisitions market more than a hedge fund manager?

When he came on the line, he said, "Been following the stock, Russ?"

"Yes, I have. I was wondering what you were thinking about our current price," I said.

"It's an aberrant, but nothing to concern yourself with," he replied.

"You are not smelling anything? Warren Buffet or Carl Icahn stalking Food Basket?"

"Could be. I've let it be known in certain corners of the financial world that I would accept a fair offer. And thanks to you, things are heating up around here."

"Okay, did it occur to you to let your CEO in on this little strategy?" I asked.

"No, why would I?" Bob asked.

"Well, for one thing, I might have had a couple of good candidates. Secondly, my enthusiasm for this task would have been considerably less had I known it was a temporary patchwork," I said a little more forcefully than I had intended.

"Well, there was no hidden plot afoot here. I figured you had enough to handle when you took over," he said.

"Okay, Bob, thanks for bringing me up to speed. I'll talk to you soon."

It must be the contrarian that beats deep in my body, but whenever someone says there is no hidden plot, that's when I start to suspect one.

CHAPTER 38

Back to the Future

I was back in my own building, the food brokerage building that Hartman and I had built with our own hands and what minds we had left. It was odd that I felt more comfortable on the sell side of the business than the buy side. I'd spent five times as many years in grocery stores, but maybe this current assignment as CEO of Food Basket was going to tell me that I had left that side at the right time. Perhaps it was that I felt like a nomad in the current scheme looking at the eye chart of the future with one hand over one eye and seeing nothing out of the other. I'd have to consult with my psychiatrist, Holly, and sort things out.

Meanwhile, I was listening to a story by Hartman, wondering where and when this huge, odd fellow would reveal the key line.

"I was at an account with a new rep," said Hartman. "And I had given him the books. It was his call to make. We'd been in a training class that week where the instructor had showed the newer members a way to try to keep a conversation alive when the customer was ready to walk away. The instructor said to use the phrase 'Could you tell me a little bit more about that?'

"So my new guy is in trouble. The veteran buyer is trying to be civil but firm when he says, 'Charlie, it's just this simple: your dead net (price) stinks!'

"You see the light go on in Charlie's face when he looks at the crusty old buyer, and in his most earnest voice, he says, 'Could you tell me a little bit more about that?'

"The buyer throws his hands in the air, gets his face about eight inches away from Charlie's, and yells, 'Yeah, your price sucks!'

"I can't help it," Hartman says. "I just crack up, which in turn cracks the buyer up."

"Poor Charlie," I said almost to myself.

Hartman agreed but told me that the buyer walked Charlie out of the office and told him if he became a little more competitive, he would take another look at our item.

I loved that story. It's so typical of the northeast United States—no subterfuge or polite nonsense. One would have to be both blind and deaf not to know what to do to close a sale. In today's terms, this part of the country was transparent.

I looked at Hartman and asked, "Do you have some time to talk about our future?"

"Definitely," Hartman said. "Have you started to form a plan?"

"Yeah, I'm working my way there. I will bounce it off you and the big boss."

"Great, I started thinking about the future and a weird thing happened," Hartman said.

"Tell me. I like weird," I replied.

"I went back twenty-five or thirty years to see if that would lead to any type of pattern to predict the future. A big change occurred in the eighties, and I experienced it firsthand. When I was recruiting MBAs for P&G, we were the top dog along with companies such as IBM. All of a sudden, we fell out of the top spot because we made things. The MBAs were chasing Wall Street—investment banking, M&As, hedge funds, REITSs, and the latest gadget bond," Hartman said.

"Okay," I said, not knowing where Hartman was going with this.

"Let me ask you something," Hartman continued. "What did Made in America mean to you back then?"

"The best product available in the world," I responded.

"And what about Made in China or Made in Japan?" Hartman asked.

"Fun stuff. Cheap crap that fell apart before nightfall," I said.

"While we were enthralled pursuing the money trail, a guy named W. Edwards Deming took Japan to the top of the product quality ladder. Dr. Deming is one of ours, but we didn't pay any attention to him until it was too late. This is way too much of a simplification, but his promise was that productivity increases with improvement of quality. Stick with me now, Russ."

"I'm sticking," I said.

"So Japan starts turning out quality stuff, cars come to mind, while our unions had piled so many benefits on the Detroit carmakers that it cost US automakers $13,000 a car more than Japan or Germany. China steps up in the early nineties with a labor rate of less than 50¢ an hour. So we send all our manufacturing capability to China, and presto, we have what I call ghost industries. They are gone. We're converting factories into condo lofts."

"Let me see if I got this," I said. "Made in America doesn't exist. Japan's and Germany's quality leapfrogs us so even in the car industry, where we actually do still make things, we are making a vastly inferior product. China has taken over our manufacturing capacity, and our best and brightest are chasing fraudulent mortgage packages on Wall Street."

"You got it!" Hartman said as his huge paw of a hand gives me a thunderous pat on the back. "But guess what? All of a sudden the Chinese labor rate escalates to about 65 percent of the US rate, fuel prices increase dramatically, and a recession hits. So now building something or making a product is back in. Ford, GM, and Chrysler are on the comeback trail making vehicles that equal our global competitors in quality. Just one little problem—we've got eleven million people unemployed, and the majority of them are not cut out for Wall Street or inventing software."

"Are you saying history will repeat itself and we will move back to manufacturing as the backbone of industry?" I asked.

"We're going to try. How successful we become is still a question. But Mercedes-Benz has seventeen plants in the United States and employs half a million people. I don't think we'll be making shoes anytime soon in Brockton again. But I'm seeing startups making upscale watches, a high-end sock maker using all American wool, surfboards, and car mats. Apple has invested a hundred million dollars making product here, and Walmart and GE are saying they will be investing billions of dollars manufacturing here in the United States. What the hell, maybe the Maytag repairman may come back!"

"I didn't know he left," I said. "I love this review, but how does it affect us?"

"Well, for one thing, if I were you, I wouldn't be too anxious to jump ship. Food Basket is not a ghost industry. We make things, we ship things, no hedge fund mumbo jumbo in this industry. This megastore in Fall River / New Bedford / Taunton could become the focal point for this revolution to return Made in America as a top-notch priority in the rebuilding of American industry.

"Hundreds of wind farms nine miles off New Bedford—who is making them, and why aren't they being made here? Furniture—we've got Jordan's here. Why can't we make their stuff? Let's land a gambling complex. Think of the infrastructure and the boots with tool belts it would put to work. How about a Walmart or Target distribution center? Who else needs to build cars here besides Mercedes? Let's get some of that GE largesse. Let's get out front of this thing and bang the drum for our marketing area."

"Who knows," I said, starting to warm to Hartman's theme, "maybe we merge with Galetti and give the big boy a run for his money."

"A good thought. Maybe the three of you combine and take on Walmart," Hartman said.

"So can I take away from this conversation that you are okay with our current situation of me at Food Basket and you running this business?"

"Five by five," he said. "You were always a very astute fellow. Also our business, Food Brokerage, has taken a page out of the change process. It is not a boutique business with commissions of 5 percent of sales. In the mid- to late nineties, it looked like good times for us because national companies discontinued their retail sales forces. But right behind that Walmart began demanding that their suppliers reduce costs. Manufacturers no longer wanted to deal with a myriad of boutique brokers. They wanted to streamline costs. Clorox went from sixty-five brokers to one, and three major US food brokerage companies emerged, consolidating the small brokers into three huge companies. Commissions were cut from 5 percent to 2.5 percent.

"But we've stayed away from the hangmen because we have great headquarters people, superior technology, willing support from inside people like the Planogram Department, quality research and local knowledge, and terrific retail coverage."

"But, Russ, we're flying under the radar. We've survived quite nicely, but one of those three national brokers wants our nuts in a jar. We are the exception—not the norm.

"All is not gloom and doom: if we decide to sell or move under the national broker roof, we'd have a nice payday. From a selfish standpoint, I love what you are doing right now as CEO of Food Basket. Hell, maybe we sell your stock in Food Basket, sell the food brokerage, and hang it up."

"Bill, I appreciate your attitude and friendship more than you know," I said.

"I know you do," Hartman replied. "But I know what I've got with you—straight shooter and integrity first, last, and always, and don' forget, one of the nicest, smartest, and most beautiful wives in America. I'm not a bit afraid of you, Riley, but I'm petrified of Holly!"

"You're kidding," I said.

"I am. But I'm reminded in life that you don't meet that many couples where all four people really like each other. And you and Holly are in that very select group with Jenny and me," Hartman said.

"What a nice thing to say," I said. "We obviously feel the same about you guys. One thing struck me when you concluded your historical business lesson. I'm wondering if we shouldn't sit down with

Joe Galetti and talk him through it. If he gets behind it, we could see some strong results when he schmoozes with these kingmakers that have eluded us for thirty years."

"Great idea. You make a fair point about us as well. It must have something to do with the cut of our jib or that our pants don't have cuffs. But it doesn't matter if Joe is representing our interests. Listen, Russ, you need to hit the road. It's bad enough that you're a CEO of a supermarket chain and a partner in this food brokerage, but what will the FTC say if they see us plotting together?" Hartman asked.

"Maybe it'll be like running for president. I'll have to put my partnership here in a blind trust," I said.

"Some would say you've reached that point already— deaf and dumb as well," Bill concluded.

"Good-bye, Bill."

"So long, Russ."

CHAPTER 39

If It Seems Too Good to Be True

Alan Cummings had never expected to hear from Lucy Santone, but it didn't surprise him that her life might be in danger. He had thought from the beginning that the trail to Bruno Jethroe was too easy. It was obvious to him that Bruno, who wasn't the brightest person on the planet, may have been in way over his head. But it was the incongruity of this couple that had made no sense to him from the start. She was on the make, but she was high fashion, well-read, married into one of the prestigious families in the state. Bruno just wasn't her cup of tea. He was shots and beer, played the ponies, and bet pro football. All of that aside, for all of Bruno's bluster, he told anyone that would listen that he did not kill Alex Santone, and Alan Cummings, for one, maybe the only one, believed him.

At that moment, O'Malley led Lucy Santone into his office and Cummings said, "Hello, Mrs. Santone. Have a seat. Can I get you anything?"

"Water, please," she replied.

"A bottle okay, or would you prefer a glass?" he asked.

"A bottle would be fine," she responded.

Cummings felt that Lucy Santone had lost that self-assured, cocky attitude he had seen in her the last time they met. Maybe that was the result of beating murder one but facing two counts of perjury. He brought her a bottle of water, sat at his desk, and waited for her to speak.

After what seemed like an embarrassing silence, Lucy said, "I think I need protection or I won't make it to the perjury trial."

"I'm going to need more than that, I'm afraid," he said.

"Off the record?" she asked.

"No, I can't do that," he said. "But how about you lay out a hypothetical plot for me?"

"You'll be able to protect me based on a hypothetical plot?" Lucy asked.

"Depends on what I hear," he said.

"Okay, I trust you, Cummings. Your girlfriend, not so much," she said.

"It's just you and me," he responded.

Lucy took a deep breath and said, "Hypothetically speaking, the person convicted for murder was set up. The woman's role in this was to have the convicted murderer fall in love with her while her accomplice set up clues that a blind squirrel couldn't miss."

A shot of heat thrust its way right up his body to his forehead, and he suddenly felt as if he would break out in a sweat. "Goddammit," Alan thought to himself, "I knew...I knew...I knew it was too pat. Fuck!"

"Go on," he said as calmly as he could. "Give me an example."

"Jesus, Cummings, who the hell leaves their love letters around for the cops to find?" she asked. "You might not think the accused was too swift mentally, but would he leave his gun in plain sight after killing someone?"

"Okay, sticking with the hypothetical, why would his beautiful accomplice pretend she only knew him slightly?"

"C'mon, Alan, You obviously didn't have the breakfast of champions this morning. How could she say she was intimate with someone that the police suspected had killed her husband? She was the grieving widow, not an accomplice to murder."

"How could she not see perjury as a major threat to her freedom?"

"You'd have to ask her. But my guess is when she was in the middle of a plot that saw her husband murdered and was subsequently charged with murder one, perjury never made it to the checklist."

"But why now? What's changed?"

"Connect the dots, Cummings. I can't do everything," she said.

"Okay, let me take a whack at this made-up scenario. What is making you particularly jumpy is the murder of Joe Snyder," he said.

"Bingo. There's hope for you, Captain," she said.

"These two murders, which could be considered random, both have Food Basket as the common link. And they definitely aren't random," Cummings surmised.

"Don't forget, Captain, this is hypothetical, so using Food Basket and real names is dragging us where I don't want to go," she said.

"Okay, hypothetically, what else?"

"That's all I know. But I am a threat because I'm not scot-free, but instead I could be sentenced to a minimum of eight to ten years. So if I'm unhappy and people think I'm going to talk because I have jail time to serve, I become a liability—hypothetically."

"I'm sold. Stay out of any dark alleys until I can convince some people that you need to be protected at the taxpayers' expense," Cummings said.

* * *

I have managed to capture some one-on-one time with my wife. The kids are buzzing around the house, but both are headed out to see friends, and Juicy is busy destroying that right-footed slipper that somehow had eluded her until now. I had escaped early from work and prepared dinner featuring my juice of the onion smasher potatoes that are laced with heavy cream and cream cheese.

Holly hit the back door at precisely six fifteen looking fresh as a daisy.

"How do you do that?" I asked.

"Do what?" she replied.

"You look as if you just stepped out of a spa, ready to start your day," I responded.

"A snare and a delusion, my dear. Wait a minute. Am I smelling smashers and a fabulous dinner prepared by a worldwide renowned sous-chef?"

"The very same," I said.

"Well, if you can hold the fort here a little longer, I'm going to go upstairs and shuck off this business garb. And if you can manage it, I'll take a glass of wine on my return," Holly said.

"Done your way," I replied. "But don't stand in front of the window when you are shucking."

"Russ, there isn't a house within five hundred yards of us," she said.

"You never know who is out there lurking with binoculars," I said.

Ten minutes later, she was back, and I handed a glass of red wine to her, and for such a ladylike-appearing person, she took a very greedy swig and then said, "Aaaah, yummy. Now the world is right where it should be. I'm home with you, having a glass of wine, and about to embark on a wonderful dinner. Perfect!"

"What's your take on the market?" I asked.

"We're in a bull market, but this bull has a nervous tick," she said. "If there is even a whisper of the government abandoning its stimulus package, the Dow sinks like a rock."

"Aren't they going to have to pull the needle out at some point?" I asked.

"Yes, but hopefully, the economy will be stronger and quantitative easing will disappear without a ripple."

"Do you really believe that?" I asked.

"Absolutely not," Holly replied. "But enough about me. What do you really think about me?"

That always made me laugh. "I wanted a chance to bounce some things off you about work, Hartman, Bob Santone, and get your take on how I should be looking at some of this stuff."

"Okay, sounds like fun. But while I've got you, give me a big hug," she said.

"Absolutely, my pleasure. Everything okay?" I asked.

"It is now."

And she reached up and gave me a wonderful, long, passionate kiss.

"What were we talking about?" I asked.

"Can't remember," Holly said.

Now that we had that straightened out, I had Holly set the table while I served dinner. We toasted each other, clinked wine glasses, and all that was heard for quite some time was silverware doing its thing—always a good sign. I received an "I'm starved" and "This meal is fabulous," so I was a happy cookie. I always wanted to be that guy in the old Westerns, Cookie, feeding the ranch hands from a covered wagon. But it ended badly. Somehow Cookie always had a drinking problem and ended up driving himself off a cliff in his covered wagon, leaving nothing to eat for the surviving trail hands.

Coffee was in the living room, and Holly was ready to chat, completely relaxed and well fed.

"What is buzzing around in that head of yours?" she asked.

"Well, my contract is about up, and I need to make a decision as to my future," I said.

"Russ, we already talked about this. You need a face-to-face with Bob and Bill."

"Half accomplished. I've talked with Hartman," I said.

"Tell me about that," Holly said.

"He completely surprised me. He gave me a very concise history of the last thirty to forty years. Basically, he said when we stopped making things, Japan and China started making them, and Made in America disappeared from the landscape. We became snake oil salesmen and software peddlers, and we lost our moral compass with derivatives and default swaps. But Hartman says America is back into the manufacturing and making quality products again."

"What's his point?" Holly asked.

"He thinks I should stay as CEO of Food Basket. Supplying food is not a shadow industry, it's real. We make things, we ship product from warehouses, and we wouldn't know a default swap from a dandelion."

"He can cook, he's fun, and, Russ, he's one smart son of a gun. You are lucky to have him. He's right. You're not selling mortgage-backed securities that are worthless—you're selling stuff."

"Not the most articulate definition of my work," I said.

Holly laughed. "Even Hartman thinks you should stay. Bob Santone is going to press you very hard to sign a long-term contract."

"You're right, and that's what I want to discuss with you," I said. "The stock took a big jump, and Arnold felt that part of the jump could be the fact that Food Basket is up for sale."

"Arnold's not wrong," Holly said.

"You know something?" I asked.

"Remember me?" Holly asked. "I cover your industry for one of the largest mutual fund companies in Boston."

"So that's what you do," I said with feigned surprise.

"It's been up on the block since Alex Santone was killed," Holly said.

"That's funny," I said. "I asked Bob about it today, and he basically told me yes, it was, and that it was none of my business."

"What was your reaction to that?" she asked.

"I told Bob that if I had known that my employment was a rent-a-job CEO, I probably wouldn't have taken it," I said.

"How did that go over?"

"Not well," I said. "I was listening to a dial tone less than a minute later. So what do you think?"

"Off the top, a couple of things to think about. First, take Jenny, Bill, and me out to dinner. What an advocate he is. Second, call Bob Santone and get in front of him one-on-one. I don't mean to be crude, but he should be kissing your ass in Macy's window. He obviously has a burr in his saddle, and you need to find out what it is. Once that's known, I think your future employment picture will be a lot clearer.

"What are you doing for the next thirty minutes, sailor?"

"Making love to you, gorgeous," I responded.

CHAPTER 40

Loose Ends

Cummings smiled as he trudged down the long hallway to Donna Mitchner's office. How their relationship had changed. He remembered entering her office several months ago slightly intimidated, trying to sell her on setting up the original wiretaps between Bruno Jethroe and Lucy Santone. She was now his intended, and he felt as happy and satisfied with life as he had in a long, long time.

But he wasn't bringing good news. He had been duped; they both fell for the head fake, but he should have been more insistent at the time. All the clues were just a little too helpful in leading him to a culprit. What kept going through his mind was a favorite saying of the New England Patriots football coach: "It is what it is."

He gave a light rap on her door, and she called out, "Enter at your own risk."

Cummings entered her office, and Donna was standing, bending over a document. Just for a second, he was stunned with her physical presence. Even in a skirt and blouse, she looked as if she could burst around the desk, take three strides, and dunk a basketball.

While he was imagining this feat of athleticism, she looked up and said, "Hello, big fella. You just made my day."

"Thank you. Frankly, you not only make my day, you make me a full-time happy guy," he said. "I just hope you are still in that frame of mind when we finish this little chat."

"Sounds serious. What's up?" Mitchner asked.

"Lucy Santone came to my office and gave me a hypothetical that will blow your hair straight back," he said.

"Frankly, I think she's a little sweet on you, Alan," she said.

"To that point, she told me on the phone that there were a few things she'd like to do to me, but knowing you were lurking close-by that she'd keep them to herself," Alan said.

"I'm not shocked at that at all. I totally believe her. I also think she's had more bodies pass over her than a body scanner at Mass General. She is a full-contact sport all by herself," Mitchner said. "What is she selling, and why is she selling it?"

"First of all, she seemed different. She wasn't cocky, and I honestly feel she is fearing for her life. In a nutshell, her story is that she and a party or parties unknown set Bruno up for the fall. Second, Joe Snyder's murder is connected to Alex Santone's death as is the money that was going directly to the basement in one of the Food Basket stores."

"Okay, I get all that, but why is she in danger?"

"Two reasons. First, she thinks that the mastermind is tidying up any loose-end participants of this plot. Secondly, she feels that if she was going to be set free, she'd still be okay. But now that she's probably going to be doing time, the real killers feel that they have to handle her as an unhappy office seeker."

"So her angle is she'd rather do the time than be on one of the state's refrigerated slabs in the morgue," Mitchner concluded.

"It's not much of a choice, all in all, but yeah, that's her thinking."

"So this puts the CEO and Food Basket into the spotlight, yes?" Donna asked.

"Certainly Food Basket is the common thread. I don't know about Riley. From what I gather, he has turned the business around since Alex Santone's death, so I can't see how another murder would help his cause in the public's eye," Cummings said.

"Is it bigger? Mafia, money laundering, what?" she asked.

"Honestly, I don't know. Here's what I think. I think she's scared, and I think she's telling the truth. How does that affect you? We could have the wrong guy doing life," Cummings said.

"Details, Alan. You know you told me you smelled a rat, and I didn't listen. This one is on me," she said.

"I feel terrible," Cummings said. "I should have put my foot down much harder than I did."

"Hell, if you had, that size 14 brogan would have crushed my dainty little feet," she said.

"Dainty, hell, I think you wear a 7, but an 8 feels so good that it could be an 11," he said with a smile.

She laughed and said, "At least when they saw me coming at the shoe store, they didn't issue me shoeboxes instead of the shoes that came in them."

"Okay already, enough with the foot jokes," Cummings said. "I thought you would really be upset, especially with me because I didn't act on my hunch that Bruno was the foil."

"Not at all. This is no trumped-up-evidence case. We didn't make it up. We just got snookered. I'll go to the AG, tell him what we have, and we will do nothing until we get to the bottom of it," Donna Mitchner said. "What have you done about protecting Lady Santone."

"I've asked to have a team assigned to her, but I haven't heard back on that one yet," he said.

"I'll give that a push," Mitchner said. "I will talk with her, but if you see her first, tell her we can't do anything for her because she hasn't given us anything yet. Call it women's intuition, but she knows who the next guy is up the ladder, and it's eight to five that she's boinking him."

"So beautiful, so suspicious, so relentless."

"You'll do well to remember that," she said with a hearty laugh.

* * *

I'd called the meeting on very short notice. It would behoove me before I met with Bob Santone to get up to speed on where Food

Basket was going and what was driving it. Arnold Cable inside the company perspective at headquarters and the stores, Larry Baldwin, the new CFO that Dave Williams found for us from within the ranks, and Bill Hartman to give us a look at ourselves from outside the front gate perspective.

Larry Baldwin went first. After he handed out a single piece of paper, I was sold on whatever he was going to say. When was the last time I'd heard a CFO give a presentation with a single exhibit? Easy. Never.

"This quarter is about halfway finished, and I can tell without fear of contradiction that it will be the best quarter in the history of this organization, so good, in fact, that I'd like your permission to start pushing some of the volume and profit into the next quarter."

"Jesus, Baldwin, you sure know how to kick off a meeting," Hartman said.

"What's driving these numbers?" I asked.

"Health and beauty aids and pharmacies," Baldwin responded. "Pharmacies are all new business, so they are jacking up our year-to-year comparisons. Also, four to five million dollars a quarter is going into the registers, and not the basement of the Warren store. Most encouraging is that baby food, disposable diapers, and baby needs are running well ahead, indicating that we are drawing a younger consumer than in previous years."

"Thank you, Larry," I said. "Love that report. Love one exhibit instead of the NYC phone-book-sized binder we usually receive, and it's the first time I've heard a CFO use the wording 'jacked up'!"

"You're welcome, Mr. Riley," he said. "If I could, I'd like to excuse myself as I have a meeting with a couple of other geeks to save us about six million a year in administrative billing."

"Go in all haste with our blessing," said Arnold Cable.

As soon as Larry departed, I said, "I really like that kid!"

"Let's wait until he brings you a crappy forecast to see how much we like him," Hartman said with a straight face.

Cable jumped in, matching Hartman's apparent "wait and see" attitude by being a hard-ass and saying, "I like him. I don't know if I love him."

"C'mon, you guys, get the broomsticks out of your asses," I said.

They both smiled and admitted they were just practicing the hard-ass, take-no-prisoners approach and that Baldwin was, in fact, a keeper.

Arnold was next, and I challenged him to be as transparent as our CFO, to which he responded, "Why in hell would I do that? If you think this stuff is easy, you'll hire some college kid for a third my salary and send me packing."

"How about one-tenth your salary?" Hartman said.

Ignoring that remark, Arnold launched into his presentation.

"First at headquarters, with fine work from the supervisors, the stores are following headquarter directives and merchandising plans rather than making up their own, which is what we faced when we took over. Sales, gross profit, and attitude/morale are up. Union grievances and Department of Health violations are down. The buying department and the warehouse have worked seamlessly to cut out of stocks to below the national average, and shrink has dropped significantly. In truth, the shrink or stolen merchandise has declined in the main because we closed up five stores that were beyond saving. Interestingly, we have found work for almost everyone from those five stores, and we will use a bunch of them to staff the Fall River–New Bedford–Taunton megastore.

"Areas to improve upon—prepared food departments aren't drawing customers, our delis need to be expanded, the lighting needs to be improved, and a number of storefronts need a modern touch. They look like the old Bohack stores in New York in the midseventies. I think we might need Shirley Macober to square away prepared food departments and the delis. Back in the day, she was hell on wheels in this area at store level."

"Thanks, Arnold. Baby steps you talked about previously seem to be second nature so that we might now be able to do something creative. Have you seen the Woonsocket store that Brewster and Hartman created?"

"Yes, I saw it, and I loved it. But the hardware and setup may be too expensive," Arnold warned.

"Hell, we are spending millions on the megastore. Pick ten stores, go to Larry Baldwin, and see if he wants to take the money out of this quarter to implement the Woonsocket plan," I said.

"Jesus, Russ," Hartman said, "Baldwin said he'd like to move some out of the quarter but into the next quarter. *Capisce?*"

"What do I know?" I said. "I was a liberal arts major."

"I like it actually," Hartman said. "All part of our master plan to drive competition nuts trying to figure out what we are up to next and what we are going to be when we grow up."

Just before I was to turn the meeting over to Bill Hartman to tell us what he was seeing and hearing from the supplier side, Melissa stuck her head in the door and said, "Artie Brown from Colgate is on line 1."

Without really thinking, I put my finger to my lips, pushed the button, and said, "What can I do for you, Artie? I have you on speaker and our vice president of procurement, Arnold Cable, is with me."

I didn't want to mention Hartman because at one time he was a direct competitor of Brown's at P&G, and people in jest were calling our brokerage business Food Basket Food Brokerage, intimating that Hartman had more access to Food Basket than he should have. Guilty as charged, but Bill never mentioned that to the FTC police he kept threatening me with at the drop of a hat.

"I wanted to call you to apologize for my behavior the other night. It was uncalled for, and frankly, your operation is one of the good ones. On a more practical matter, if Shirley hadn't steered Pondorf away from me, I could be pushing up daisies right now," Artie Brown said.

"We've all been there, Artie. I know I've made an ass out of myself and regretted it later," I said. "Maybe someday you can return the favor and give us a heads-up when we are about to screw up."

"Will do. Thank you for your understanding, and also thank you for the new item," he said.

"My pleasure. Have a good day," I said.

"Talk about turning the other cheek," Arnold said. "Maria Galetti taught me that one. I remember her saying that at some point a product will go on allotment, and if you've done a turn for someone like Artie Brown, you would get what she called your fair share advantage."

"Okay, Bill, what are you hearing and seeing?"

"Well, the best measure might be the year-to-date business figures from our brokerage house. Food Basket is up 14.2 percent. That's a monster increase. And importantly, it points up one significant fact: your business isn't just up, as Baldwin pointed out, because of the pharmacies, but I do think there is a direct correlation between the pharmacy business and the increase in H and BA. Business is up substantially, even when you take pharmacy out of the numbers. Guys on the sell side are excited that a customer has risen from the dead. Believe me, it's nerve-wracking when your gains are only coming from one account—Walmart. They are so big that they could snuff your business out by accident and never know it until you showed up in a body bag."

"Thanks, Bill, Arnold. How about we head out for a cold beer?"

"Can't fly on one wing," Arnold reminded us.

"Okay, two beers and home," Bill opined.

On the way out, I said to Melissa, "Would you please make an appointment for me with Bob Santone?"

"Will do, Chief," she said as we exited the office.

CHAPTER 41

Martha Stewart and Singing Like a Bird

She rounded the corner and entered the parking garage after shopping at her favorite boutique. He stepped out in front of her, blocking her access to her two-door Mercedes.

He startled her, and she said instinctively, "What are you doing here? You told me to make no contact with you, but here you are."

"I'm here to deliver a warning, and you had better pay close attention," he said.

"Are you giving me the treatment that Whitey Bulger gives witnesses for the prosecution?" she asked.

"What does that mean?" he responded.

"You remember, the guy who was going to testify against Whitey was poisoned and found dead two days before his big day in court."

"It would be less obvious, but the result will be the same. You will be dead," he answered.

Lucy was frightened, but she tried not to show it.

"What brings us to this very unpleasant meeting?"

"You've been spotted in the police headquarters, and we are curious as to your affinity with this building," he said.

"I'm not going to lie to you. If I get ten to twelve years in a maximum security prison, I'm going to sing like a bird," Lucy said.

"I told you I was working on it. I can tell you now that you are going to the same country club where Martha Stewart did her stretch," he said. "But I don't have an update on what the judge is thinking about the length of your sentence."

"This is like waiting for the results of a biopsy to see if I have cancer," she retorted.

"Only a week to go," he said. "Be smart and keep your head down and maintain a low profile. You have some very influential and dangerous people concerned about you."

"Yeah, well give them a message for me. If they can't mitigate this sentence for me, I'm not going down alone. I was a good soldier. I did my job, and instead of walking away, I'm looking at a decade of prison time. Now get out of my way because I know you are not going to kill me in a shopping center garage."

She stepped by him, entered her car, and drove out of the lot without looking back. When she edged onto the highway, she immediately pulled over to the side of the road and started to shake uncontrollably. She felt as if she was in way over her head. Who was this guy, making wild love to her on one hand and threatening to have her killed on the other?

When he drove out of the same garage, he stopped immediately and used his cell phone.

The response on the other end was a terse "Yeah."

"She's going to sing like Mario Lanza if she doesn't get probation," he said.

"She's got to have balls to reach the notes Mario used to hit," the other man said.

"Enough with the jokes. She sings, I'm fucked," he said.

"It's your bed, baby, sleep in it," came from the other end of the line. "But before you do anything, my guy on the inside says she has police protection starting today."

"Those guys couldn't find their dick with two hands," he said derisively.

"Not to worry. She'll find it for them."

CHAPTER 42

Managing One Up

I was escorted into Bob Santone's office at precisely 9:00 a.m. by a very vivacious assistant named Tiffany. It started me wondering as to what percentage of the population in the Providence metropolitan area was named Tiffany. Less than the average around the United States was my guess.

Bob closed a computer he was working on, stood up, stepped around his desk, and shook my hand.

"Welcome to my world. It's a tad more esoteric than your world of grocery stores."

"How so?" I responded.

"All we do up here is trade paper. You provide a real service to the consumer, otherwise they would starve to death."

"I suppose. But trading paper and making obscene amounts of money—did you forget to mention that part of the deal has its fan base also?" I asked.

"Touché, mon ami," Santone said. "Let's talk about where these two elements meet. That's right at the place where my hedge fund, the paper example, lends Food Basket 250 million so they can continue to service their customers."

"I have two items I'd like to throw out on the table as well," I said. "First is the name Santone and Food Basket appearing with increasing frequency on the daily police blotters. Second is my contract. I have three months to go, and I haven't had an indication from the chairman of the board—that would be you, Bob—on what the future holds."

"Fair enough," Bob said. "Let's do my subject first, and that might give some perspective to your two items."

"Done," I replied.

"First, I need to pay down our loan of 250 million as fast as we can. Some of my hedge fund bets are leaking oil, and I need money," Bob said.

"I can't do that, Bob," I said. "I have empathy for your situation, but that money is committed to projects that are currently underway."

"It's my ball and, in this case, my money, so I'm not offering you a choice. I will have a ramped-up schedule of payments on your CFO's desk in the morning," Bob said.

"But, Bob, among other things, that means stopping the mega-store project and perhaps forfeiting millions of dollars. Tell me your hedge fund is not a Ponzi scheme," I said.

This meeting had started cordially enough, but it was deteriorating very quickly. Bob's face turned crimson, and veins were popping out of his neck when he said, "Ponzi scheme? How dare you! You are the CEO of Food Basket, Russ, but don't you ever forget that you are an employee. No wonder Joe Galetti fired you. You've got a fresh mouth and the tact of a bulldozer."

"Listen, Bob, I may be an employee, but my contract says I get to call the shots. Additionally, the 250-million-dollar loan has an agreed-to repayment term, and you won't send my CFO anything about rearranging it," I said.

"For your information, I can garner the votes to fire your ass. And that, perhaps, will answer your question about your future employment," Bob said.

"Very bad bluff, Bob," I said. "I'm there every day, and I have the majority of the votes, and I have a one-year option to continue on this job. Additionally, the organization has two murders on its hands and another Santone about to be incarcerated for perjury, so firing your CEO right now, unless you have a death wish, isn't going to go over too well with your employees or your stockholders."

"You got it all figured out, don't you, Russell?" Bob said.

"Actually, I didn't until now. But this meeting should have been about thanking me and the Food Basket management team for pulling this chain out of a deep tailspin. We are now competing on equal footing in the industry, our employees' morale is sky high, and the stock has tripled in less than a year. Instead, what do I get from you but a shit sandwich. That leads me to the conclusion that you wanted the chain to fail," I said.

"Of course I don't want it to fail," Bob said. "You've done a terrific job, but goddammit, Russ, I want to sell it and get it out of my hair. I can't draw a buyer when my ratio of debt to equity is as high as it is now."

"Bullshit," I said. "C'mon, Bob, I might be a liberal arts major, but I'm not an imbecile. We are making money now, not losing it, so any prospective customer would see that there is no chance of this loan being forfeited because the chain didn't have the resources to pay it off."

"It's not that simple," Bob said.

"Well, break it down for me because it smells. Providence, in its day, led the nation in per capita murders. This chain is funneling money into a basement under the auspices of a board member, and the chairman ends up with two matching bullets in the back of his skull. If I were Captain Alan Cummings from Homicide, I'd be spending all my free time with you. Two people on my management team think money laundering for someone was going on here."

"You've got detectives on your management team?" Bob asked.

"Of course not. But I have one local who keeps his ear to the ground, and a fifty-year legend as a consultant who knows what's shaking in the shadowy world of money manipulation and payoffs," I said.

"Here it is, Russell," Bob said, "with the bark off. Both of your people are seeing an Indian behind every tree. I made some bad bets in the hedge fund that I thought I could correct in the short term.

At the same time, you came to me for the loan, and I borrowed the money from a group with egregious repayment terms. To date, I haven't been able to institute corrective measures for the fund, so I'm sinking into the sunset quickly. Of course, if I could sell the chain, I'd generate the cash necessary to bail myself out."

"Okay, Bob, thanks for giving me the straight-talk version. Where do we go from here?" I asked.

"Well, you may be right or you may be wrong about what I can do legally, but I know that I can't afford to be tied up in a legal battle. So I'm going to rely on you to help with this repayment once you've looked at the numbers. As to your continued employment, let's circle back to that in a month or so," Bob said.

"Okay, Bob, I'll call you when I know something," I said as I stood, shook his hand, and left.

When Russ was in the elevator, Bob picked up his phone and said to his secretary, "One by one, get me the people on the board at Food Basket."

"Yes, sir," she replied.

CHAPTER 43

Count/Recount

I was back in my office after my call on Bob Santone, and I had a bad feeling that he didn't take kindly to my refusing to pay back the loan faster than the agreement called for by written contract. Acts of less consequence than that were responsible for me being canned twice at Galetti, so the only thing that made sense to me was to try to seek counsel from the person who had fired me twice, Joe Galetti.

Joe picked up the phone on the first ring and said, "What can I do for the big boss today?"

"Talk about role reversal! How are you? What have you been doing to move the business ahead?"

"I'm doing okay for an old codger. I have news from Joey, the son that doesn't listen to me. He's moving his business to Fall River, buying a house in Westport, and asking his pals in the business to move down here. He's thinking along the lines of a mini Silicon Valley," Joe said.

"Amazing. Good news. He was always a favorite of mine, as you know," I replied.

"He did something else that you don't know about," Joe said. "And after I tell you, you still don't know about it. *Capisce?*"

"I can't wait to not hear this one," I replied.

"Well, it was kind of my fault," Joe said. "I took him to the newly renovated Food Basket store in Woonsocket."

"Okay," I said with just a little trepidation.

"While he's in the store, he whips out his cell phone and calls his cousin."

"Trip?" I asked. "Are they still close after the court battle?"

"Tight as ticks," Joe responded. "They don't compete anymore except in racquetball, and Trip uses all of Joey's software in his stores."

"Cozy," I said, pimping Joe a little.

"What do you want," Joe responded, "a first cousin duel with paint guns at twelve paces?"

"What do you know about paint guns? We got off the subject. What shouldn't I know?"

"He told Trip, based on a limited sample admittedly, that he should buy Food Basket," Joe said.

"You're kidding," I said. "I just found out from Bob that he's anxious to sell it and that's what I called you about. We had a conversation that was just barely civil. His hedge fund has made some bad financial moves, and he wants me to pay our loan back a lot faster than the terms of the contract. I had the distinct impression that part of the loan took place in a pool hall with an egregious interest rate attached to it."

"What else?" Joe asked.

"Well, to tell the truth, I was expecting an *attaboy* or two, an extension of my contract, and maybe even a bump in pay," I said.

"And?" Joe asked.

"None of the above. And he didn't know that I have the option in my contract to re-up for another year at the same compensation plus 10 percent," I said, "something my financial advisor inserted into the small print."

"Holly?" he asked.

"Yep," I said, trying to match Joe's short responses.

"Want my advice?" Joe asked.

"Of course I want it," I responded.

"You have two choices: First, resign gracefully and go back to your brokerage business. In my experience with you, I have to say that your skill set precludes any action defined as graceful," Joe said.

"Jesus, Joe," I said, "why don't you tell me what you are really thinking?"

"Hey, kid, I'm not too graceful myself now that I think of it," Joe said.

"No shit," I responded.

"Okay then, let's stop for a minute and think what a man would do when he has his tit in a ringer and a recalcitrant employee is telling him to blow it out his butt," Joe said.

"A cement suitcase?" I asked.

"A possibility, but no," Joe said. "There's too much of that kind of thing hanging over the Food Basket business right now. Knocking off the CEO gangland style isn't in the cards, even for a desperate man."

"Get rid of me another way?" I asked.

"Bingo, Russell. It's six to five that he has or is currently talking to your board to garner the votes to fire you. No question in my mind."

"Ouch. How's that going to work out?" I asked. "I have results on my side."

"You do. But some of those people are either loyal to Bob or owe him big time," Joe said. "This is a job for me. It's clandestine, below the belt, a rabbit chop to the neck—all the things I specialize in. I'm going to start using the phone. A couple of these folks owe me big time, and we have the element of surprise on our side because Bob doesn't know about my influence with these folks. You take Garth Brewster and the new CFO. Is he a board member?"

"Thanks, Joe. I'll get to work on those two because Larry Baldwin is a board member. One ramification for you that might not have occurred to you—the first thing that will be stopped is the construction of the megastore complex because that is taking literally millions from the pot right now."

"Son of a bitch! No way that's going to happen," Joe responded.

"Listen, Joe, if you had guys chasing you that deal in 80 percent interest who specialize in broken body parts, you'd put the arm on everybody you know to get out from under," I said. "Megastores, hitting up ex-wives, selling pencils on the street corner, anything but digging your own grave while two people watch over you with Glocks at the ready."

"Okay, as I promised you, I did look at the Santone connection, and Alex Santone was not connected to the local mob, but he was pretty deep into their pockets, and he was just barely paying the vig when he was killed."

"You were going to tell me about it when?" I responded.

"Probably never unless it became germane," Joe replied.

"Who else knows about this?" I asked.

"Arnold Cable knows, and Garth Brewster knows, and to my knowledge, none of the board knows," Joe said.

"Why were you guys withholding this information from me?" I asked. "I'm the CEO. I'm supposed to know what the hell is going on."

"Because you are the CEO," Joe responded.

"What? I don't get it," I said.

"Look, once Joe Snyder got popped and after Lucy Santone's obvious connection to Food Basket, we figured that someone from law enforcement would want to talk to you and that you should remain Mickey the Dunce on all matters to do with the case and specifically the mob."

"Okay, Joe," I said. "But it was a bad call. And here is why: You guys acted like the individual stores did when I got here. They didn't adhere to headquarters, everybody running their own deals. The team is the thing here."

There was a long hesitation at the other end of the phone, and then Joe said, "Russell, very strong logic and very good point. I apologize. I'm still treating you like you were a kid back in the original store."

"Apology accepted, Joe. What are you thinking?"

"Let's take them in order. First, we need to start working the board immediately, and then I'd like a shot at seeing if I can get a backup loan just in case," Joe said, "in case Bob has the votes from the board or if we have the votes forcing Bob to fold his tent with his hedge fund."

"Good deal. I'll get to work. Glad you are on board, Joe, as I feel a little out of my depth here."

After hanging up with Joe, I called Garth Brewster.

Garth answered by saying, "I'll listen to any reasonable offer to buy my vote at the next board meeting."

"Shit," I responded.

"You're going to have to do better than that," Garth said.

"I'm guessing I'm second to the dough dish," I said. "What is Bob asking you to support?"

"Shit-canning you and paying the loan back pronto," was Garth's concise answer.

"What did you tell him, if I may be so bold?" I asked.

"Well, the first thing I asked was why couldn't we pay back the loan and keep our current CEO," Garth said.

"And?" I asked.

"He said basically that he wasn't willing to work with a 'disloyal prick' and that you have to go."

"Man, that smarts a little," I responded.

"I hear that," Garth said. "But remember, he's not a czar like Joe Galetti was. This is a public corporation, and if the board votes for you, Bob is going to have to find another way."

"Which way are you leaning?" I asked.

"You may be so brazen," Garth said. "I'm voting for the guy who started this party about nine months ago. And don't bother calling our newly minted CFO or Harry Hopkins because they are voting for you also."

"Joe is making calls too," I responded. "And thanks for your support. I greatly appreciate it."

"You're welcome. Well deserved."

One thing was clearing up for me: Hartman had been right, as usual. I wanted to stay as CEO and leave on my own terms. I truly believed that long term I'd return to my own company, but not now. And I had to reconnect with Holly. She had pushed me into this job and then worried that I was in over my head and not enjoying myself.

She was one for two: I was definitely in over my head, but I was enjoying the hell out of it.

CHAPTER 44

Money Talks, but It Don't Sing and Dance

The result of Lucy Santone's perjury trial was predictable. She was found guilty on two counts, and surprisingly, the short trial garnered almost no publicity. But today was different—very different. The courtroom was filled to capacity to hear the judge's sentence. If Las Vegas was involved, I thought the heavy money would be on a maximum sentence. The scuttlebutt in Arnold Cable's Lawyers Weekly group was that Lucy Santone would receive the maximum sentence because she had "skated" on the murder one conspiracy charge.

Probably an overused term, but the moment of truth had really come for Lucy Santone. The judge had finished her preamble, and then she looked at Lucy and said, "Not more than twelve months on each count of perjury."

I looked at Donna Mitchner, and one could read the sharp disappointment in her face. I was pretty sure she was thinking an eight- to ten-year stretch for Ms. Santone. Donna, like many others, was hoping the judge would assign a heavy penalty as a "makeup" for having Lucy walk on the murder conspiracy complaint. Lucy Santone wasn't smiling, but I think she knew that she couldn't have had a much better outcome. It reminded me of the old philosopher Neil Diamond and a specific lyric that says, "Money talks, but it don't sing and dance, and it don't walk." In this case, I was guessing that Lucy was nine to thirteen months from walking with good behavior.

The judge gave her sixty days to put her affairs in order before her incarceration. That gave me a thought, but I needed Captain Cummings to hear it to see if it made any sense at all. I usually wasn't this ambivalent, but I wasn't even supposed to be at this sentencing. I had no background in Cummings's chosen field of endeavor, and I had a job that at least one person wanted to separate me from quickly and with as little fanfare as possible. And that part, the job volatility, reminded me to make a mental note to call Arnold Cable. Holly often told me that my mental notes weren't that reliable given the source, but I was going to hang on to this one.

I called Alan Cummings and asked him to come to my office at his convenience. When I came back from lunch, his large frame was spread out in my office, and he was reading the *Wall Street Journal.*

When I came in, he said, "I hope you don't mind, but Melissa told me to make myself comfortable."

"Not a problem," I responded. "I have a guy who comes into my office, takes off his shoes, thumbs through my inbox, and sometimes fluffs up the pillows on the couch and takes a nap."

"Sounds like the guy was brought up in a barn," Alan said.

"Well, it's a special guy. He was my boss for thirty years in another lifetime," I said.

"What can I do for you, Russ?" Cummings asked.

"I've got some information that may or may not be germane, but I want to share it with you and let the expert, you, in this case, decide. But before I do that, I wanted to ask you how your lovely fiancée was feeling after the sentencing of Lucy Santone today."

"Russ, I'm not full of specifics because I'm giving her a wide berth myself until I see her tonight. But I can tell you that it's one of the few times I would feel sorry for any person whom she's trying to prosecute today. God help the poor bastard!"

The way he said it made me laugh. I think he might be slightly intimidated by his bride-to-be.

"What I'm going to tell you may seem as if it's self-serving, and maybe it is. I'll let you be the judge. I'm currently in a struggle with Bob Santone. He wants to have a 250-million-dollar loan he arranged for Food Basket paid back faster than the agreed to terms. I said no way are we going to do it because we have the money committed to projects that we'd have to stop in midstream."

"Like the megaplex store near Fall River?" Alan asked.

"How do you know about that?" I asked.

"Donna knew about it. She's quite a fan of yours actually, so perhaps I better keep a closer eye on you," he said with a smile.

"Okay, I admit it. Donna is gorgeous, but I'm very happily married, and I certainly would try to avoid any behavior that would make you take a special interest in me."

"I'm only kidding you, Russ," Cummings said with a smile. "Get me back to the loan."

"Yeah, okay," I said. "During the course of this rather unpleasant conversation with Bob Santone, he said he had some heavy losses in his hedge fund business and had borrowed some money from people who don't take kindly to late payments."

"Mafia?" Cummings asked.

"Haven't a clue," I responded. "But if I'm right, it looks like we will have a board of directors vote to see if he can fire me while persuading the board to change the terms of the loan."

"Okay," Cummings said. "But how does that help me?"

"Maybe it doesn't. But here are the pieces I'm putting together, mostly because I watched the trial instead of working for my stockholders. First, Alex Santone is murdered by a professional. Jethroe is not a professional, and I can't understand Lucy Santone's attraction to him. In the meantime, money is flowing into the basement of one of his stores, and his money guy, Joe Snyder, is murdered, and another Santone, Lucy, in this case, gets a ludicrously light sentence."

"Okay, unbelievably circumstantial, but you are saying the common denominator is the Santones and money."

"Yes, but here's the kicker: I was in court today, and I noted that Lucy has sixty days to settle her affairs," I said.

"I see a certain irony to that phrasing, but so what?" Cummings said not unkindly.

"You put someone on Lucy 24-7 and see who she takes you to, especially if it's some out-of-the-way meeting spot."

"Riley, you may have missed your calling. Here's why," Alan said. "Lucy Santone came to me and painted a hypothetical that showed Bruno Jethroe was set up. She was working me for protection. She thought if she received a long jail sentence, she would become a liability. We put her under a security blanket, and nothing happened, so I figured she was just being a little paranoid."

"Maybe not. Just maybe your security detail was too tough to crack," I said. "But that works for you now because she feels she's not under surveillance, so she can go wherever she pleases."

"Why is this information self-serving?" Cummings asked.

"Because I'm about to get into a lethal shit fight with Bob Santone, and think how distracted he'd be if he thought he was a person of interest in this case? But honestly, the thing that brought it all together for me was having Lucy cruising around town for another sixty days."

"Russ, it's way out there," Alan said. "But it would be within reason for you to ask me what else I've got going on in this case."

"What else have you got going on in this case?" I asked.

"Bubkes," Cummings responded.

"Okay then, I'll talk to you later?" I asked.

"You will indeed," Cummings said. "Thanks for the chat."

Immediately after Alan left my office, I was on the phone to Arnold Cable.

"Arnold, I'm assuming that you've heard about what's coming," I said.

"I have. Is there no job out there that you can take that doesn't find you on the lam or terminated?" Arnold asked.

"Apparently not," I said.

"I can't keep coming out of retirement to help you if you can't keep a job," Arnold said, then he thought about that for a moment and said, "Wait a minute, maybe I could. Work a year, you get fired again. Off for an indeterminate period and back to work when someone else hires you. At this rate, I won't have to take social security until I'm seventy."

"Okay, Arnold, but I need you to see if we can make a skate save for me now," I said.

"What exactly do you need?" Arnold asked.

"I'm thinking of a little grassroots support for our management team. We have a board of directors meeting the fifteenth of next month, and I was thinking about an employee rally outside the meeting."

"Jesus, who the hell do you think you are, Walter Reuther? When did you become such a rabble-rouser?" Arnold asked.

"When I saw someone trying to kill our forward momentum for no apparent valid reason," I responded.

"Didn't Shirley Macober and Pondorf do something like that for you when you were fired at Galetti?" Arnold asked.

"Yes, they did," I responded. "But I'm looking for two or three hundred folks with placards. I think it might influence board members who are on the fence to vote with us."

"Let me work the stores. If there is some enthusiasm, I'd say we do it. But, Russ, if the folks are apathetic, I'd say we think of something else. I don't want to be in the middle of a crowd that is ambivalent or feeling as if they were forced to participate."

"Fair enough," I responded. "I'm hoping that they feel as if Food Basket is on the rise, that their jobs were in jeopardy until we came along, and that they have the resources to compete on an equal basis with competition. On a more personal note, Arnold, if they are ambivalent, we'll know it's time to leave and put you into that indeterminate period you mentioned between assignments."

"I like the sound of that temporarily. I'd trade in my florescent tan for some real sunshine as I sink my toes in the sand on the beach."

"Yeah, but, Arnold, how long can you take that kind of boring existence? Beers in a cooler, a Jack Reacher head-banging novel in your lap, women walking by in all kinds of abbreviated outfits, and the smell of a steak cooking on the grill."

"At least six months. This idea of a rally for the team is intriguing. I'll know in a week or ten days which way the troops are leaning," said Arnold as the line went dead.

Melissa stuck her head in the door and said, "Holly on two."

I picked up the phone and said, "What a nice surprise."

"I was thinking about you, so I decided to call you up and tell you that I love you," Holly said.

"Best thing that's happened to me all day by far," I responded.

"Tell me the not-so-good today," she responded.

"Let's see, Bob Santone wants his loan paid back faster than the contract specifies. I said no. He's working the board of directors to vote me out. I had a visit from Alan Cummings at my office, and I think he thinks I could be a halfway-good detective. I talked strategy with Joe Galetti on the board vote, and I've tasked Arnold to see if we can get some grassroots, store-level support for our team by means of a rally at our next board meeting."

"That's enough action for any person for one day. I'm on my way to you right now. Here's the plan: a dual spa massage, dinner for two at an exquisite restaurant, and home to bed. What do you think of that plan?" Holly asked.

"Hurry," I said and hung up.

As I packed up my business bag that I knew I wouldn't open tonight, I thought about Holly. And the one thing that flashed through my mind was even a blind squirrel finds an acorn every once in a while.

CHAPTER 45

Close Encounter

They had been drinking in his living room when she was suddenly taking his clothes off at a very rapid rate. The high acceleration of passion produced a number of couplings between a man and a woman that made it hard for him to recall after the fact. But what he did remember was her pure brute strength, throwing him around like a sack of groceries. This was a high-wire act, pitched intensity and pure passion that he could only hope wouldn't fade in time.

When they eventually unraveled from each other, he said, "Not that I would wish this on you, but if you ever receive a screwball sentence for someone you prosecuted again, call me right away. I want to be sure and be home when you arrive from work."

Donna Mitchner laughed out loud.

"I didn't hurt you, did I? You're right. I brought the office home with me today, and you were the recipient."

"Benefactor would be more apt," Alan Cummings said.

"Believe me, Alan, it wasn't all one way. I enjoyed it immensely, but justice was not served today. I don't think I'm being too cynical when I say some cash passed hands today on that sentence. I know you're a little sweet on her, but Lucy Santone might as well have walked today. I was counting on eight years, but instead she'll be out in eight months," Donna Mitchner said.

"Speaking of people you are sweet on, I had a nice chat with Russell Riley today," Cummings said. "By the way, he said you were gorgeous."

"What did you say?" she asked.

"I told him he was working his way up to twenty-four-hour surveillance for hitting on a homicide captain's intended."

"Okay, scratch one of my admirers. I do think he's a sharp guy in a platonic kind of way," Donna said.

"Right answer," Alan said. "But he called me to tell me he had a theory about the case. He has followed the case very closely and has been in court on numerous occasions. Interestingly, he's running parallel to us in that he thinks Bruno was set up and that Alex Santone's and Joe Snyder's murders are connected to some type of money-laundering scheme. He believes this because Bob Santone came to him and wanted to speed up terms on a loan Santone had made to Food Basket. Apparently, Bob Santone has made some bad picks for his hedge fund and needs money now."

"Interesting. I told you he was good. Riley is nobody's fool, and he has given us motive in Bob Santone's case that we didn't have an inkling of through our channels. What else did he say?"

"He said it wouldn't be the dumbest idea in the world to put a tail on Lucy for the next two months to see who she pals around with."

"He's right," she said.

"Phone taps?" he asked.

"Slim chance," she said. "She has already been convicted and sentenced, and her coconspirator is in prison. Listen, if she leads us to someone or something that would help to convict the hierarchy of the mob, then maybe I could sell a tap."

"Fair enough," Alan said.

"Now what were we doing before this current conversation?" she asked.

"Counting backwards from a hundred," he said.

"One hundred, ninety-nine, ninety-eight, ninety—oh, oh—ninety-two—oh, Alan, don't stop."

CHAPTER 46

Fox in the Henhouse

Jim Sneed was sitting at my secretary's chair when I arrived at my office at 6:45 a.m.

I looked at Jim and said, "Melissa is going to kick your butt if you are going through her stuff."

Sneed smiled and said, "What kind of banker hours are you keeping, Russ? I thought you grocery types were up with the roosters."

"Actually, if you have to know, I've been in two stores, checking the shelves and sell-by dates," I said, somewhat indignantly.

"Really?" Sneed said.

"No kidding," I replied.

"I'm impressed," Sneed said as I led him into my office.

"Do you know how to make that coffee machine work, or should we just go directly to the cafeteria?"

"Ye, of little faith," I said. "Contrary to the word out on the street, this CEO can fend for himself. I can make coffee, turn out a three-minute egg, and take out the trash."

"I like it. Most CEOs are waited on hand and foot and, as a result, are not good at attending any kind of basic task," he said.

"But, Jimmy, you didn't come here to admire my omelet-making skills. What's up?" I asked.

"Really sour news—the worst kind. You've got a fox in the hen-house," Sneed said.

I brought Jim a cup of coffee, settled into a chair across from him, and said, "You mean a rat."

"A classic rat. Makes Benedict Arnold look like a patriot," Sneed responded.

"I don't need this right now with a board meeting upcoming," I said. "Say it ain't so, Shoeless Joe."

"You told me to canvass the board of directors that I am either a member of or ones that I am instructing on best practices, remember?" Jim said.

"I do," I said. "Tell me that it's not Garth Brewster."

"It's not Garth Brewster," Sneed replied. "It's Joe Galetti."

"Bullshit! I don't believe it," I said a little too loudly.

"Don't shoot the messenger," Sneed said.

"Sorry. You have got to understand, Joe is supposed to be out there collecting board of directors votes for me."

"Kiss those votes good-bye. He is working the other side of the street," Sneed said.

"But why?" I asked.

"Here's the story: Alex Santone discovered that Bob Santone was laundering money through his stores and threatened to go to the authorities."

"I thought Alex Santone was an incompetent drunk who didn't know shit from Shinola," I said.

"I'm not sure about that, but I'm guessing he had to be some-what coherent if he was running an eighty-store supermarket chain—clever enough to catch his nephew with his hand in the cookie jar. In the meantime, Bob is having a fling with his uncle's wife, and she in turn is boinking Bruno Jethroe. So Bob cooks up this plot to knock off his uncle but calls Joe Galetti to find a suitable replacement for Alex Santone once he is eliminated."

"Tell me Joe didn't have anything to do with the murder of Alex Santone," I said.

"That's not clear. But what is clear is that Joe Galetti is won-dering why Bob has called him for a candidate for CEO when Alex is still alive. Once he's murdered, it doesn't take an engineer from Purdue to figure out who did it."

"So at that point, Joe extorts his way into the Food Basket larder?" I asked.

"Bingo. Also, what I tell you next is a little hurtful to your ego, but I'm not going to sugarcoat it," Jim said.

I refilled our coffee cups and closed my office door as people were now arriving to work in force.

I turned to him and said, "Go."

"According to my sources, Bob wanted to hire someone who would complete the task that his uncle had started of driving the chain into the ground," Jim said.

"But why?" I asked.

"He wanted to drive the stock down to a dollar or less and then take Food Basket private with Joe Galetti running it. Joe tells Bob that he thinks you'd be the perfect guy for the job," Jim said.

"C'mon, they picked me because they thought I'd fail?" I said.

"Yes, Joe Galetti apparently said you spent money with reckless abandon."

"But what now, Jim?"

"Oh this is the beauty of it. They are screwed. The stock has gone from $5.50 a share to $16.00 a share. No way they can take it private with you at the helm. They aren't really concerned about the loan. They just want to get rid of you and hire someone without much on the ball. Oh, man, you have really messed up their plans royally!"

"Thank you for the heads-up, Professor. One thing for you that you probably figured out early on—the police are going to talk to you before this is all over," I said.

"Yep," Jim responded. "What can I do to help out?"

"Get me a head count of the board of directors. What kind of shape am I in, and who do we need to work? Is there anyone on the fence that we can swing to our side?" I asked.

"Will do," Jim said. "I hate to drink your coffee and run, but I have to go."

* * *

After Jim Sneed left, I had to talk with Bill Hartman.

He was in the building, and I asked him to come to my office. He showed up in a great suit, clean-shaven, hair all smoothed back, and smelling like the perfume counter at Bergdorf Goodman.

I said, "What's up with you, Hartman? You look like Mitt, and you smell like a French whorehouse."

"Got a shot at some new business. I'd send my partner to close this one, but he's otherwise *ocupado*," Hartman said.

"That stings," I said.

I told Hartman the whole gruesome Joe Galetti story, and he said, "It doesn't surprise me a bit. I know you like him, Russ, but I think he's a horse's ass, and I don't trust him as far as I can throw him."

"But what now?" I asked.

"From the look of it on the surface, it seems as if my partner will be back at the firm earlier than anticipated," he responded.

"Seriously, Bill, this puts Joe right in the middle of this sordid affair with murders, money, and mobsters. He could be facing extended jail time," I said.

"Just what he deserves. I thought he should have gone to jail twenty years ago when he was messing with Maria's money. Goddammit, Russ, he's a crook," Hartman said with some emotion.

"But he's family," was all I could think to say.

"Send him some homemade chocolate chip cookies in jail," Hartman said. "Let's look at this strategically. He thinks he's conning you, but thanks to Jim Sneed, you have a chance to turn the tables. So the first thing to do is not to tip your hand. Call the son of a bitch right now. He's supposed to be gathering votes for you from the board. Check him out."

I reached for the phone, called Joe Galetti's cell, and he picked up on the second ring and said, "Russ, what's shaking?"

"I'm just checking in, Joe. Any progress on influencing board members to vote for the good guys?" I asked.

"Very slow progress, Russ. It's not going as smoothly as I thought it would, frankly."

"What about Andrews and Kelly? I thought you had pictures of them in bed with a giraffe."

"I do, but I think Bob Santone has them in bed with each other. I'm getting a lot of 'I'm still chewing on it, Joe.' You know what I mean?"

"I do," I said. "Keep swinging, Joe. My job is up for grabs here. You remember what it felt like when they took your stripes away as CEO."

"Sure do. It still smarts. I built the place brick by brick, and they sent me out to pasture," Joe said.

"Are you going to let them do that to me?" I asked.

"I'm trying, Russ. I'm giving it all I got," Joe said.

"Try harder, Joe." And I hung up.

"Well?" Hartman asked.

"Jim Sneed is spot-on. Joe is working for the other side. He and Santone must be laughing their asses off that I went out on my own and hired Joe Galetti. Andrews and Kelly owe their careers to Joe Galetti."

"You remember the old count/recount back in the day?" Hartman asked.

"I do. They were a licensed to steal money from the manufacturer for very little effort," I said.

"Well, we need an accurate one and before the next board meeting," Hartman said. "I'll go capture that new business, but you need to gather Cable, Larry Baldwin, Garth Brewster, and Jim Sneed at my place tomorrow at noon. We'll be cooking burgers and counting votes."

"I'm on it," I said as Hartman wheeled out of my office and headed out to add more products to our food-brokerage business.

CHAPTER 47

Strategy, Secrets, and Sugar Lips

We were all gathered at Hartman's house on Craigville Beach early the next morning. Somehow, the view off Hartman's porch of ocean meeting the blue, blue sky at the horizon gave me great peace of mind. We had had to scramble to get everybody here on this kind of lightning timing, but equally important was my attempt at subterfuge; I didn't want anybody to know where we were. I really believed in the element of surprise, but trying to hide the whereabouts of six executives who had a myriad of people reporting to them wasn't easy. Hartman, Cable, Brewster, Baldwin, and Sneed all pushed aside plans to be at this meeting, and that by itself would send up smoke signals that something was up.

Everybody settled in around a fabulous poker table in the center of Hartman's living room, and I opened the meeting by thanking them for dumping their regularly scheduled activities to be here and added, "I think it's safe to say that the stakes that are up for grabs in this discussion are several times larger than any game that Bill has held at this table."

Hartman gave us the "maybe, maybe not" hand signal, which made us all chuckle.

"Without further ado, let me turn the meeting over to Jim Sneed to give us his best guesstimate on how the board will vote on the fifteenth of next month."

Jim handed out a single sheet of paper with two columns as follows:

For (Good Guys)

1. Riley
2. Brewster
3. Hopkins
4. Baldwin
5. Nock

Against (Not Good Guys)

1. Andrews
2. Kelly
3. Santone
4. Little
5. Schoch
6. Duer

Undecided

1. Valera
2. Simpson

"Net, gentlemen, they need only one of two undecideds, but we need them both."

"Wasn't Simpson a business associate of yours at one point, Garth?" Cable asked.

"He was, but we agreed to disagree, and I bought him out at a very fair price," Garth said.

"Can you schmooze him over to our side?" Jim asked.

"Maybe. But it's no better than sixty-forty, not a sure thing," Garth said.

"Okay, what about Valera?" I asked.

"Nancy Valera is the one mystery guest. She owns a string of high-fashion boutiques, and she is very successful," Sneed said. "The only thing I could find out was that she was a good friend of Alex Santone's first wife, Olivia."

"Good intel, Jim," Arnold Cable said. "How about we put Holly and/or Jenny Hartman on her? This could be a break for us if she isn't that crazy about who succeeded her friend as Alex's second wife."

"What about Olivia herself?" Larry Baldwin asked. "Anybody know her or know anyone that does?"

"I'm guessing Bob Santone is the only one that knows her," I said. "But what about combining these two ideas and having Holly and Jenny try to contact Olivia Santone? I'll call Melissa to see if we can get a phone number."

"We are still odds on to come up one vote short," Hartman said. "Anybody have a worst-case scenario plan?"

"I do," Cable responded. "I'm working with store personnel right now to see if we can't pull off a rally of employees—three or four hundred strong to march on the board meeting on the fifteenth showing their belief in the current management."

"How is that working out?" Garth Brewster asked.

"Too early to tell," Arnold replied, "but we've had some positive vibes, and, Russ, Pondorf, Macober, and Williams insist on being a part of the rally. I told them they had the wrong food chain, but they insisted that we had the right guy to rally around."

"Crazy bastards, I love them!" I said. "We still have two weeks until the meeting. Garth, you work Simpson, and Hartman and I will see if Holly and Jenny can contact Olivia Santone and, in turn, Nancy Valera. Arnold, you've got to scramble to rally the troops, and, Larry, why don't you take on the logistics of transporting three or four hundred people to the meeting site with placards. Anything else?"

There was no response, so I said, "Let's get back to where we are supposed to be today. Many thanks."

We must have been in emergency mode. It was the first time in recent memory that we didn't savor goodies cooked on Hartman's very weird cooker.

* * *

O'Malley was in a place he wasn't familiar with, and he had no place to hide. He was parked on a long beach road that ran parallel to the ocean and in front of some large cottages in Watch Hill, Rhode Island. He had followed Lucy Santone from the city, where he had plenty of cover, to this godforsaken spot, where all he could see was sand stretching in front of him for miles. He took the number off the mailbox, moved out of sight of the cottage, and called it in to headquarters. Using the clerk at police headquarters to do a reverse address lookup, he found that the cottage belonged to Bob Santone.

He then had his call transferred to Alan Cummings, who picked up his phone and said, "Cummings."

"O'Malley, Captain. I'm in Watch Hill, Rhode Island, as we speak."

"Pretty upscale neighborhood for a police detective, isn't it, O'Malley?" Cummings asked.

"C'mon, Alan," O'Malley said, "I wouldn't be anywhere near here if I wasn't working. I followed Lucy Santone here, and the house is owned by Bob Santone. But I'm really exposed here. There is no place to hide."

"Okay," Cummings said, "bring it on in. You've done enough good work today."

"Copy that. Thanks, Chief," O'Malley said.

* * *

Inside the house, Lucy Santone was lying naked, gasping for breath, after making passionate, all-out love. She was frustrated, she was too long deprived, and as a result, she had made love with a vengeance. She wanted Bob to cry out. She wanted to hurt him.

"Jesus, you almost killed me!" he gasped.

"You had it coming to you, you son of a bitch," she said.

"Had it coming?" he said. "People should have enemies like me. I got you a sweetheart of a prison location and eight months when you could have done twelve years."

"That's mighty generous of you, but why am I doing time at all when you did the crime?" Lucy asked.

"We didn't see the perjury backdoor trap coming. But I've hustled my ass for you, not to mention nearly a half million dollars it cost me to put the fix in."

Lucy was dressing when she turned to Santone and said, "You're not getting any more of this for almost a year."

"Don't worry, I'll be waiting for you at the jailhouse door, sugar lips."

Lucy walked out to her car, started the motor, and drove away. As she left the driveway, she thought to herself, "Sugar lips, my ass. You're going down with a thud, Santone."

CHAPTER 48

Preplanned
Spontaneous Rally

I had called Donna Mitchner because I was curious to know if Captain Cummings had shared the information I had learned from Jim Sneed about Joe Galetti's involvement in the Santone murder. She said she had talked to Cummings about it and that, although she couldn't share the specifics, another piece of the puzzle had fallen into place. I had really called to see if they were going to move against Bob Santone anytime soon because only ten days remained to the board meeting where I could find myself sliding down the sidewalk unemployed. But Donna was tougher than scoring a ticket to a Bosox playoff game when it involved releasing information.

In the meantime, I was busily checking with my sources to see where we stood with the undecided board members, Valera and Simpson. I called Garth first to check on his former business partner, Matt Simpson, and he said, "He's still on the fence, Russ. I know what appeals to him—money, so I tried to stress what happened to the stock since you have taken over. But I have no way to know if that argument holds water because I don't know if he has any stock, so I'm sticking with sixty-forty. He wasn't unfriendly, but he was noncommittal. What's working against us is that Bob Santone could make him the same argument and slip him some cheap stock under the table."

"Not without Larry Baldwin knowing about it. I will alert him. Thanks for the effort, Garth."

I had already talked to Holly, and she had arranged, through Olivia Santone, Alex's first wife, to meet Nancy Valera for tea, which would take place the day after tomorrow.

I called Jim Sneed to tell him that my gut feeling was the board would be deadlocked with one abstention, or we would go down by one vote.

He listened and said, "It could be your lucky day, and you could win by one vote."

"Are you willing to bet the ranch on that prediction?" I asked.

"No, I'm not," Sneed replied. "I think we need the intimidation factor—the blue-collar uprising. What is Arnold saying?"

"He's next on my list," I replied.

"Talk to you later, Russ," Sneed said as he hung up.

I buzzed Arnold, and he trotted over to my office.

He came through the door with a placard that read, "Riley rules. We support our CEO."

"I see Larry has been busy down in the sign-making shop," I said.

"Indeed he has," Cable said. "I've got good news and bad news."

"Bad news first," I said.

"The union shop steward says you have to pay time and a half for the people who participate in the rally plus a travel allowance."

"Travel allowance?" I said. "We are providing the transportation."

"That's what I said," Arnold responded. "He let that one ride."

"What's the good news?" I asked.

"Over six hundred people want to go to the rally!" Cable declared.

"Yahoo!" I replied. "Great job, Arnold."

"I'd like to take credit, Russ, but honestly, this was like shooting fish in a barrel. I think what we forgot is that their pensions are tied to our success as an organization. It hit a nerve with the workers."

"Arnold, we are going to need them. So use your contacts to get the proper paperwork so that we can rally and keep it on the down low," I said.

Arnold burst out laughing. "Down low. You are becoming a shadowy character."

"I still don't have *vig* clear in my mind. All I remember is that your lunch money in elementary school was vig."

"I'll get right on it. Larry Baldwin has arranged for the transportation, and he's made an ample amount of signs. You're telling me it's a go, no exceptions."

"It's a go. We need this distraction," I replied.

Just before leaving the office, I received a call from Captain Alan Cummings at police headquarters.

I said, "Hello, Alan. What can I do for you?"

"I told you not to fool around with my girlfriend, didn't I?" he said.

"Ahhh, I don't—what do you mean? I'm sure you have the wrong fellow," I replied.

I heard this booming laugh from the other end of the line.

"Only kidding, Russ. How are you doing?"

"Better now," I said.

He chuckled again and said, "I owe you one. For God's sake, don't tell Donna I told you this, but we made the connection today between Bob and Lucy Santone."

"My lips are sealed," I said. "Without giving away the keys to the city, do you have any idea when you will move against Bob Santone?"

"Unless we get a major break, not anytime in the next couple of weeks," he said.

"Thanks, Alan. I really appreciate the information."

CHAPTER 49

The Girls

Holly Riley, Jen Hartman, and Olivia Santone were in a private parlor at the Wayside Inn in Sudbury awaiting the arrival of Nancy Valera, one of the two undecided votes on the board of directors. They were a contrast as they sat at an elegant table with the requisite wherewithal for drinking tea. Holly was tall, slim, and possessed a beauty that made you double back for another peek to verify what you already knew. Jen Hartman was tiny, but not like a china cup—more like a marathon runner with short blond hair, quick movements, and a dazzling smile. Olivia Santone looked every bit of her chronological age, but she was elegant and comfortable around people and in just about any situation. She had laugh wrinkles and crow's crinkles in all the right places.

Olivia looked at Holly and Jen and said, "Relax, ladies, this is going to be fun. Nancy Valera is a hot shit, a self-made millionaire who has the business acumen to put together a string of very successful high-end boutiques. They are my personal favorites to shop. Her merchandise is awe-inspiring—so much so that you don't even look at the price tags. You just want to buy it before somebody else sees it and steals it away from you while you're not looking. If I don't miss my guess, she'd much rather have a Manhattan than a cup of tea."

"How should we approach her?" Holly asked.

"Look, I'll get the ball rolling. If I know her, she already knows what we want. Holly, and you too, Jen, are going to tell her why she should vote to maintain the current management. You can do that, right?" Olivia asked.

"I can," Holly said.

Nancy Valera arrived fashionably late, dressed all in red, including a floppy hat reminiscent of something Greta Garbo or some other publicity-shy well-known person would wear. She sparkled in gold and diamond accessories, and she had a handbag that would cover the rent for a month at a good-sized condo on the east side of Manhattan. She was sixtyish, looked early fifties, but had had more tucks than a bottom sheet on a king-sized bed. She was medium height but looked taller in high heels, and she was in shape—odds on to have a personal trainer and an equal chance that she was a runner.

Olivia Santone jumped up, hugged her, and said, "You look great for an old bag!"

"Speak for yourself, sweetie. Chronologically, I'm spinning my way back to thirty-nine," she said with a laugh that a partially deaf person could hear from fifty yards away. She then looked at Holly. "There, that's the look I'm trying to capture. You are Holly Lansing and you are gorgeous."

"Thank you very much, Mrs. Valera," Holly said.

"Nancy. Mrs. Valera sounds way too formal. I've been a fan of yours for years. And oh by the way, over the years I've made a fortune investing in your fund," Nancy said.

"Thank you again," Holly said. "I'd like to introduce you to Jen Hartman, an old and dear friend of mine. Our husbands worked together before Food Basket stole Russell, my husband, away to try to resuscitate their business."

"A pleasure to meet you, Jen," Nancy said. "This is a lovely place, but the sun is over the yardarm, and the booze is flowing like glue around here."

By this time, this foursome looked like a meeting of old friends. Olivia hustled out into the hallway and signaled to the business planner.

When he arrived, she said, "Get me a bartender and remove the tea set."

"Yes, ma'am, right away."

Olivia reentered and said to the group, "The purveyor of colored water is on his way."

"Excellent," Nancy Valera said. "Now tell me what you folks are up to besides the usual."

"We will," Holly responded. "But first tell us about your fantastic boutiques. What would Jen and I need to start our own boutique?"

"Lots of money and don't plan on a life away from your business. It's like the restaurant business in a way. Everyone thinks if they can't do anything else, they can open a restaurant. The mortality rate is over 90 percent," Nancy said.

"You are telling me nine of ten restaurants fail?" Jen asked.

"Exactly," Nancy said. "My guess is that you two guys, if you had the money and the time, would be successful because you have innate good taste. Speaking for myself, I'm about to marry husband number four, and I have no children or grandchildren, so be careful what you ask for."

"Husband number four! Jesus, Nancy, you are working on a Liz Taylor streak," Olivia Santone said.

"Yes and no," Nancy said.

"What's the 'no' part?" Olivia asked with a laugh.

"Husband number four was also husband number two," Nancy revealed.

The table burst into laughter just when the bartender arrived with drinks.

Holly proposed a toast, "Here's to Nancy. She's going back to husband number two as she winds her way back to age thirty-nine."

The ladies clinked glasses, and Olivia said, "Holly, why don't you take Nancy through the purpose of this get-together."

"Okay, I'll do my best. Maybe the best way to explain it is that I bought a bunch of Food Basket stock a little less than a year ago when my husband became CEO, and my investment is up 300 percent to date," Holly explained.

"Whoopee!" Nancy shouted. "That means I was in on that windfall because I have gobs of that fund. Why did you buy it, besides great faith in your husband's abilities as a top flight executive?"

"Every portfolio manager has quirks or things they see as buy side tells. For me it is CEOs. For instance, as soon as I see that some high-ranking executive from General Electric is becoming CEO at Account XYZ, I buy the stock. If he's been trained at GE, he is going to be successful elsewhere."

"Fascinating," Nancy remarked.

"Nancy, I'd like to give you some perspective on Food Basket from the supplier's point of view," Jen Hartman said. "At my husband's food brokerage business, the Food Basket business year-to-date is up 14.2 percent, reversing a five-year downward trend. Food Basket is kicking some butt, and morale is sky high."

"Okay, so what's the issue?" Nancy asked.

"Bob Santone ordered Russell to pay back a 250-million-dollar loan much faster than the terms of the agreement stipulate. Russell said no."

"Why?" Nancy asked.

"Because it meant shutting down multimillion-dollar projects in midstream, for example, the megastore being built in the Fall River marketing area."

"Okay, Olivia, you haven't said anything," Nancy noted.

"I can't add anything to the current situation, Nancy, because I know nothing about it. But I will say that my ex, God rest his soul, was paying little, if any, attention to the business the last few years of his life. A number of my friends have stopped me in the street to tell me that Food Basket is a pleasant shopping experience again."

"If I vote for current management and against Bob, what assurances do I have that they will stay in place?" Nancy asked.

"You have no assurances," Holly said. "But I think a pretty good indicator is that Russell and his team are ready to fight it out in court if they have to. Another indicator is that he's put three of us on you to try to schmooze you to vote for his team."

Nancy chuckled at that and said, "Olivia, you three folks make an awesome team. Bob has been working me all week, but this is clearly a case of 'if it isn't broken, don't fix it.'"

"So we can count on your vote?" Holly asked.

"It's in the bag," Nancy said. "How could I vote against the husband of a person who has made me wheelbarrows full of money? Now let's talk about something important. Olivia, who are you sneaking up your back staircase after dark?"

The foursome broke into laughter, and Jen signaled the bartender for one more round.

CHAPTER 50

Firsthand Account

Lucy Santone was walking towards Donna Mitchner's office for a chat that could decide her future well-being. Ironically, Lucy was going to call Donna Mitchner when she had been summoned to the assistant district attorney's office. Donna greeted Lucy at the door of her office and showed her to a seat in front of her desk.

As she walked around her desk to sit down, she said, "Okay if I call you Lucy?"

"Absolutely. You're holding all the cards, so you can call me anything you want," Lucy responded.

She thought she saw Donna blush a little when she said, "Okay, you may not have the cards, but call me Donna. We have very recent information that in some ways parallels what you told Alan Cummings in your hypothetical story— two things that are related. First is that the local mastermind behind these murders is Bob Santone, and if that is true, then we feel Bruno Jethroe was set up."

"Okay," Lucy said.

"Cummings and I feel that you can confirm for us that Bruno did not kill Alex Santone."

"What's in it for me?" Lucy asked.

"It depends on what you know. Remember, with two counts of perjury on your sheet, you don't qualify as witness of the week."

"Why talk to me then?" Lucy asked.

"Because you may be key in obtaining freedom for a man who is now serving a life sentence," Donna said.

"Trust is an issue here," Lucy said. "You have already back-doored me with this bullshit perjury case."

"I understand that, but if you could get an innocent man off the hook and further lower your sentence to house arrest, would that interest you?" Donna asked.

"Yes, if all your cards are on the table. When I look at you, I'm always looking over my shoulder for the boogeyman," Lucy said.

"No tricks up my sleeve," Donna said.

"Okay, first, I know nothing about the murder of Joe Snyder. I never met the man. But I was standing in the kitchen of my house when Bob Santone shot my husband twice in the back of the head."

It took all of Donna's self-control not to jump up in the air and signal touchdown!

"Lucy, I'm going to bring in a stenographer and have you dictate your story to her and sign it, okay?" Donna asked.

"Yes," Lucy said, "I feel better already having told somebody what really happened."

"Do you know if anybody else is connected to this money-laundering operation?" Donna asked.

"Bob never talked to me about these things. Our relationship was purely physical."

"Okay, let me go get that stenographer."

* * *

Miles away, Russell Riley placed a call to Alan Cummings.

After opening pleasantries, Alan said, "What can I do for you, Russ?"

"A quickie, a nugget, maybe nothing. Remember the guy I told you about who takes off his shoes and snoozes on the couch in my office?"

"Yeah, you said he was your old boss," Alan replied.

"Right, well, in this board fight I'm having with Bob Santone, I've learned that this guy, Joe Galetti by name, is actually working with Bob against me," Russ said.

"Okay, so?" Alan responded.

"I was just thinking if Joe Galetti is working with Bob Santone, how much does he know, and when did he know it?"

"I like it, Riley," Cummings said. "One more clue like that and you'll earn an honorary badge!"

"I'll take it," Russ said and hung up.

CHAPTER 51

Orange Is the New Black

I knew it was a bit self-serving, but this was the board meeting day, and we had twenty buses of employees on the way with signs and placards supporting the current management team and, specifically, the CEO, me! Hey, it's my livelihood as well as pride of accomplishment that's on the line. If I'm going down, I'm going down swinging.

Holly, Jen, and Olivia had delivered Nancy Valera to our side of the ledger. So we were all square, six votes a piece. But Garth Brewster's erstwhile partner, Matt Simpson, was no sure thing. My plan was simple but logistically difficult. Our meeting was at two at a downtown bank building. Arnold Cable had secured the permits to legally demonstrate, and he had found a place that could easily hold twenty buses of placard-carrying Food Basket employees. Cable had even arranged to provide police traffic coverage for the six hundred folks to move to the boardroom location. I asked him how he had managed that but received a garbled message that he totally meant to be incoherent.

The members of the board were starting to gather and mingle at about one thirty. Everybody was cordial on the surface, and last-minute schmoozing was not apparent. I was beginning to get a little nervous that Arnold and his troops had hit a snag when Bob Santone sidled over to me and asked, "Have you got the votes, Russell?"

I shook his hand, smiled, and said, "I'm not sure, but I think I'm close enough for government work."

"You can still get out of Food Basket in good graces by just relenting while continuing to work as CEO."

"I'm not a good graces type of guy, Bob, but—"

Suddenly, a deafening racket was taking place off to our right.

"What the fuck?" Bob said as we all rushed over to the window to see what the ruckus was all about.

One floor below us, six hundred people, many carrying placards, filled the streets and square. They were a noisy bunch. They were chanting "We want Riley" as they surged towards our building. I noticed off to my left that the local TV station's news trucks had been tipped off and were on the scene. It was pandemonium, and the message was clear: don't fix what ain't broken.

I called the meeting to order at precisely 2:00 p.m. and addressed the board.

"We are here today to address the matter of dismissing me because I will not pay back a loan to Bob Santone faster than is required by contract. It's really that simple. So let me open up the floor to the board."

A number of hands shot up, and I called on Matt Simpson.

Matt stood up and said, "I move that we adjourn this meeting, delaying a vote to a time and place that is a little less hostile."

"Second?" I asked.

"I second the motion," said Nancy Valera. "And I would urge this group to reconsider replacing a management team that has tripled our value in about a year."

"All for adjourning? Twelve to adjourn," I said. "The motion is carried, and we will announce the new date and time shortly. This meeting is adjourned."

Santone raced over to me. His face was crimson in color, and veins were sticking out of his neck.

"You son of a bitch! I know you planned this dog-and-pony show. But you are only delaying your own execution."

"Bob, I needed to delay this meeting because I was fairly sure that you had the votes. But there was another good reason as well," I said.

"What was that?" he asked.

"I think by the time we have the next meeting, you will have traded in your tweed jacket for an orange jumpsuit."

With that message delivered, I left the room to let Bob ponder his future.

CHAPTER 52

The Fall of an Icon

T hings moved quicker than I thought possible. Seventeen days after our board meeting, Bob Santone was arrested for the murders of his uncle, Alex Santone, and Joe Snyder, former CFO of Food Basket. The city of Providence and the state were shocked at these revelations, and the only winner was the former mayor of Providence, whose morning talk show received a rocket-booster ratings increase because people really believed he had the inside scoop on murder, corruption, and all local nefarious shenanigans.

Imagine my surprise when I was riding to work one morning, listening to the radio, and the mayor's special guest was Arnold Cable. The mayor introduced Arnold as president and second-in-command of Food Basket, taking a swipe at me by saying that he had tried to get me for the show, but I had not returned his calls. Absolutely untrue.

The mayor went on to explain that he and Arnold were childhood friends and that he was grateful that someone had come forward from Food Basket to "face the music."

It was early, but the mayor was already giving me heartburn. Arnold responded to that comment by saying, "Now, buddy, let's not paint a corporation with a giant brush because of the actions of one person."

The mayor jumped on that immediately. "Wait a minute, Arnold. This chain had been heading for bad, bad times for at least three years."

"Okay," Arnold responded, "let's concentrate on the family then. Alex Santone was somewhat distracted during the last years of his business life."

"*Distracted* may not be a strong enough word. His focus was entirely on his bombshell of a wife thirty years his junior," the mayor responded.

"You know what they say when people ask, Why does George Clooney date women that are under thirty?" Arnold asked.

"No, what?" the mayor asked.

"Because he can," Arnold responded.

That drew a big guffaw from the radio host while at the same time sending the mayor in another direction.

"What about your boss, Russell Riley?" the mayor asked.

"What about him?" Arnold responded.

"He seems like the Teflon man. He's an interloper from another state, and he flies under the radar. His wife is a big-time portfolio manager in Boston, and I'm wondering if he looks down his nose at us. You know, Providence is home of the AAA Pawsox while Boston boasts a bona fide major league contender," the mayor said, stopping only because he was out of breath.

"Well, you are right about one thing, Mr. Mayor, he has a sizeable proboscis."

The mayor laughed heartily at that.

"C'mon, Arnold, you're making me work too hard, even though it's very enjoyable."

"Okay, okay, first of all, his wife is from Cumberland, and Russell Riley and his team have absolutely turned Food Basket around in a year. Their volume is up, profit is up, and most importantly, morale is sky high. I don't know if you noticed, my old friend, but six hundred employees marched on a Food Basket board meeting when it was rumored that Bob Santone was going to replace Riley and his team. If it weren't for Riley, half of those people would have been laid off, and they knew it."

"Okay, okay, he's ready for sainthood," the mayor said.

"Maybe not. But if you had bought the stock when he took over, you'd be up 300 percent year-to-date."

"How does the absence of Bob Santone from Food Basket play?" the mayor asked.

"I don't know if you picked up the story yet. I just happened to see it on the *Today Show*. But the FTC has halted any transactions on his hedge fund, which usually means a Ponzi scheme isn't far behind."

"Arnold, you are full of bon mots today," the mayor responded. "What are you picking up from your Lawyers Weekly crowd?"

"Not much really," Arnold said. "A rumor is floating around that the police will make one more arrest in connection with the Santone murder, but my sources say it has more to do with money laundering."

"Folks, you've been listening to Arnold Cable, local boy made good as he is now president of Food Basket. We will be back with Arnold after these messages. Don't touch that dial."

I pulled into the office and missed the rest of the interview. I thought that I'd better give Arnold a raise. I didn't know that he was president of this operation.

Later that day, Arnold Cable appeared at my door. I immediately looked up and said to him, "Mr. President."

"I have to admit it," Arnold said, "I really liked that part. I've known the mayor forever. He's really a good guy when you get by all the fancy watches and expensive cars."

"I'll say this—he certainly had his hands filled with you today. I thought you were masterful."

"Thanks, Chief. Hey, I've got some information for you that will hit tomorrow," Arnold said.

"Okay, fire away," I said.

"Joseph Galetti is going to be picked up by the police tomorrow, and he will be charged as accessory to murder after the fact," Arnold said.

"You can't be serious!" I said. "Joe is a tough old bird, and he's smart. The state hasn't a chance of proving that, and he's no virgin when it comes to being hauled into a courtroom."

"You're right," Arnold admitted. "But my sources say they are going to squeeze him, hold him without bail, and make his life miserable."

"But why? The guy's eighty years old, and he's not a flight risk," I said.

"They want Joe to give them the skinny on the money laundering and Bob Santone's role in that piece of the business. That way they have Santone coming and going for murder, money laundering, and probably extortion somewhere along the way," Arnold explained.

"Arnold, I know Joe isn't on the top of our hit parade right now," I said, but Arnold jumped in and said, "Hit parade, my ass! You hire the guy in good faith, and he fucks you in the ass, if I can be so crude."

"Okay, okay," I said, relenting to Arnold's emotion. "But I feel I should tip the old bastard off."

"Like you said, he's smart. He'll figure it out. But he's between two really bad choices. If he tells the police the ins and outs of the money-laundering scheme, he is probably indicting himself. If he doesn't, he goes to trial as an accessory," Arnold said.

"His only out is to obtain immunity from prosecution for himself on the money-laundering charge," I said.

"But think about where that leaves Donna Mitchner. Her star witness against Bob Santone for murder has been convicted of perjury, and her witness to the money-laundering scheme has been given immunity," Arnold said.

"You're right, Arnold. You would have made a hell of a lawyer. This looks like it's headed for the 'tangled web' department to me."

"Yeah, but think of the good news," Arnold said.

"Give me some," I said.

"The board meets in two weeks, and you get a 12–0 vote," Arnold said.

"Couldn't have done it without you, Arnold. When those six hundred folks marched into the square with their placards, it was a sight to behold. I had goose bumps," I said. "Oh by the way, even though you aren't the president of this organization, you'll find an enhanced value in your next paycheck and the one after that and the one..."

"Thank you, boss," Arnold said. "I'll use the new cabbage to buy some more stock in this pop stand!"

* * *

I had one final piece of business to complete. He met me at the Barker Tavern, and when I arrived, he was already there, and my Bloody Mary was waiting for its owner.

I looked at Joe Galetti and said, "What's your deal?"

"Same as always, trying to make a buck," Joe responded.

"Are we talking a clean, legitimate dollar?" I asked.

"You always were a bit of a Boy Scout, Russ, holier-than-thou type," Joe said matter-of-factly.

"If you mean I do things on the up-and-up, I'll plead guilty to that. And guess where I learned business ethics?" I asked.

"Where?" Joe asked.

"From your dad and your brother and, until now, you. Is it true that you told Bob Santone to hire me because you thought I'd fail and you could pick up the chain on the cheap?"

"Absolutely. I was sure you'd step on the throttle, push it to the floor, and drive Food Basket to a deserving grave," Joe replied.

"How'd that turn out?" I asked.

"Not well," he said. "You learned finesse, and more importantly, you took advantage of my old operation with Macober, Pondorf, and Williams. You trumped that with Sneed and Brewster while dumping the real deadwood, Joe Snyder, and putting that bright kid, Baldwin, in as CFO."

"You must have laughed your ass off when I called you to put you on board here at Food Basket," I said.

"I have to say it seemed like a piece of good fortune. But, Russ, it wasn't all bad. I did some good work—the megastore being but one example," Joe said.

"Yeah, that was great, Joe, almost as good as you working for me to secure votes from the board of directors."

"It's just business," Joe said.

"See, it's not just business, Joe. It's business with two murders, money laundering, Ponzi schemes, extortion, and who knows what else. It's dirty, Joe. You're a smart guy. In your heart of hearts, you have to know it's just not business," I said.

"I have no connection to any of that," Joe said.

"You're connected right up to your ears. Further, the police, specifically Captain Alan Cummings, has you in his sights," I said.

"How did that happen?" Joe asked.

"I tipped him, Joe," I said. "I wanted you to know how you got on their radar."

"You son of a bitch! After all my family has done for you over the years," Joe said.

"Joe, all by yourself you used up all the goodwill I felt for the Galetti family. It's sad, Joe, that you have really lost your way."

"They'll never pin anything on me," he said.

"Maybe not, but let me cover one logistical piece of business. Your ride home tonight is the last you will have with the car and driver. But don't worry, the state will provide a ride for you tomorrow."

I stood up, turned around, and left the room to let Joe contemplate his future. The Bloody Mary never secured an owner.

CHAPTER 53

All Is Well as the Curtain Falls

I t's been three months since Bob Santone was indicted for murder and money laundering. Things have gone from bad to worse for Bob as the FTC has halted any trading on his hedge fund, strongly suspecting a Ponzi scheme. Arnold, with his good ear to the ground, says a plea may be brewing, but at this point it's only speculation. The trial hasn't begun because Bob asked for a change of venue, and his lawyers are saying they need more time to prepare the case.

On a brighter note, Arnold's fearless forecast came true: I was elected for another year by a 12–0 vote. The business is starting to roll now under its own momentum, and Garth Brewster was rewarded by the drug industry as their man of the year for his work at Food Basket. Bill Hartman is okay because he knows I'll be back at the food brokerage at some point, and Jim Sneed has a year to find my replacement.

Joe Galetti has been charged with money laundering, but because of his age and the fact that he will be a key witness in the

Bob Santone trial, he escaped jail time. The fact that he was charged with a felony had to be a low point for Joe and the Galetti family.

Holly and I are putting on our best stuff to head to the North End this weekend for the wedding of Alan Cummings and Donna Mitchner.

Right now, I'm sitting at my favorite steak-and-cheese place that has a front window view of a Dempster-Dumpster, waiting for my luncheon companion. He hadn't arrived yet, so I ordered two extra-large steak and cheese bombs, fries, and two sodas.

He walked in, looked at me, looked at his meal, and said, "Are those fully loaded?"

"Ye of little faith. Is there any other way?" I asked.

"Who is buying?" he asked with some suspicion in his voice.

"Bought and paid for," I replied.

"You can't have Macober, Pondorf, and Williams again," he said.

"Not asking," I said as part of my sandwich slithered down my chin on the way to the plate.

He took a major-league bite out of his sandwich, but it was clean; he didn't spill a drop.

"C'mon, Russ, you're killing me. You've got that crazy look in your eye. Something is brewing in that noggin of yours," he said.

"One word, Trip—*acquisition*," I said.

"Not merger of equals?" he responded.

"Acquisition," I repeated.

"Let's chew on that for a while," Trip said.

What's Next for the Property Brothers of the Food Industry?

Bill Hartman said it best when he told me that the Cummings had tumbled off the social ladder altogether when they started hanging out with us. The six of us were inside Hartman's cottage because the fall wind had a definite chill to it. I don't know much about wind direction, but I think it was blowing from the north and east. The reason I clung to this dubious fact was that the horizon extended well beyond where I thought ocean and sky usually met. I imagined I was seeing Nantucket, but that was doubtful, as well as it was some fourteen miles away. We cling to these half-truths with tenacity, and if we repeat them often enough, they become our reality.

Alan Cummings loved our little neighborhood and, specifically, Craigville Beach, as he plotted and planned for a place of his own.

"Do you think the real estate folks around here would be suspicious if I plunked down three-quarters of a million in cash that I 'light-fingered' from the evidence locker at the station?" he asked.

"Don't worry about the real estate people, I'll have you in a holding cell before sunset," Donna Cummings replied.

We were all laughing, but we knew the assistant district attorney was not kidding.

"Not to make a pun, but I think you better cashier that plan, Alan," Hartman said.

Jenny Hartman jumped in and said, "Speaking of cells and cash, what is going on with everyone post the Santone skullduggery era?"

"I can't help thinking of the irony produced by the top line of this case and how it played out," Holly said.

"What are you talking about, my beauty?" I asked.

"Well, think about it. The guy who had nothing to do with Alex Santone's murder draws a life sentence. The woman who was standing next to Bob Santone when he pulled the trigger walks," she said.

"Okay, not our best day," Donna Cummings admitted, "but the modern-day Detective Clouseau got it right…eventually."

"Wait a minute, you guys. This isn't like fitting a guy for a new suit and finding out it doesn't quite fit. So he goes back to get another one or has the original one altered. Bruno Jethroe was fitted for a life sentence," Hartman said. "And Lucy walked because you can't try her for the same crime twice."

"You're right, Bill," Donna said. "But I have to credit Alan for turning this thing around. He felt it was a setup early on, and that really helped us get it as right as possible in the end."

"Amen. Never mind would of, could of, or should of," Jenny said. "Where is everybody now that the smoke has cleared?"

"Okay, here's what we know," Alan Cummings said. "Bob Santone will be serving two consecutive life sentences, no parole. He is still in court, trying to defend his hedge fund wrongdoing, but that is slipping away from him quickly."

"What does he care?" Holly asked. "With two consecutive life sentences on the horizon, I wouldn't think his assets would mean much. Further, he's not going to be paying back his stockholders with his earnings from the prison laundry."

"Second ironical twist," Bill Hartman said. "He somehow, not pointing any fingers at the judicial system, obtained a creampuff facility for Lucy Santone and an unbelievably light sentence for perjury. But he received the maximum— twice—and there's not a damn thing he can do about it."

"Good point," Donna said. "Just between us chickens, I'm investigating that whole area."

"Let's see," Alan continued. "Bruno Jethroe is a free man, and Lucy Santone is as well, although she is on probation. My information is that they have purchased a restaurant near Worcester, but I can't confirm that."

"I can," Donna added.

"I never saw them as a couple," I said.

"I didn't think it was a match either, but stranger things have taken place. Sophia Loren and Carlo Ponti, Miller and Monroe, Liz Taylor and the Mormon Tabernacle Choir— all of them. Lucy may have grown weary of grasping for the gold ring and falling short," Jen said.

"What about Joe Galetti?" Holly asked.

"He didn't do time, but he was convicted of a felony," Alan said. "He helped to bring down the largest money laundering organization in state history."

"I talked to Trip Galetti a few days ago, and he says Joe has dropped completely out of sight. As a felon, his charity and philanthropy work has ended. He's toxic even among his family. His career and his legacy have been damaged to the point beyond recognition," I said.

"Sad end to a storied career. But I have no empathy for the man—zero," Bill Hartman said. "He became a sleazy criminal in the end and, in so doing, destroyed not only his career and legacy, but severely tarnished the Galetti name."

"Okay, what about the business?" Alan asked. "Is all the good your team has done with Food Basket going down the drain? You can tell us. We won't spill our guts to the local grocery rags."

"Yes, indeed," Donna added. "I can always resurrect that holding cell if I don't start hearing the latest moves by the property brothers of the grocery industry. The last update I had, Russ, was that you were about to lose a board-of-directors vote followed by a hasty exit."

"Hey, we're not holding out on you, but the playing field is changing, and we are facing some pretty stiff winds in the brokerage business. The day of the boutique food broker has ended as three national broker houses have combined to eliminate the little guy. As an example, Clorox once had sixty brokers around the country. Now they have one. We are surviving quite nicely, but we are bucking an inevitable trend," I said.

"As a result, Russ and I are thinking of selling that business and starting another food brokerage in the food service business," Bill Hartman said. "P&G had a division in food service when I worked there. Its nickname was Flop and Slop because we sold to hotels, restaurants, and bakeries."

"That's all well and good," Donna said. "But, c'mon, guys, how far is this conversation going to go before we talk about a multi-billion-dollar business that you guys saved and sent soaring. What about Food Basket?"

"I'll take that one," Holly said. "In my rounds at the mutual fund water cooler, I'm hearing merger between Galetti and Food Basket. If it happened, they would be on an equal footing with the number one volume chain in New England."

"It's a learning experience for me," I said. "But this last year and a half have been a blast, working with quality people with integrity who really want to win. No way this would have happened without the team: Jim Sneed, Garth Brewster, Larry Baldwin, Arnold Cable, Pondorf, Shirley Macober, and Dave Williams, just to name a few. Bouncing things off Holly and Bill was invaluable, but in the same breath you have Bob Santone, Joe Snyder, and Joe Galetti, where greed controlled the play. They had a chance to do the right thing, but you can't buy integrity. I hope I never forget what really counts."

"A lesson for all to follow, no matter what endeavor you are connected with," Donna said. "But, Russ…"

"Yes," I responded.

"Surely, you two guys can't do two jobs at once," Donna opined.

"Stay tuned," I said.

Kirkus
Reviews

TITLE INFORMATION

Checked Out
A Russell Riley Novel
ISBN: 978-1-68213-493-1

BOOK REVIEW

Harris (Blood Feud, 2012) spins a rousing whodunit set in the lucrative supermarket business in this second series installment.

Russell Riley, former president of the New England—-based Galetti Supermarkets, is back to sort out more familial unrest involving the greed and deceit running rampant throughout the "food brokerage business." Unceremoniously fired after a three-decade tenure with Galetti Supermarkets for not keeping the business profitable throughout a "two-billion-dollar family food fight," Riley receives a life-changing call from college-baseball buddy Bob Santone. Santone's multistore Rhode Island supermarket family business, Food Basket, had been recently thrown into turmoil after his uncle Alex, the company's extravagantly bankrolled CEO, was murdered in his living room. Santone dangles a lucrative one-year position in front of Riley in a desperate attempt to rescue the business from financial ruin. After conferring with business partner Bill Hartman; lifelong friend Arnold; doting wife Holly; and even Trip, CEO of Galetti Supermarkets, he accepts the challenge. Police Capt. Alan Cummings, who's investigating the case, is ably assisted by hardnosed Assistant District Attorney (and passionate love interest) Donna Mitchner, who is trailing suspected killer Bruno Jethroe, as well as other suspects, including Alex's widow. The action builds as shady life-insurance policies, fiery courtroom antics, money laundering, and double-indemnity plots abound. Meanwhile, Harris keeps even his peripheral characters multidimensional and the dialogue sprightly. Without question, Riley is the star throughout and, together with the detectives, soon fleshes out the intricate details of the twisty murder plot. Harris, who draws great inspiration from over 30 years in the food business himself, once again writes an energetic, high-stakes yarn of greed and betrayal navigated by the charmingly quirky Russell Riley and leaves room for more possible antics to follow.

A satisfying blend of intrigue and corporate mayhem helmed by a playful, foodie do-gooder.

About the Author

Daniel Harris is a 32 year veteran of Procter & Gamble who spent the majority of his career calling on Food Industry customers. He is a graduate of the University of Virginia where he majored in English. He served as a Lieutenant platoon leader in Vietnam. He and his wife Joy live south of Boston, have two adult children, and three grandchildren. *Checked Out* is Harris's fourth novel, *Blood Feud*, (2012), *Capital Crimes*, (2001), *Goodbye Dearie*, (1999), and the second novel in the Russell Riley Series which focuses on working in closely held Family Businesses. Harris's published short stories include "The Closer" (2012), and "The Cowboy" (2011).

Acknowledgements

This novel, *Checked Out*, is a sequel to the one that just preceded it, *Blood Feud*. The person in charge of trying to manage the simultaneous promoting of *Blood Feud* while I was writing *Checked Out* was my sister, Carolyn Harris. Even Angelo Dundee, the irascible and humorous manager of Muhammad Ali, could not keep as many balls in the air as my sister. Her decade of training at Simon and Schuster held her in good stead as she schmoozed a better print ad price than was first offered (clergy discount anyone?), worked her way through dozens of book promotions to pick one that actually worked, and took on social media when she knew I didn't speak URL.

And that was just with *Blood Feud*! On *Checked Out*, she was the part-time editor and proofer. Additionally, she worked with the very talented Justine Ives to produce a cover and an interior of the book that we all felt very good about.

But most important, she felt *Blood Feud* was a quality book that people would really enjoy. Her opinion was seconded by Kirkus Review, who gave it a wonderful review and featured it in their publication, where less than 10 percent of their reviews are featured.

To my friend, neighbor, traveling buddy, and sailing companion, Jim Mead, retired management consultant, who helped me visualize the process of hiring people at the highest level.

For George Ganzenmuller, who I hired out of Fordham University, who lent expert advice on the food brokerage business. In a fun twist of the dial, he married the daughter of the man who hired me.

I have to mention Larry Corthell, who risked life and limb to take photographs for me outside a supermarket window at night, standing in a grocery cart, hoping it wouldn't start rolling while he was photographing. Larry also created the cover for my previous book, *Blood Feud*, but he wasn't recognized for it at the time, so we are applauding that effort here.

Professor Bill Schoell, who encouraged us at every turn and had a nose for turning down promotions that seemed to be too good to be true and, in fact, were too good to be true.

For Cindy Taber, who typed all 73,000 words numerous times without a single complaint. Her high skill level was the key in finishing this novel on a timely basis.

And of course, to Joy, who thought up the title of this book while spelling innumerable words for me as she passed by my desk on her way to another part of the house. *Checked Out* would have never been written if Joy hadn't convinced me to publish the first book in the series, *Blood Feud*. It languished on the shelf for a year ,but her persistence eventually won the day.

CPSIA information can be obtained
at www.ICGtesting.com
Printed in the USA
BVHW071729081221
623537BV00004B/300